hen **Virginia Heath** was
ges to fall asleep, so she m
ead to help pass the time w
e ceiling. As she got older the stories became more
omplicated—sometimes taking weeks to get to
heir happy ending. One day she decided to embrace
er insomnia and start writing them down. Virginia
ves in Essex, with her wonderful husband and two
enagers. It still takes her for ever to fall asleep.

THE
UNCOMPROMISING
LORD FLINT

Virginia Heath

MILLS & BOON

First Published in Great Britain 2018
by Mills & Boon, an imprint of HarperCollins*Publishers*
1 London Bridge Street, London, SE1 9GF

© 2018 Susan Merritt

ISBN: 978-0-263-26879-9

MIX
Paper from
responsible sources
FSC C007454

This book is produced from independently certified FSC™ paper
to ensure responsible forest management.
For more information visit www.harpercollins.co.uk/green.

Printed and bound in Spain
by CPI, Barcelona

For Monique Daoust,
who gave the French part of Jessamine her voice.

Chapter One

Late May 1820

'English pigs!'

The wrought-iron bars rattled again as another hailstorm of stale breadcrumbs hit him squarely in the face. She might well be a traitor and a termagant, but Lady Jessamine Fane's aim was reliably accurate.

'I'm sorry, my lord. Had we known she was stockpiling her rations to use as weapons we would have relieved her of them.'

Lord Peter Flint dusted the latest baked embellishments from his lapels and smiled tightly. 'Pay it no mind, Captain. This is an unusual situation for all of us.' It wasn't every day that a Royal Navy frigate became a floating prison for one inmate and a female one at that. Nor did he, in the usual run of things, find himself the reluctant gaoler of one, tasked with dragging her foul-mouthed and fiery carcass back to London. A job that he was now prepared to concede might not be as simple as he had first thought. Lady Jessamine did not strike him as one who would go meekly. Or even quietly. The blasted woman had been hurling abuse at them for the better part of half an hour. Hell, she'd been yelling from the moment he boarded the ship and they had set sail an hour ago. A constant tirade of pithy, imaginative and noisy invective issued alongside the flying food from her nest in the shadows.

'Can we bring some more lanterns down here?'

The brig was unnecessarily dark and forbidding, the heavy, windowless timbers of the hull creaking as they rocked on the tide. Her collection of missiles would be more easily avoided with the addition of some light and he wanted to know exactly what and whom he was dealing with and, no matter what she had done, it seemed a tad cruel to keep her in the dark.

Flint was yet to see her face properly. It was buried in a ratty tangle of dark curls. All he could properly ascertain was despite her strength she was small, judging from the petite size of the grubby hands which gesticulated wildly in a Gallic fashion. Yet her surprisingly sultry French-accented voice and impressive repertoire of insults suggested she was no girl. Not much of a lady either, but then what had he expected?

Lady Jessamine might have once been the daughter of an English earl, but a decade had passed since she had been ripped out of her British life by her traitorous French mother. A mother who had fled England to live openly in sin with her French lover. The Comte de Saint-Aubin-de-Scellon had been one of Napoleon's biggest supporters. He was still one of his most loyal supporters, if their intelligence was to be believed, and the lynchpin of the French side of the smuggling ring they were yet to destroy. In view of her bohemian and scandalous upbringing, her lack of morals hardly came as a shock. Nor did the treason. As the Comte had had more of a hand in Lady Jessamine's upbringing than her own father, it was hardly a surprise that her allegiance was staunchly with the enemy.

Like mother, like daughter.

Except the loud-mouthed Jessamine had done more than share a bed with the enemy. If the mounting evidence was to be believed, she had committed all manner of atrocities which had seen good men die. Men he considered friends as well as comrades in arms. Once she had served her purpose and spilled her secrets she would likely hang. And rightly so. All Flint had to do was deliver her to Lord Fennimore, the courts and the lawyer Hadleigh and then he would be shot of her and her foul temper.

Above him, he listened to the sounds of the huge canvas sails snapping in the wind and knew the next few days would not be pleasant despite their fast speed. Aside from this ocean journey, he would then have to spend days stuck in a coach with her. It couldn't be helped. He was between missions and the rest of the King's Elite were either in the thick of it or on honeymoon. His friend and fellow spy Jake Warriner had been the first to fall into the parson's trap, something which still came as a shock considering Jake had always been a committed and cheerful rake determinedly averse to settling down. He had been closely followed by Seb Leatham, who had gone and married an effervescent incomparable despite his painful shyness around women. As both friends had been working on the same mission to catch exactly the same smugglers as Flint, their sudden and unexpected plummet into marital bliss was a worry. Two good men down. A state Flint wanted no part of.

Not this side of fifty at least. Perhaps when he was older and beginning to creak he might welcome the presence of a wife. And then again perhaps not. Merely considering it made him frown.

It wasn't so much the institution of marriage he took issue with, rather the inevitable tribulations which came along with it. As the youngest of six children, five of whom were female, he'd had quite enough feminine machinations, hysterics and interfering nosiness to last a lifetime. He'd been hen-pecked, mollycoddled and driven to the furthest limits of his sanity for his first twenty years. Those scars still ran deep. Too deep to plunge headlong into marriage any time soon. Women were born conditioned to find ways to control and confound the men they cohabited with. A fact he understood only too well.

He loved all his high-strung sisters dearly, was hugely proud and protective of them in equal measure, but also spent a great deal of time wanting to strangle the lot of them. Despite all now happily settled with good husbands and families of their own, they still devoted a huge and wholly unnecessary amount of time meddling in his life.

In the last two years that meddling had become considerably more unbearable than it had been in his youth—before he had discovered the sweet taste of freedom—because now they had collectively decided their little brother was in dire need of settling, too. In their minds, seven and twenty was precisely the right age for a man to marry. He couldn't return home without an attractive and eligible female being unsubtly wafted under his nose.

Last month, when another mission necessitated a protracted visit to his estate, his troublesome sisters had conspired to procure three potential brides who just happened to be invited to every dinner he was home to eat. And he had been purposely non-committal about his possible attendance at *all* meals—yet those eligible girls were there regardless. One of whom was so enthusiastic Flint had had to keep his wits about him for a whole week to avoid being caught in a compromising situation. That chit had been hellbent on being ruined and his sisters, and his own beloved mother, had encouraged her ardent pursuit! It was a sad state of affairs when a man's house wasn't a safe haven.

Thank goodness the wandering and unpredictable life of a spy had given him a convenient excuse to avoid his siblings for months out of every year. They lived in Cornwall, miles away from anywhere, and he cheerfully resided in London in bachelor lodgings, blissfully female-free. A situation which suited him perfectly. As he knew to his cost, all women—family or otherwise—really couldn't be trusted.

A hard chunk of well-baked crust caught him on the temple. 'Do not dare try to ignore me, English pig! Let me out of here! You do not know what you have got into. They will come and they will kill you. Every one of you!' He dodged the next doughy projectile and rolled his eyes. All this combustible feminine emotion was tiresome. She saw it and became most fervent, her small hands curling around the bars and her dark eyes wide beneath the tangle of curls.

'Do you seriously think they will let me set one foot on English soil and not be there waiting?'

Something he and his superiors were counting on and the real reason why she had been held tantalisingly on this huge ship, conveniently anchored within plain sight of the beach at Cherbourg for almost six days.

Lady Jessamine was bait.

A tasty morsel to lure her fellow traitors out of the woodwork. 'You are overreacting, madam. Before you know it, you will be stood firmly back on English soil, in the dock and found reassuringly guilty and we'll all be much happier for it.'

Her hand went straight to her neck as she stumbled back a step and he felt a pang of guilt at being so brutal before he ruthlessly quashed it. So what if she was a woman? She didn't deserve his compassion and any residual, instinctually protective ideals about the fairer sex did not apply here. She was a traitor. A criminal.

She might not have wielded the pistols that had killed, but she'd had a hand in loading the bullets and reaped a share in the ill-gotten profits. Shamelessly co-ordinating the smugglers for the elusive Boss, a man the King's Elite had been desperate to arrest for over a year. The callous and invisible criminal mastermind behind a plot to restore Napoleon to power. His network had infiltrated the upper echelons of the English elite and flooded the market with smuggled brandy, the proceeds from which went straight into the enemy's coffers.

Alongside the Comte de Saint-Aubin-de-Scellon, the petite Lady Jessamine was his partner in crime. The Boss's assistant across the Channel. Every covert, coded message they had intercepted in the last few weeks had been written in her pretty, looped handwriting. Times, places, shipments, vessels, corrupt English peers complicit in the widespread and dangerous treachery—Lady Jessamine was privy to it all. In fact, she had assisted in orchestrating it. Always had. There were three other convicted traitors languishing in Newgate awaiting execution who had repeatedly testified to as much.

A midshipman arrived with a lamp and the damp brig was suddenly bathed in golden light. Another pang of pity troubled him as she flinched in pain and shielded her eyes. She'd been kept in the dark too long. Her skin had the grey pallor similar to that seen on long-term prisoners.

Now he could clearly see her body, the evidence of her rough treatment appalled him. One sleeve hung limply at her elbow, ripped nearly clean from the bodice. Finger-shaped bruises marred her upper arm. Her dark hair was matted. Her small feet bare. The remnants of her gown stained and filthy. The coarse, utilitarian fabric surprised him. Flint had expected silk and lace—the obvious trappings of wealth and ill-gotten privilege—not dull, patched serge.

A disguise? It had to be. Once her hideaway had come under siege, it made sense she would don the garments of a servant and attempt to flee capture. But still…

'Send for soap and hot water, Captain. Some fresh clothes and a hairbrush.' Whatever she had done, Lady Jessamine was still a human being. 'And arrange a screen out here so she can bathe in private. The guards can wait outside.' She was also the sole woman on a ship filled with lusty men who spent the majority of their lives on the ocean with other males.

'If we can't see her, there is no telling what she might do! The blasted chit has tried to escape three times already!'

'The anchor has been weighed and we are miles from shore. Unless she swims underwater with the speed of a dolphin, where exactly do you think she will go?' Flint turned at the same moment she brushed the dark curtain of hair from her face.

Beautiful.

That was the only thought he had and one that certainly wouldn't do. He'd been bewitched by traitorous beauty before and had trained himself to be immune since. As her deep brown, almond-shaped eyes locked with his, he abruptly turned on his heel, a little staggered at the odd emotions the sight of her conjured. He had thought he hadn't needed Lord Fennimore's stinging reminder about his previous gullibility—now he clung to those insightful words gratefully.

'Don't let her wiles waylay you. Remember what happened the last time.'

As if he could forget? His father had almost died as a result. But that had been years ago when he had still been green around the gills and had assumed that all women were like his sisters—over-emotional but good inside. That particular prisoner had duped him with her tears, capitalised on his familial obligation to protect and then thoroughly seduced him into dropping his guard. To then watch helpless as she had shot his poor father with Flint's own pistol had been a hard way to learn his lesson—but learn it he had. What she looked like and how his body responded had nothing to do what his mission. The mission always had to come first. 'Get yourself cleaned up. We will talk again in an hour.'

Jess watched him leave. Watched the Captain and her two surly guards follow closely behind, then sank to the floor. The last few weeks had been terrifying and exhausting, but tears had no place now. Self-pity was an indulgence she couldn't afford—not yet at least. Perhaps soon she could curl up in a ball in a safe little room far, far away and cry for a month to let it all out. Until then, she needed to hold the tears back, knowing instinctively that if she started then she wouldn't be able to stop.

Everything was going entirely to plan.

Not that she really had any more of a plan now than she had when all this had started a few weeks ago. It was more a series of events and opportunities created out of necessity and desperation and a large sprinkling of unexpected luck, but at least she was out of the run-down *pension* which had been her prison for the last month and was heading home, albeit as a prisoner again.

She hoped this ship was fast.

The more miles between her and Saint-Aubin the better. Cruel, callous and with the single-minded determination to crush anyone or anything that got in his way under the heel of his

glossy boots, that monster had stolen too many
years and sucked all the joy out of her soul. Oh,
how she hated him! Except now he had an excellent reason to turn all that venom towards her.
She hadn't just escaped, she had destroyed the
documentation he would need to fill the void she
had left. Every name, every contact, every supplier carefully recorded in her mother's leather
journal now languished somewhere at the bottom of the harbour in Cherbourg. It would take
him weeks and possibly costly months to piece
it all together again—unless he found her first
and forced the details out of her.

Torture, then death.

Neither appealed. Once she was in sight of
the English coast, Jess would find a way to escape properly and disappear, never to be found
again. A new life and a new identity, miles from
the shore, ships and the smugglers who had stolen her old ones.

The only hatch to the brig opened, followed
by the tell-tale smell of boiled cabbage and stale
sweat, and the same toothless sailor who had
watched her lasciviously for the last week, carried steaming wooden buckets of water. Over his
shoulder were tossed towels and fresh clothes.
Behind him came the other guard, not quite as
hostile but no more compassionate, with a small
tin bathtub filled with folded sheets which the

pair of them suspended from the low ceiling like a sail. Then with a snarl, the toothless one produced a key and undid the padlock of her cell, warily watching Jess as she sat unmoving before him.

'Your *bath*, your *ladyship*. Not that traitors deserve baths as far as I'm concerned. If it was down to me, I'd leave you to rot in your own filth.'

'As you do?' Bating him was probably not sensible. The toothless one was free and easy with his fists, but Jess couldn't bring herself to cower subserviently. She had experienced worse. 'You stink.'

His lip curled and he raise his hand, then dropped it. A first for him. Something must have changed to make him resist. He threw the soap and hairbrush into the straw in front of her.

'Once you're finished, the *illustrious* Lord Flint wants to see you in his cabin while *we* get to clean up the mess you've made.' Something which clearly disgruntled the old sea dog immensely. 'Don't try any funny business! There's another guard up there with a loaded musket and orders to kill if you don't do as you're told. Bath. Dress. And be swift about it.' Threat issued, they retreated up the narrow steps to the main deck and the tiny hatch slammed closed once again.

Lord Flint.

So that was his name? It made sense he was an aristocrat. Every aspect of his being—from the inscrutable expression on his handsome face, the arrogant stance and the impeccably tailored coat he filled so well—all pointed to as much. His obvious physical attributes aside, the privileged, pampered English male was always the same no matter what magnificent shape or size they came in. Cold, detached and uninterested in any opinions which contradicted their own.

Jess hadn't been exaggerating when she had warned he was in danger. Saint-Aubin would have them both torn limb from limb and their entrails fed to the dogs in a heartbeat, yet Lord Flint had brushed off her concerns with rude indifference. She hated that.

She remembered her father's same indifference all those years ago when her mother declared her intention to leave him and take their only daughter with her. Like the arrogant Lord Flint, he hadn't believed a word of it and lived to rue the day. Or more likely, as it turned out, he had simply been glad to be shot of her and hadn't rued it at all. The manner of her leaving had certainly given him a valid excuse to dissolve the marriage with impressive haste, disown his only daughter and rapidly find a new wife to finally give him his longed-for son. Cold, detached and uninterested peers of the realm were so at odds with her experience of their French aristocratic counterparts. Saint-Aubin had been hot-headed, suspicious and terminally cruel. While she might have been fleetingly attracted to the man, Lord Flint's staid, emotionless demeanour had been reassuringly familiar.

He hadn't bothered introducing himself, not that she'd really given him much chance to or cared overmuch who he was. It wasn't as if she intended to spend much time in his company. Jess had ranted and raved for all she was worth. If one of Saint-Aubin's men were on this ship—and she wouldn't put that past him because he had his poisonous tentacles everywhere—then Jess needed to appear outraged and afraid at being captured rather than relieved. It was relief tinged with a healthy dose of raw terror, but again that emotion was so familiar nowadays, always lurking menacingly in the background, that she had ruthlessly trained herself to ignore it unless absolutely necessary. Right now, while she was bobbing in the middle of the English Channel, it wasn't necessary.

If they came in little boats in the dead of night to fetch her and drag her back, her only chance at living to see another sunrise depended on her fighting her new captors tooth and nail while lying through her teeth. Once she set foot on English soil, Jess was a dead woman walking.

Saint-Aubin or the Boss would have highly paid assassins waiting to eventually erase her from the world unless she outwitted them first.

Until—if—that happened, she could console herself with one not insignificant achievement. Her trail of crumbs had been followed and she was out. That alone was cause for celebration.

Allowing herself a small smile of satisfaction, she rose and dragged the tub to a position which she hoped afforded her the most privacy and emptied the steaming buckets in. It was a meagre bath by normal standards, the water merely a few inches deep, but it was hot and wet and the first proper bath she had been allowed in months. Even conditions in this dank and humid brig were a considerable improvement on her rat-infested prison in Cherbourg or the same, compact four walls in Saint-Aubin's claustrophobic and oppressive chateau.

All in all, things were looking up. Jess would not weep today. If she was destined to die in the coming few days, then she would take whatever small pleasures she could in the interim. Jess closed her eyes, inhaled slowly and deeply, tucking the constant fear into the little box in her mind where she stored all the bad things, then stripped off her filthy dress, kicking it back into the cell. It was the last vestige of Saint-Aubin and she was done with all that.

From this moment on she was in control of her destiny and nothing and nobody was ever going to get in her way again The call of freedom and survival was too strong. She took a moment to inhale the sweet, fresh scent of the soap before she gratefully stepped in the tub and lowered herself into the water, revelling in the glorious sensation of soothing, clean water enveloping her skin.

Délicieux!

Paradise.

It was the little things, the things people took for granted, that she had missed the most. The hot meals, the heady aroma of fresh air, this warm bath. The unfamiliar sound of her first language spoken once again and the odd yet comforting way it felt coming from her own lips after all these years. Everyday luxuries she would rejoice in until she gasped her last breath because she was tired of hating herself and determined to begin her life afresh.

The handsome Lord Flint and his aristocratic arrogance could wait until her bath chilled and her skin shrivelled before she deigned to grace him with her presence. If he was to be the latest in her long line of temporary gaolers, it was best he found out early that Jess had never been partial to following orders.

Chapter Two

The harridan had made him wait two hours already. No doubt she would have made him wait two more had he not dispatched someone to go fetch her. He would allow her that petty victory. He'd used the time constructively, going over the prearranged route to London and writing messages to send to every fashionably busy inn along the way, cheerfully appraising them, and anyone else who intercepted the missives, of the exact dates and times he expected to arrive at their establishment. Lord Flint and Lady Jessamine would require two rooms next door to one another, but not a private dining room. The more witnesses who saw her pretty face, the better.

The rap at his cabin door had him pausing mid-sentence. He kept his head bent and his pen hovering as the guards shepherded Lady Jessamine in, ignoring the way his body seemed to sense her.

'The prisoner, sir. Would you like me to attach the manacles?'

'That won't be necessary.' Flint didn't do her the courtesy of looking up. He could play silly games, too. Till the cows came home if need be. 'Leave us.'

Both guards hesitated, then let go of her elbows. 'As you wish, sir. We'll be outside.'

He scratched out another few words, then dipped his quill in the inkstand before continuing to write, leaving Lady Jessamine standing like a naughty student at his desk. In his peripheral vision he took in the sight. Bare feet, clean this time, and several inches of shapely, naked female calf poked out from beneath the striped sailor's breeches she had been issued. The overlarge linen shirt had been gathered to one side and tied in a jaunty knot, cinching the masculine garment tightly around her slim waist and displaying the obvious feminine shape of her rounded hips and bottom to the world. The collar was undone, the graceful curve of her neck and delicate collarbone yet another reminder of her sex—not that one was needed. Her long, tousled, jet-black hair was completely loose and tumbling down her back and around her shoulders. A beautiful, dark-haired temptress who might have been expressly designed by God to specifically appeal to his particular taste in women—damn her.

She looked scandalous, sultry and, to his shame, Flint's body had never wanted a woman more. But he wouldn't be waylaid by the physical. Beneath the perfect veneer, the wood was rotten. He gripped his pen so firmly as he formed the next letters, it would take a miracle to prevent the crew hearing the sound of it squeaking against the parchment up in the crow's nest. Sheer pride made him grit his teeth and continue regardless. Let her think he was furious, which he really was now—but at his own uncontrollable and wholly unwanted lust rather than at her.

Arrogant to the last, without waiting for an invitation, she wandered to the comfortable armchair across his cabin and lowered herself into it. For good measure, she crossed one delectable leg over the other and lounged with an elbow propped upon the arm and stared at the top of his head insolently.

Totally relaxed.

Totally galling, when he could feel the intoxicating power of those beautiful eyes all the way down to his toes.

Flint waited another couple of seconds before he carefully laid the quill down and faced her, his face a perfect mask of blandness that took all his years of training to muster. 'Your friend—The Boss—I need his name.'

'Straight to the point? No small talk, Monsieur Flint?' Dropping his honorific was an obvious insult, not that he cared. In his line of work, where he was paid to be a chameleon, he rarely got to use it anyway.

'You are to stand trial for treason, Lady Jessamine. A crime, as I am sure you are well aware, which carries the death penalty. Your co-operation now might encourage the courts to be lenient with their sentence should you be found guilty.'

She snorted and tossed her head dismissively. 'There will be no leniency nor a fair trial. Your courts will hang me regardless of what I say or do not say. I have been tried and found guilty already. *Non?*'

'Perhaps that is the way they do things in France, but back home…'

'Spare me your superior English lies. I am not a fool, Monsieur Flint. My confession makes your job much easier, yet it will not help me. You have your supposed witnesses so I am doomed either way. Whether it is by an English hangman or a French assassin, my life is soon to be taken from me.' Her dark eyes locked with his and held. Beneath the façade of insolence he saw sadness and fear and wished he hadn't. She was easier to hate when devoid of all human feelings. Knowing she possessed some made it difficult to offer false hope.

'Confession is good for the soul, or so I am told. You will meet your maker knowing you repented at the end.'

'My maker knows the truth already, Monsieur Flint. I have nothing to prove to him.'

'Perhaps you do not understand the gravity of what you have done? Are you aware of the consequences of your actions?' He didn't bother pausing for an answer. 'This year alone, eighteen men have been murdered thanks to you. Granted, many of them had it coming. Seduced by the easy riches that come from smuggling, they were lured to participate in high treason and reaped the rewards. When you dance with the Devil, you inevitably get burned. However, ten of those men were servants of the Crown whose only crime was doing their duty. They were murdered in cold blood.'

'Not by me. I am merely the messenger!'

Instantly annoyed and determined to control it, Flint stood and braced his arms to loom across the desk. 'They were simply doing their duty, yet your people reacted as true cowards always do. They killed innocent men to save their own corrupt skins.' He opened a drawer in his desk and pulled out a sheet of paper. He didn't need the list. Their names were engraved on his heart for ever, but he appreciated the gravitas of an official document as well as the bolster to his resolve to remain unmoved by her.

'Allow me to tell you about them. Let's start with Customs Officer Richard Pruitt. His throat was cut when he boarded one of your ships before Christmas last. He is survived by his wife and three small daughters, none of whom are old enough to remember their brave father.' Flint refused to look at her to see if his words had hit their mark.

'Then there was Corporal Henry Edwards and young Jack Bright of the Essex militia, who likely stumbled across a boat unloading while doing their routine night patrol of the sea wall at Canvey Island. I say likely as we'll never know what happened, except to say with some certainty that your smugglers garrotted both and tossed their bodies over the wall into the estuary. Edwards washed up on the beach in Southend a few days later. Bright's rotting corpse served as fish food for three weeks before he floated up the Thames to be found bobbing in Tilbury dock. One had a fiancée, the other an aged mother who relied on his income.' A quick glance showed that her face had blanched, but she still met his gaze dead on. 'Shall I continue?'

She shrugged and turned her head away from his gaze. 'You will do as you please. No doubt.'

'You have blood on your hands, Lady Jessamine.'

Her mouth opened as if to speak, then clamped shut, her eyes now fixated on a spot on the floor. Temper had him reeling off three more names just as coldly. Each was met with stoic silence. Her body was as still as a statue and her composure just as hard. 'Are you proud of yourself, Lady Jessamine? Do you feel no shame for what you have done? No compassion for the lives you have destroyed? The widows and innocent children left bereft and impoverished by your greed and avarice?'

Her head whipped around and those untrustworthy eyes were swimming with unshed tears. 'You know nothing about me, Monsieur Flint! Nothing! And I shall tell you nothing. You can name every dead man. Every member of his family. Blame me for every travesty. And I shall reward you with my silence. My secrets are mine to take to the grave! A grave I am fully aware I might lie in soon.'

One fat tear trickled over her ridiculously long and dark lower lashes and dripped down her cheek. Flint had seen enough female tears to be unaffected, but the matter-of-fact way she swiped it away and proudly set her shoulders got to him.

His words had hurt her. Deeply. He knew it with the same certainty that he knew his own mind. Lady Jessamine had a conscience. Something he didn't want to know. 'Tell me his name.'

Her eyes lifted to his. They were miserable. 'I don't know it. I am just the messenger.' And, God help him, against Lord Fennimore's voice screaming in his head, Flint believed her.

'You're lying.' Of course she was—Flint had now changed his opinion. Behind the beautiful, deceitful face, she had a soul as black as pitch and blood on her hands.

Her eyes drifted back to the riveting spot on the floor and her slim shoulders slumped for the first time since he had seen her. 'Have it your way. You will regardless.'

Alone, in the relative privacy of her cell, Jess fought the tears. Hearing those names, imagining every man and picturing his family, literally broke her heart. *Ah, quelle horreur!* She had always known the smugglers were ruthless, known deep down that there were others suffering worse than she was, but personalising it made those dark, shadowy, distant thoughts starkly real. She hated Lord Flint for holding the mirror up to her face and forcing her to acknowledge the gravity of it all. For the last year she had loathed herself. Hated what she was forced to do and hated that she continued to bend to Saint-Aubin's will because she was weak. For the whole time she had plotted and schemed and tried to fight back, only to cave in when the blind terror overtook her and she begged for mercy.

Of course, Lord Flint would see her eventual acquiescence as guilt. To him, she supposed her involvement made her a traitor—and perhaps now she knew the full extent of what she had unwittingly been involved in, perhaps she was. There *was* blood on her hands. She hadn't known that before.

It didn't matter that every message she had written had been done under extreme duress or that she had been oblivious to the full extent of her mother's treachery until it was too late to flee. Or that Saint-Aubin had specific and horrific punishments which had broken her resolve to resist. She should have been braver. Stronger. Resolute despite the brutal punishment he was prone to dish out. Whether she had or hadn't committed outright treason—and she still desperately wanted to believe she hadn't—those tragic names would haunt her for the rest of her days. Days which frankly would be significantly numbered unless she could escape this boat and the hateful Lord Flint who had just broken her heart.

Sitting here, feeling sorry for herself, wasn't going to make that happen. Nor was it going to change the past or bring those poor men back. To learn she had been unwittingly responsible for murder was a terrible burden she would have to carry for ever. It added to the deep well of self-loathing that festered within. She could weep for them every night once she had her freedom. Search out their families and send them money—not that she had any—but she would earn it and she would share it with them. Make amends as best she could. Right now she could not indulge her sadness or her guilt. Right now she had to plan, because if Saint-Aubin caught her then his revenge didn't bear thinking about—and she knew without a doubt she couldn't bear it again. Because despite all the talk, all the bravado and all the defiance, she wasn't strong enough—and he knew it. Jess ruthlessly set aside the spectre of that retribution and forced her mind to focus.

When the guards had first come to fetch her earlier, Jess had purposely sauntered to Lord Flint's cabin. She had gazed at the clear blue sky, sniffed the sea breeze and trailed her fingers lazily along the wooden railings. In part it had been purposeful dawdling—her rebellious nature wouldn't give anyone the satisfaction of seeing her jump to attention—but she was also taking careful stock. The size of the deck, the number of sailors, the position of the openings used for the gangplanks. When she had been brought on board bound, kicking and screaming, it had been dark. The frantic scan she'd made then had been superficial and she didn't trust it to save her skin when the time came to run—or swim. Jess needed to be prepared for every eventuality should an opportunity to escape present itself.

Several seamen, shirtless and dressed in only the striped breeches from their uniforms in deference to the glorious spring sunshine, paused in their work to watch her. Jess memorised every interested face as she purposely undulated past, maintaining eye contact with the boldest with the knowing half-smile she had often seen her ridiculously beautiful mother deploy to great effect. Jess wasn't averse to flirting her way to freedom, not when it had proved to be an invaluable tool already. She might have little in common with the woman who had birthed her, then selfishly ripped her from her life and plunged her into a new world of war and danger, but if everyone who had known her then and commented upon it was to be believed, Jess was the spitting image.

Before her polite interrogation had begun, she had also memorised the layout of his cabin.

It was spacious and bright and airy. Two large windows flooded the space with light. Windows which had hinges and latches and opened on to the ocean. Windows she could just about fit through. All she needed to do was think of a way to be alone with one of those windows before the ship reached its destination.

That created a whole new problem.

Jess had been denied knowledge of the port they were headed to now they had finally left Cherbourg, so had no idea how long the crossing would take. She also had no way of correctly knowing the time without asking the guards. After her indulgent long bath and painful visit with the emotionless Mr Flint, all she could estimate with some certainty was that several hours had passed since they had set sail.

From what she recalled of the journey all those years ago when she had been dragged to France, it had taken for ever. But a child's concept of time was very different from an adult's. She knew Saint-Aubin's ships made the crossing easily overnight, leaving in the early evening, unloading in the small hours when it was less likely they would be seen and blithely returning home during the morning. If one bore that in mind, she was now probably closer to English waters than French. She needed a plan immediately.

* * *

Half an hour and much pacing later she called for the guards. 'I wish to speak to Monsieur Flint. *Tout de suite!* Take me to him!'

'I can fetch him.' The toothless sailor folded his arms belligerently. 'Then again perhaps I can't. I don't take orders from you, traitor.'

'Suit yourself. But I shall tell his lordship you refused to allow him to hear my confession when we dock. I doubt he will take it well. He is an important man, *non*? One your Captain takes orders from…'

As she had hoped the man scurried off and several fraught minutes ticked by before he returned. 'Lord Flint will see you in his cabin.'

Jess stood patiently while the sailor unlocked the bars and allowed him to grab her upper arm without tugging it away or complaining. Only her complete compliance would lull him into a false sense of security. That and the shameless display of flesh on show. She had rolled up the breeches to sit on her knee. All the spare fabric in the billowing shirt had been gathered up so that her figure was on full show and the upper swells of her breasts were clearly visible above the wide V of the open collar. He had allowed her to linger on the deck the last time because his shipmates had enjoyed the spectacle of a scantily clad woman. For her plan to succeed, she needed to be a spectacle once again.

He climbed the steep steps first and offered his hand down the hatch to assist her. She took it with her mother's smile, making sure she emerged into the late afternoon sunlight gracefully. Then took a moment to stretch.

Men were such predictable creatures. Every eye swivelled to her, raking her body up and down. Some had the good grace to be surreptitious. Most openly ogled. One bold seaman winked and she winked back, causing much bawdy laughter and back slapping. To them she was sport and did not deserve the gentlemanly good manners reserved for ladies. One or two made rude gestures in the air, miming what they would like to do to her. Beyond, the Captain and his officers joined in the laughter. They wanted to humiliate her, too.

That was fine by Jess. Humiliation had gone hand in hand with incarceration for over a year, yet they had all failed to crush her soul. For this next bit to work, she needed them to be lusty dogs.

A burly man near the rail played right into her hands. 'If you get lonesome down in the brig or fancy making it your last request, I'd be happy to keep you company.' He raised his eyebrows suggestively. 'A decent bit of English might do you good after all those Frenchies.' He bucked his hips, the message clear.

She let her eyes take in the broad chest and muscled, folded arms before shrugging off her toothless chaperon and walking slowly towards him.

'What is your name, handsome?'

Chapter Three

Flint heard the whooping and catcalling and shot to his feet. Whatever she had done, he couldn't sit by and allow the crew to abuse her like that. He was still riddled with misplaced guilt for reminding her she would be hanged. There had been genuine terror in her lovely eyes then and that fear, and the knowledge he had put it there, did not make him feel like much of a man. His fingers reached the door handle the same moment the noises beyond changed from bawdy to shocked, as the laughter quickly turned to what sounded like blind panic.

He strode on deck into chaos. The entire crew seemed to have simultaneously run starboard. All along the rail, men clamoured to peer over the edge. Those that couldn't find a spot ran left and right like startled deer. 'What the blazes is going on?' He caught the arm of an officer.

'The prisoner has escaped!'

As they were in the middle of the English Channel it didn't take a genius to work out where the minx had escaped to. Even so, Flint pushed his way to the rail and was rewarded with the sight of Lady Jessamine speeding through the waves. The blasted woman swam like a fish.

Next to him, he could hear the Captain issuing rapid orders. A couple of sailors were in the midst of lowering a rowing boat. Another was untangling the ladder to toss over the side. Someone else was hunting down rope. She had caught them on the hop and now the lot of them were behaving like headless chickens without a single working brain between them. Meanwhile, she was putting some serious distance between herself and the frigate.

On a withering sigh, Flint shrugged out of his coat and tugged off his boots. Catching her was the first priority. He'd worry about getting her back on the boat afterwards. As soon as the last button was undone on his waistcoat he dragged himself to sit atop the rail to stare in disgust at the briny water below. Lord, how he loathed sea bathing. The lauded benefits of salt water never outweighed the awfulness of the experience. It stung the eyes and tasted foul. Almost as foul as the knowledge that she was in the sea in the first place because he had been soft. Damned woman. That would teach him to feel mercy towards the vixen. She was every inch the duplicitous, self-serving, self-centred, untrustworthy traitor he knew her to be. Another harsh lesson learned.

The icy water came as a shock, robbing him of the ability to breathe for long moments until he acclimatised. Then he set off after the veritable mermaid in the distance, his anger at both of them propelling him more effectively than the inept sailors in the wobbling dinghy could row. She was fast, but thanks to his strong arms and longer legs he was faster. Despite that, it took him a good ten minutes to come within twenty feet of her.

Sensing someone close by, she turned and then panicked, breaking her stroke to cough up the wave she had accidentally swallowed. Flint used it to try to talk some sense into her.

'This is pointless. Land is a good five miles away!'

Undeterred, she set off again, her bare feet splashing wildly as she kicked for all she was worth. Twice he came within a hair's breadth of one and twice she evaded his grasping fingers. On the third attempt, he caught her ankle and earned a kick in the stomach that winded him and made him swallow a mouthful of seawater as well. It was then that his anger turned into outright rage and he lunged once more, plunging them both underwater, but this time he wrapped his arm tightly around her waist and held her firmly against his body.

'*Salaud!* Let go of me!'

She wriggled like a hooked salmon and was twice as slippery. Her flailing knee came within inches of his groin before he twisted her out of the way. Backwards she was marginally less dangerous, but only marginally. She lashed out, using her nails like claws, scraping them hard whenever they encountered him. Her black hair, floating on the surface like seaweed, felt like a whip as it lashed repeatedly against his face. 'Hold still, damn it!' The hand he was using to help keep them both afloat joined the other around her body, pinning her arms against her ribs. Still she fought him.

'English pig! *Imbécile! Tout ça ne sert à rien!*'

'We are both going to drown!'

'At least I will take you with me!'

Flint managed to move his hand a split second before her teeth clamped around it and tilted his weight so that she was lying on her back down the length of his body. Then, with the last strength he possessed, he kicked towards the rowboat.

It took the three of them to get her into the thing as it rocked dangerously from side to side. Once they did, he happily allowed one of the sailors to tie her hands behind her back while the other restrained her. There was no telling what damage the wench could do in such a confined space otherwise. Tethered and impotent, that riotous mane of hair plastered all over her face and shoulders, she began snarling and insulting them, alternating seamlessly between French and English as they rowed back to the ship. He got the gist. He was an idiot and he would die.

'We'll winch her up.' It struck him as a simpler solution than coaxing her up the rope ladder. The fact that it served to send her into an outraged rant after she had made a fool of him was a bonus that went some way to making Flint feel better. If she had been a man, he would have punched her back there in the water and dragged her sorry, unconscious carcass back. Because she was a woman, and he couldn't seem to get over that inconvenient yet ultimately minor detail no matter how hard he tried, he had suffered every blow—and there had been rather a lot of them. The saltwater was stinging the numerous scratches her nails had gouged in his hands and arms, his throat was raw, his eyes rawer and his ribs hurt like the devil. He would add feral to the growing list of adjectives he already had to describe her, alongside traitorous, beautiful and infuriating.

Flint sat back in the rocking boat to steady it and happily allowed the others to wrestle the rope around her middle, then saluted her as she was lifted kicking and screaming out of the boat.

She was going to be a handful.

Typical, really. He spent his life trying to avoid feminine histrionics and manipulations, yet fate kept throwing them at him regardless. At least he would be shot of this one within the week. He was stuck with his exasperating family for life.

The cheer from the deck signalled her safe arrival and was closely followed by another tirade of insults, this time all in French. Despite the fruity tone, Flint preferred the French. Her voice was seductive. Breathy and earthy. If he let it, the sultry sound made the hairs on the back of his neck and forearms stand to attention in a wholly pleasant way. Something he was determined to quash indignantly. He didn't deal well with difficult and emotional females. Aside from the obvious obstacle of her impending date with the hangman, he preferred his women sedate and calm. Like a mill pond. If he were to compare *her* to water, Lady Jessamine Fane was akin to the crashing waves on the rocky Cornish coastline near his home in winter. Unpredictable, noisy and very, very dangerous.

The men were now jeering above him. The whistles and inappropriate comments were getting out of hand. She didn't deserve that. Nobody did. Until he was shot of her, she was his responsibility and he wouldn't see her abused— verbally or otherwise. With a weary sigh he climbed the ladder. The crew had circled around her, baying like wolves tempted with the scent of fresh blood. The rope they had hoisted her with was still wrapped around her body and held firmly by the belligerent toothless sailor who had been appointed her guard. The malicious glint in the fellow's eye sickened Flint. To be a bully was bad enough. To bully a helpless woman was deplorable.

'Stop.'

He didn't shout or snarl. The icy stare he had perfected in his youth when his womenfolk had pushed him too far always served him well. He shoved himself past the wall of men to stand in the circle. 'Does this make you all feel better? Does humiliating a shackled woman make you feel proud?'

Flint allowed his gaze to slowly meet every pair of eyes. Most dipped in shame. He turned and purposely glared at the Captain who had been lounging against the rail with his arms crossed, a laughing spectator who should know better. 'Deal with your crew. They are a disgrace, Captain.' He let his expression convey the fact that he also lumped the officers in with that criticism.

Couldn't they see that beneath all the shouting she was terrified and cold? Her slim body was quaking with the force of her shivers. 'Might I remind you all that we serve the Crown and we do so with honour. A crown that prides itself on its adherence to the doctrine of *habeas corpus*. The prisoner is presumed innocent until she stands trial and all the evidence has been heard. Until such a time as that happens, she will be afforded the same respect as any other *human being* on board this ship. It is not your place to be judge and jury, nor is it ever appropriate to treat a woman like an animal.'

He snatched the line of rope from the toothless sailor's hand and untied it, then gently led her by the elbow through the parting line of subdued men as the embarrassed Captain began issuing a litany of orders. For once, she came quietly and waited patiently for him to open the cabin door before quickly rushing through it to sanctuary.

'Thank you…for that.'

So, there were manners beneath all that pithy hostility? Oddly, he would have preferred there weren't. Manners made her likeable and likeable was dangerous. He nodded curtly and made a show of locking the door behind him and pocketing the key. Only then did he go to the bonds still on her wrists and untie them. It wasn't an easy task. In the struggle, the men had caught the over-long sleeves of the linen shirt she wore in with the rope and both materials were now hopelessly knotted together. As soon as they were free she instinctively lifted her arms to rub the area. One of the sleeves dropped to her elbow, revealing a band of scarred red skin encircling her wrist. It had been irritated by the rope, but not caused by it. She saw him stare at it and hastily covered it before standing proudly to meet his eye.

'You are not the first man to imprison me, Monsieur Flint, but you will be the last.'

Probably true. Once Flint delivered her to Newgate she wouldn't have long left. The charges were drawn. They had witnesses, albeit dubious ones. Conclusive evidence. The trial, at this stage, only a formality. Still, he hated seeing the signs of mistreatment on her body. A body that was still shivering violently. 'If it is any consolation, my lady, I am as reluctant to be your gaoler as you are to be my prisoner. Let's try to make the best of it.'

'By that, you mean you want me to comply and not try to escape again? I can't promise that.'

'Nor would I in your position. Unfortunately, as I am in charge, I have no intention of allowing you to do so.'

'*C'est la vie*. Then I suspect the next few days

will be interesting—*non*?' As she spoke she unconsciously reached up to gather her sopping hair to one side, wringing it out like wet washing matter of factly. The thin wet linen stretched taut over her body, almost transparent and leaving little to his imagination. Dark pebbled nipples shifted slightly as she moved. His instant physical reaction angered him. That she had done it on purpose angered him more.

'I won't be seduced as easily as those sailors.' But damn him, he was. Just as with that prisoner all those years ago, her blatant femininity affected him. She was like a siren. That voice. That body. That fiery spirit.

'Seduced?' She appeared genuinely baffled until he gestured to her full breasts with his eyes. Like the consummate actress she was, Lady Jessamine did an excellent job of being mortified and instantly clamped her arms tightly over her chest.

More shaken by his reaction than he cared to admit, Flint stalked to the washstand and grabbed a towel. He tossed it to her unceremoniously and then rummaged in his own bag for dry clothes. He'd scarce packed enough for his own use, but figured the more he covered that delectable, ripe body with the better. Breeches, another shirt and a waistcoat were a good start. A large sack and a thick eiderdown might be better, although he already knew the image of those dusky nipples would be seared on his brain for ever. An image a man who had to put duty before all else, who knew only too well the dire consequences, had to ignore. 'Put these on!'

For good measure, he took himself to the other side of the cabin and, because he had no idea how to behave without appearing riddled with unfathomable need, stood with his hands planted on his hips, hoping he looked unimpressed and in control rather than suddenly consumed with unwanted lust.

'Do you intend to watch me?' Her eyes were wide and that sultry, accented voice a little high-pitched. When he didn't move, those dark eyes became darker and convincingly sad to purposely manipulate him. '*Ah.* I see. Everything you said out there was a lie. I am not to be afforded the basic dignities of a human being after all.' Once again she stood proudly. Five feet of shivering, strangely noble femininity that did weird things to his emotions. He wanted to protect her. Why? 'These wet clothes will do well enough, I think.'

The unspoken insinuation stung. 'Unlike you, I don't lie, Lady Jessamine. I meant every word I said to those men. While in my charge, I will respect your right to dignity and no harm will come to you. Not of my making anyway. But I am not your friend. Nor will I be manipulated like those fools out there, or succumb to your wiles and you would do well to remember that, too. Do not confuse basic decency with stupidity. The best you can expect from me is indifference.' He fished in his pocket for the key and turned to the door. 'Get changed. We dock within the hour.'

Slamming it behind him made Flint feel marginally better. He locked it and marched away in search of dry clothes. He'd been so flummoxed by the sight of her, so ashamed that she had basically accused him of being a hypocritical voyeur, he hadn't had the wherewithal to collect any for himself. It took him less than ten minutes to dry and dress, and by the time he strode back across the deck the ship was once again back on course and riding effortlessly across the waves, the Devon coastline looming large on the horizon.

The Captain beckoned to him, clearly intent on making amends for the gross dereliction of his duty and supremely aware that Flint worked for Lord Fennimore—a man with not only the ear of the First Lord of the Admiralty, but the King as well.

'Despite our little detour, we should still reach Plymouth before the afternoon tide turns, Lord Flint.'

Little detour! The captain had allowed his men to abuse the vixen while he had stood by and watched the entertainment. If the shocking innuendo and insulting whistling Flint had only just witnessed coming from the crew were anything to go by, Lady Jessamine had been violated twice this hour alone. It was hardly a surprise she had flung herself over the side. How much more had she endured in the five days before he'd arrived? The woman was a walking advertisement for gross mistreatment. Those bruises on her arms were fresh. The marks on her wrists were old…

'Still—no harm done, eh? We've been at sea months. Seemed cruel to deny the men a bit of sport.'

'Do you have a wife, Captain? A mother? Sisters?' Flint's tone was bland and measured. Those that knew him well, knew that was always when his temper was closest to the surface.

'All three, Lord Flint—but we're not comparing like with like, now, are we? She's naught but a traitor and deserves all that's coming to her.'

'*If* she's found guilty!' Despite all the evidence to the contrary, a little nagging voice in his head wanted to believe she wasn't guilty. In all likelihood it stemmed from his own disgust at finding himself overwhelmingly attracted to a criminal once again and attempting to justify the attraction by attributing noble qualities to her that she did not truly possess. Even so, there was still something in her eyes and the proud set of her shoulders. Something that called to his heart and his head. Either that, or at her contrived behest the contents of his breeches had taken over all rational thought—which made him little better than the entire ship's crew. Unpalatable food for thought. 'Until such time as that happens, she will be treated with the respect and consideration due her. Keeping her in the dark, in that festering brig, allowing your men to be rough with her and talk to her like a harlot is not what I, and no doubt the rest of our illustrious superiors, expect from the Royal Navy!' He turned on his heel and left the Captain standing with his mouth hanging slack at his furious tone.

The toothless guard snapped to attention as he approached his cabin.

'What's your name, sailor?'

'Foyle, sir... I mean your lordship.'

'You are dismissed, Foyle.'

'But I've been assigned to keep watch over the traitor till we make port. You've seen for yourself how wily she is. There's no telling what she'll do without a constant watch on her. Them's the Captain's orders...'

'As I outrank the Captain on this voyage, take it from me you are not only dismissed, but you will confine yourself below deck until *Lady Jessamine* is safely off this ship. Until then, I will be her only guard.' Because it went without saying, Flint was the only man within a mile he trusted with the task. He might well be overwhelmed with unwanted attraction, but at least he knew exactly what she was about and would never fall for it.

'But, sir...'

'Thanks to your negligence, she escaped. I could have you court-martialled for that alone. Get below deck and spare me the sight of you else I change my mind!'

The sailor didn't need to be told twice and practically ran away. Flint took a moment to compose himself, then politely tapped on the door. 'Lady Jessamine, are you decent?'

No reply.

He knocked again, louder this time, and when he heard not so much as a movement in the cabin beyond began to feel uneasy. She wouldn't? Couldn't, surely? His fingers fumbled with the key and Flint flung open the door. The spacious cabin was silent save the gentle lapping of the waves against the hull. One of the tiny windows was wide open, a knotted rope of sheets, blankets and Flint's own spare breeches dangled from the ledge where they had been secured and flapped in the sea breeze.

Chapter Four

With the beach now firmly in her sights, Jess began to relax. For a little while the turning tide and her own newly crushing guilt had almost beaten her and sent her careening towards the rocks, but she had fought it like she fought everything and escaped a foamy death by the skin of her gritted teeth and through sheer stubborn determination.

She'd lost sight of her floating prison long ago as that same tide had taken her briskly around the rocky headland and sheltered her from sight. Only then had she removed the makeshift turban she had fashioned out of a green-velvet cushion cover and that had undoubtedly helped her dark head to blend into the vast expanse of ocean. Close up, she was a ridiculous woman with a cushion on her head. From a distance she was merely one of the many kaleidoscope colours that made up the English Channel.

Later she would take a moment to selfishly congratulate herself, right now she had to drag her exhausted body to the beach and find a place to hide. The last few months, and Saint-Aubin's cruelty, had taken a toll on her body and, despite religiously exercising every day in her cell to maintain her fitness should an opportunity present itself, the laboured swim had pushed her to the limits of her endurance.

Every stroke made the muscles in her arms and legs scream in rebellion. The partially healed welts on her back stung thanks to the salt water. Even her lungs hurt—but she was free. That heady feeling superseded all others and spurred her on. When her feet finally scraped shingle, she stood gratefully and, with the last of her severely depleted energy, dragged her aching body the last few yards, then collapsed exhausted on her knees to catch her breath before the next leg of her journey. She daren't hang around too long. Lord Flint would be furious when he realised she had duped him and would have that ship sailing up and down the coastline searching for her.

Jess allowed herself a triumphant smile which slowly slid off her face when she took in her surroundings.

Incroyable!

The isolated and tiny beach she had washed up on was secluded. It had that in its favour.

But little else. The ragged rock formations she had seen at a distance were enormous close up and ringed her tiny bay, effectively cutting it off from everything else. Walls of solid rock loomed menacingly. The crescent cliff jutted out to sea at both ends, meaning to leave she either had to take her chances with the crashing waves again and swim around them or forge on ahead and scale the craggy wall in front of her.

As it wasn't a sheer cliff, more a haphazard collection of giant boulders on top of one another, climbing seemed the lesser of two evils. But with no rope to aid her and a life-long fear of falling to her death making her dizzy, it was only marginally less dangerous. Gelatinous, slimy seaweed coated every surface, waiting to send her careening to the ground. Aside from ignoring the fear, she would need a great deal of strength to achieve it. The muscles in her arms and legs were quivering from the exertion of her frantic swim and the dangerous, powerful waves which had done their level best to smash her against this very cliff. Jess had nothing left to climb a mountain—and these jagged rocks might as well be a mountain in her current state. They clearly displayed an obvious waterline, telling her in no uncertain terms that this narrow beach wouldn't exist when the tide turned and she would be at the mercy of the sea again—probably very soon.

The sudden urge to succumb to tears had her crumpling into a ball.

She was petrified of heights.

The thought of them left her paralysed and shaking.

Rationally she knew that fear stemmed from breaking her ribs after falling out of a tree at the tender age of twelve shortly after being displaced in France. She also knew that it wasn't so much the fall that was responsible for this persistent phobia, but the dreadful way Saint-Aubin exploited that fear afterwards. In her youth, whenever she became too rebellious, he would drag her to the roof of the chateau and use his superior strength to lean her over the ledge precariously until she promised never to defy him again. Finding a twisted and perverted delight in hearing her beg for mercy and confessing how much she feared him. Later, in Cherbourg… Involuntarily she shuddered. The beatings… The window. Saint-Aubin's mocking laughter at her fear, reminding her he would happily allow her to plunge to her death the moment she ceased to be useful or dared to defy his express instructions.

While she gave the guards the run around and defied them for as long as she was physically and mentally able, it didn't take long for her to selfishly surrender to just the beating from

Saint-Aubin, pathetically confessing that nothing in the world scared her more than him. In case he truly did send her tumbling to her death while in the grip of his all-consuming and blood-thirsty temper.

Now that she knew for certain men had died because of that weakness, did that make her a traitor? Was she more like her self-centred mother than she realised.

Now there was a comparison she had never imagined possible—that like her mother Jess had eventually complied for an easier life.

She quashed the errant thought ruthlessly as she vowed to ignore the irrational way the fear of the cliff set her legs a-quiver and her stomach lurching.

She wasn't a traitor. Not intentionally at least. And she would make amends for all her unwitting crimes, because they were unwitting and the alternative had been her own demise when her soul internally screamed she deserved to live. Just once she wished luck or God would favour her. Just once! Was that too much to ask after all the obstacles she'd had thrown in her path? All the ordeals and pain she had been subjected to. It wasn't fair!

It wasn't fair!

But whining and wailing about it was pointless. She swiped the tears away angrily. Self-pity wouldn't get her out of this mess. Neither would luck. Jess would simply have to do what she always did and endure. She hadn't come this far to fall at the last obstacle. Going up was much easier than going down, because going up meant not having to look down. Down was her nemesis after all. It wasn't that high and once the cliff had been climbed then she truly would be free and clear.

Which was all she had ever wanted.

Wearily, she stood and wrung the seawater out of her hair, then spent a few minutes squeezing it out of her clothes. By her best guess it was late afternoon, so there were many hours of daylight left, which in turn meant she could put a good few miles of road between her and the sea before nightfall as soon as she had conquered her irrational fears. Focusing on what came after might lessen the nerves.

With no idea where exactly she was and no destination in mind, common sense told her she would need to stick to the small lanes and paths rather than the main roads. From somewhere she would need to procure a hat to disguise her waist-length hair. A woman in breeches was probably still a scandalous sight in England and with her slight frame and distinct lack of height, there was a good chance she could pass for a boy. Lord Flint's fine silk waistcoat now protected her modesty, so there was no chance of inadvertently flashing her bosoms to anyone else who happened upon her. Jess was still mortified that he had seen them—or most of them. The wet linen left little to the imagination.

Of course, he had been nonplussed, the horrid man. The brief flash of temper she had witnessed when he had caught her in the water was swiftly buried under his emotionless, aristocratic expression back on deck. Only his stormy green eyes gave any indication of his mood. He didn't like her, hardly a surprise, and found her an inconvenience. But he had been kinder than anyone had in a long time and that alone made her predisposed to like him a little bit even though she hated him with a vengeance, too.

Jess turned a slow circle and considered the best route out. Neither end of the tiny bay looked better, so she went with instinct and took the one beyond the foaming rocks she had battled to swim around. The initial boulders were worn smooth by the sea, allowing her to climb tentatively up several feet before the ragged, smaller rocks above stalled her pace. Although considerably less slippery, they were sharp and chiselled nicks in her skin if she stepped on one incorrectly. She didn't dare look down, or up, or even side to side, knowing that focusing on the solid wall in front of her was the sight least likely to send her head spinning and her stomach lurching. Using her small hands wedged between the crevices or the occasional tenacious clump of coarse foliage, Jess was able to take some of the weight of her body from her feet, but not much. The saltwater dripping from her sodden breeches infiltrated the cuts and added to the pain. She ignored it. Onwards and upwards towards better things.

Midway, well past the ominous waterline, she paused on a flattened ledge and risked a brief gaze out to sea, making sure her eyes never dipped down. Still no sign of the frigate or Lord Flint. Either he had yet to discover she was missing or they had taken the direct route to land and were miles shy of her position. Perhaps God had heard her prayers and had sent the powerful currents to save her? Both things made her smile and as a reward Jess allowed herself five minutes of rest which then gave her a burst of physical and mental strength to continue upwards.

She could do this!

The final stretch was steep but easier, thanks to a thick blanket of grass which covered the rock that now gently tapered to form a hill rather than a sheer cliff. The ground beneath her feet was now reassuringly solid again.

Another blessing in a life sadly devoid of them. Finally, her time had come to escape and it felt marvellous. The cuts on her feet would heal, the scars on her heart would fade and maybe one day she would know what it felt like to *not* be terrified all the time. A staggering possibility that was becoming reassuringly more real, despite the dreadful height, with every laboured step.

As she left the sea behind, it appeared she had found the most deserted bit of England to land on. A narrow spit that jutted out to sea, completely devoid of buildings or even a path to suggest somebody occasionally visited. Another of today's fine blessings that she didn't have time to enjoy, but one day in the future she would venture back here with a picnic and simply sit and take in all the spartan beauty properly. The only signs of life not plant based were the many sea birds that swooped along the shore line and nested in the cliff.

Jess was all alone and free.

For the first time in years!

That giddy realisation caused a tiny bubble of laughter to escape her throat. She'd done it! Against all the odds and solely using her own wits and sheer damned stubbornness, she had escaped both Saint-Aubin and the British Navy. The laughter wouldn't stop, so she took herself well away from the terrifying edge and threw her head back, allowing it free rein. A minute of indulgence. Surely she had earned that?

'There she is!'

The shout from above caused her heart to stop. *Ce n'est pas possible!* But it was.

Lord Flint crested the top of the hill and was closely followed by most of the crew from the ship. The tears came then as her throat closed with the pain of defeat, like the hangman's noose choking the last vestiges of hope and all of her foolish dreams. What did God have against her? Could he not see this was all so unfair? Or did he not care? Was her soul indelibly stained with the sins of her mother and her own weaknesses despite her best efforts to make amends? Just once, she wished that God would help her. But, of course, he didn't. Because she was on her own.

Always had been.

Her wits returned in a whoosh to counter the blind panic, her head whipping from side to side to find the best escape route. She had got this far without help and she was not dead yet! Jess wouldn't allow it. The sea of grass and gorse and sailors was the only way out, unless she threw herself over the rocks behind her.

'Fan out, men! We have her cornered!'

Sadly true, but Jess had come too far to give

up all hope now. Like a banshee she launched herself forward. If she could just get past them…

She used her shoulder, hunched low, to barrel into the first man, then simply kept on running, darting sideways to avoid the grasping hands of another. Like sheep, they began to herd together and follow her, closing the distance with each stride of their legs, yet still Jess ran. Her lungs burned and she could hear nothing over the sounds of her rapid heartbeat.

Someone grabbed her collar and tugged, pulling her backwards on to the ground. The strong smell of cabbage announced her assailant better than words. For him, her capture would be intensely personal. Jess twisted in an attempt to loosen his firm grip a split second before the back of his meaty hand cracked across her jaw and stars exploded behind her eyes. After that, despite all her best efforts, she could barely keep them open.

There were shouts.

Just one man shouting.

He was angry.

Livid.

'You bastard!'

Jess heard another crack, then a dull thud. Through a fog she saw the toothless sailor lying flat on his back next to her, groaning.

Faces.

Many faces. From the past and from the grave. Her mother. Her long-forgotten father. The innocent men she had unintentionally sent to their slaughter…but only one pair of eyes. Green like the grass she lay on. Very green.

Gentle hands brushed over her forehead.

'Jessamine? Can you hear me? Can you…?' Jess felt another tear leak out of her eye and drizzle down her cheek. She didn't have any fight left to stop it.

It was all so tragically unfair, but maybe fully deserved.

Her dark eyes had fluttered open and she stared into his briefly before she passed out. A bruise already marred her perfect cheek and a tiny trickle of blood oozed from the cut on her lip. Both piqued his rage and made Flint want to pummel the toothless sailor for daring to take his hand to a woman. Then he had momentarily lost control, something he rarely did, and sent the fellow flying before rushing to her aid.

Now, with her dark hair fanned out on the snowy white pillowcase and her face pale, those fresh bruises stood out in stark relief alongside the dark shadows he now saw beneath her closed eyes. In slumber, Lady Jessamine looked nothing like the calculating traitor or the confrontational termagant who had showered him in stale bread.

She looked vulnerable and alone and painfully delicate.

Except she wasn't delicate. Far from it.

It took physical and mental strength to swim close to two miles of the English Channel, fight the current and crashing waves and then scale a small cliff barefoot and, God help him, a large part of him admired her for that. She was desperate to live and who could blame her? Were he facing a date with the hangman, Flint would doubtless react in a similar manner and would fight for his life till his dying breath. Hell, he'd even swim the channel to get back to safety if push came to shove.

The utter devastation on her face when they found her again was not something that he could easily forget either. Guilt had been his first reaction before he'd ruthlessly corrected his emotions, but the weight of that guilt still lingered and plagued him. Obviously misplaced. After all, Flint had a weakness for a pretty face and a sultry pair of eyes. Lady Jessamine had both and used them mercilessly to get her own way.

Those emotive eyes had tricked him once already. The more he thought about it, the more her initial escape from the boat seemed gallingly like a preamble. During questioning, she must have spotted the only unguarded route of escape in his cabin and then what followed had been a contrived way to get back in that cabin and be left all alone.

'I am not to be afforded the basic dignities of a human being after all.' Those manipulative and mournful eyes had brought shame on him when he should have planted his feet firmly, shrugged and informed her that prisoners did not have the right to privacy, so she could change in his presence or remain dripping wet.

Lady Jessamine had used his chivalrous nature against him and then left him to look like the biggest of fools in front of the entire crew. Once bitten, twice shy…yet his whole being was at odds with his level head and wanted those traitorous eyes to be telling the truth.

When they had tracked her down on top of the cliff, the disbelief and the horror which had skittered across her features before she appeared to glance heavenwards in exasperation had bothered him. Still bothered him nearly three hours later, truth be told, because just one solitary tear had rolled heavily down her cheek. Flint had watched her swipe it away defiantly as she refused to surrender, almost as if she was embarrassed to be vulnerable, despite the fact it was obvious escape was futile and she was clearly exhausted.

The second fat tear had unmanned him and he had felt compelled to brush it gently away with his thumb before he began issuing orders to have her battered and prone body moved. Flint had carried her the first mile himself before men arrived with the stretcher, her slight body unhealthily slim in places beneath his hands, yet her heartbeat against his own was strong and steady and determined.

It called to him and the proud memory of it held him still. Flint hadn't left her bedside, claiming that he was responsible for the prisoner, when in truth he had needed to stand guard over her to ensure that no more harm came to her. What the hell was that about?

Although it didn't take a genius to work out she had come to harm before and not just from the heavy-handed sailors on the ship. After the innkeeper's wife had undressed her and swaddled her in a clean nightrail, Flint returned with the doctor. He had asked the physician about the red scars on her wrists, although he knew, deep down, what had made them. Manacles. There had been another similar, yet considerably faded band on one of her ankles, too. At some point in the not so distant past, Lady Jessamine had been chained to something. By whom or why he had no idea. A rival gang of smugglers? Ruthless gangs wouldn't care if she was a man or a woman. All they would care about was stealing the bounty, something she was undoubtedly guilty of. Except…

He shook his head, annoyed at the overwhelming need to be chivalrous and magnanimous over the more pressing constraints of his mission, and paced to the window rather than continuing to stare at her in concern. After years of chasing the worst sort of criminals, after he had nearly lost his father to a villainess's bullet, he should be able to differentiate between a traitor and a woman. A traitor was a traitor no matter what body they happened to occupy. All his training, experience and deep-set beliefs were screaming at him. *Remember the mission. Always remember the mission.* A mantra which he fundamentally adhered to and believed in with every fibre of his being. Unfortunately, mission aside and as the only brother to five women, he couldn't overrule the instinct to protect one. Even though she probably didn't deserve it. Something he would do well to remember if he was going to complete this particular mission.

A mission that was now delayed, the well-laid plans hastily adapted to accommodate this unforeseen change in circumstances. That couldn't be helped. The life of a spy was unpredictable at the best of times and Flint prided himself on his adaptability and his meticulous ability to plan. Their route to Plymouth would be a little more convoluted and they would arrive a few hours late, but they would arrive and would still take the main road to London as planned. If anything, the short delay would give the Boss's men time to stew and become restless, which would play in Flint's favour. Every bloodthirsty cutthroat he had ever dallied with had been impatient and unpredictable. Much like the vixen in the bed.

Behind him she murmured, obviously distressed, and Flint hurried to her, his lofty mission and deep-set beliefs instantly forgotten once again.

Chapter Five

Ah, bon sang! She must be dead.

Swathing her, Jess could feel the crisp sheets as her body bobbed on the soft cloud beneath her. If this was what death felt like, then it wasn't so bad. Sheets and comfortable mattresses were a long-forgotten luxury and, like all small luxuries, deserved to be fully revelled in.

She adjusted her position, then winced as her head protested. Suddenly her throat burned raw. How typical that pain would still exist in heaven. Unless the Almighty had decreed she should go straight to hell...

'Lady Jessamine.' She knew that voice. The clipped English consonants which still felt so odd when she spoke them. The deep, soothing timbre that came from somewhere deep in his chest and made the tiny hairs on the back of her neck quiver uncontrollably. Jess forced her eyelids to open at the exact same moment she felt his big, warm hand cup her cheek again. Bizarrely, the touch made her feel safe. Something she most definitely was not. Not with him. They stared at each other, startled for a moment before his hand dropped and his mask was back in place, making her wonder if she had imagined the compassion she had seen seconds before.

'Where am I?' She struggled to sit and gave up as dizziness swamped her.

'At an inn. You hit your head. The physician suspects you have concussion.' Which explained why his face and the walls were spinning so fast. Jess squeezed her eyes shut and gripped the sides of the strange bed to steady herself. She supposed she should be relieved she wasn't dead, except knowing she was once again a prisoner extinguished that one small triumph. 'I'll fetch him. He wanted to see you as soon as you were awake.'

She heard his boots pace to the door, tried, then failed to listen to his whispered conversation, then heard the chair next to the bed creak slightly as he lowered himself back into it. 'I've ordered some soup as well—nothing too heavy. Something in your stomach might make you feel better.'

'Better for what? My impending execution?'

He ignored her croaked sarcasm. Instead, Jess

heard water being poured from a jug. 'Here—drink this.'

That comforting hand buried gently under her head on the pillow, supporting her enough that he could press the cup to her dry lips with his other hand. Jess drank gratefully, uncomfortable at being helpless—especially in front of him, the hateful man. Meeting his gaze in this state was unthinkable, so she focused on the cup instead and the steady hand holding it. Surprised that the neat, clean fingernails did not sit on the pampered hands of an aristocrat. Those hands had seen work, real work. Capable hands. Kind, too. Even when they had restrained her in the sea, he had not retaliated and hurt her when so many male hands had. He had been strong, though, more proof if proof were needed that her new gaoler did more than socialise and issue orders to his servants.

Being so close unnerved her. She could smell his skin—soap, some deliciously spicy cologne with undertones of fresh air from his immaculately laundered shirt, evidence that Lord Flint was particular about his personal cleanliness. Another luxury she had once taken for granted. Up against his golden perfection, she doubtless looked a wreck. Her own fingernails were torn and she was aware of a tender swelling on her lip. Before one errant hand went to her head to check the state of her hair, Jess pushed him and the cup away, suffering the indignity of allowing him to lower her spinning head back to the pillow. She made the mistake of glancing up at him, her eyes locking with his concerned green gaze. There it was again. That odd sense of well-being and connection, when she knew better than to trust anyone.

'Thank you.' Not at all what she wanted to say. A pathetic, heartfelt effort, when she wanted to spear him with something pithy. Something that clearly demonstrated she was not done yet and he hadn't beaten her, but those kind eyes drew her in and the intended insults died in her mouth. He smiled with genuine amusement then and her breath hitched.

'Fear not. I'm sure the politeness you are suffering is only a temporary affliction brought about by your knock to the head, my lady, and the old you will return soon enough to vex me.'

'*Oui*... I hope so, too.' Jess felt the corners of her mouth begin to lift in a returning smile and screwed up her face to stop it. Why was she responding to his charm and his undeniably handsome face? She hated him! If she ignored the flashes of compassion, gentleness and decency, this man wanted to see a rope around her neck! What was worse was there were no stinging retorts currently in her arsenal either and that wouldn't do. For several seconds, she searched her mind for something—anything in either English or French—to redress the balance and came up blank. *Incroyable!* What use was being fluent in two languages if neither served your purpose at your time of need?

'You are very lucky to be alive. Many a ship has fallen foul of those rocks you scaled. The sea was calmer today.'

Jess didn't feel particularly lucky. Hard to feel blessed when now so riddled with fresh guilt that seemed to have lodged itself between her ribs like a parasite that was doing its best to claw its way through her, reminding her that she was selfish to still be thinking only of her freedom despite the dreadful ramifications of her actions, not to mention she was back at square one. Galling when she had specifically aimed for the most deserted piece of coastline. 'How did you find me?'

'I know this area well and the good-for-nothing Captain turned out to be very good at one thing. He calculated the speed of the current and plotted your likely direction. You were either destined for the headland or the calm bay behind it. We landed there, in case you were wondering, and rather fortuitously saw you climbing that cliff as we sailed past.'

Imbécile! She should have paid closer attention to the water rather than her irrational fear of heights!

He seemed to understand her anger and its cause, and merely smiled in response. He would pay for that, once the bed stopped whirling. The knock at the door saved her from pouting like a spoiled child.

A cheerful, ruddy-faced older gentleman barrelled in, clutching a black leather bag. 'I see the patient is finally awake.' He smiled kindly as he sat on the mattress next to her. 'You took quite a bash to the head, young lady. If you don't mind, I need to examine you. How are you feeling?'

Jess wasn't going to discuss anything or suffer the indignity of being examined in front of her gaoler, allowing him to see the evidence of her weakness and shameful frailty, so turned to him imperiously. 'You may leave us, Monsieur Flint.'

He laughed then and shook his blond head, and she hated the fact he looked delectable when amused. 'Not in a million years, my lady, I believe you are forgetting who is in charge. Until you have been safely delivered to London, I'm afraid I shall be sticking to you like a barnacle sticks to a rock. From this moment on, I will be your shadow. Joined at the hip. But in the spirit of *basic human decency*, I shall step out of your way and avert my eyes.' He made a great show of moving towards the window and turned his back to stare out of it. 'You may continue, Doctor. Imagine I am not here. Both of you.'

'Twenty-four hours of bed rest!' Gray shook his dark head in disbelief. 'If word gets out she's here, we'll be sitting ducks.' They were still waiting for the other fifty men from the King's Elite to make their way from Plymouth, where they were waiting, to this remote corner of the Devon coast. It would be hours before they arrived. 'We're too close to the coast for my liking. If the Boss's men find her, they'll have her halfway back across the Channel before the others arrive!'

'That's why I've told the Captain to set sail immediately and head out to sea. I don't want anyone spotting a Royal Navy frigate lurking near the shore.' Flint had kept back a few of the crew to stand guard in the interim. It wasn't an ideal scenario, but at least with the enormous ship gone, the tiny fishing village would appear normal from a distance to anyone unfamiliar with it.

'And if someone from here talks, or has already talked? We caused quite a stir marching in carrying her on that stretcher. I don't like it, Flint.'

Neither did he, so he didn't argue. With the spring sun setting and only the one narrow lane serving as both the entrance and exit of the village, if the enemy came, they were done for. 'It is what it is. We can't move her yet. She's as weak as a kitten—albeit a feral one with claws.' Who he didn't trust as far as he could throw her despite his irrational need to protect her.

'Rather you than me, old boy. I think I'd rather take my chances with the smugglers. At least they are predictable.'

A good point. Flint glanced back at the bedchamber door, then decided that leaving her alone for two minutes, even though the windows were securely locked and the key was tucked in his waistcoat pocket, were two minutes too long. To be certain, he stalked back to the door and poked his head inside. She was sleeping just as she had been when he had left her, but in case she wasn't he left the door open a crack before returning to his friend.

'Have a carriage readied as a contingency in case we do need to leave fast, but assume that we'll be off some time tomorrow afternoon to make Plymouth before nightfall.' Being on the roads after dark would be tantamount to suicide and counter-productive. They were supposed to be bait, not a target.

Flint watched Gray leave and felt a pang of guilt for putting his comrades in danger. Not that he'd lied about the bed rest, the physician had been most specific, citing all manner of complications should they attempt to move her too soon, but because he was putting the welfare of a potential traitor over that of his men. Why should he care if Lady Jessamine became ill? But he did.

Wearily he took himself back into the bedchamber and dragged the cot the innkeeper had found for him to lay it directly in front of the door, then arranged his long limbs as best he could within its confines. Unless all hell broke loose, sleep was necessary. He would need every one of his wits completely sharpened to deal with her again tomorrow, but for now, predominantly thanks to the potent sleeping draught he had insisted the physician slip her, she was wrapped soundly in the arms of Morpheus. Decisively, he closed his eyes and joined her.

The dream was as vivid as it was erotic. Sultry eyes. Long, jet-black hair. Wet limbs entwined. The Jessamine of his imagination was as passionate as she was tempestuous. Bold and wanton, her hands explored him everywhere, greedily caressing every inch of his naked skin. In the dream Flint lay beneath her, content to let her explore, watching her lips and tongue work their way up his chest, moaning his encouragement. She smiled down at him as her fingers dipped into his waistcoat pocket…

Wait… If he was naked, why was he suddenly supremely aware of his waistcoat?

Like lightning, his hand clamped around her wrist and pulled her so that she fell sprawled across his chest, his narrowed eyes inches from her shocked, wide ones in the darkness.

'Give it back.'

'You were having a bad dream…' She attempted to rise on her knees, but he held firm.

'Give me the key.'

'I don't know what you are talking about. You were restless…' As she spoke in uncharacteristically reasonable tones, she was also carefully arranging her legs beneath her voluminous borrowed nightgown to bolt, so he twisted sharply to unbalance her and send her sprawling across his chest again.

'You were trying to escape.'

'Ce n'est pas vrai!' And she was fighting him again, tugging her arm for all it was worth. Flint wrapped his other arm tightly around her waist and rolled them to reverse their positions, only remembering that his body was hard and needy from the dream when it rested damningly against her stomach and he saw her eyes widen with surprise. He didn't want to want her, nor to have her know it, but it served her right and might

deter her from interrupting his slumber again in the coming days. Even so, he shifted position to spare them both the embarrassment.

'I won't ask again.' Her trim body felt too good beneath his. Thanks to the pale moonlight bleeding through the window, Flint was forced to notice all her silky, dark hair fanned across his pillow. The beautiful arrangement of her eyes, nose and plump mouth. Feel the fevered rise and fall of her breasts against his chest. His mouth scant inches from hers. Things he didn't want to notice. Couldn't afford to notice. 'Give me the key.'

'I don't know what you are talking about!'

He reached between them to retrieve her small, clenched fist and raised her hand to lie next to her furious face on the pillow. 'Give. It. To. Me.' Damn it all to hell, he wanted to kiss her. Badly.

'Abruti d'imbécile!'

It came as no surprise when she set her jaw and tried to heave him off her, but he was considerably bigger and easily used his bulk to pin her to the lumpy, straw mattress while his other hand slowly prised that determined fist apart. As Flint dislodged each stubborn finger to take back what she had stolen, she treated him to another stream of impassioned rapid French. He found himself smiling down at her, enjoying her hot-blooded spirit despite his better judgement. She was a glorious handful. Passionate and tenacious. Did those passions extend elsewhere? Best *not* to think about that now. Or ever.

'This is pointless, madam, as you well know.'

Typically, the minx didn't make it easy, nor did Flint truly expect her to, but using far more of his strength than he had ever used on a female before—including his exasperating oldest sister Ophelia—he finally managed to remove the key from her grasp.

Victorious and breathless, and shockingly aroused at the same time, Flint rolled off her and jumped to his feet.

'Well, that was all very unnecessary.' He pocketed the key again and she shot up from the cot like a wild cat, those vicious claws bared once again as she lunged for him. His surprisingly good mood vanished.

'*Tu ne comprends pas!* I have to get away!' Unwilling to defend himself because of that damn ingrained vein of chivalry again, he wrapped both arms tightly around her to trap her hands against the wall of his body and held on for dear life.

The insults came thick and fast, but among them she was muttering about something which Flint sensed was important, but his knowledge of French didn't extend to translating it all so quickly. When a button pinged off his waist-coat, he held her at arm's length and positively growled, 'Either rant more slowly, woman, or insult me in plain English. I know you speak that just as well!'

'He is going to kill us both!'

'Whoever *he* is, *he* doesn't know where we are!'

'It will make no difference. He has people everywhere. Well connected and powerful...' Her voice petered off as his eyes narrowed.

'Then seeing as we are now both wide awake, why don't we make a list of every one of those powerful names?'

Chapter Six

Jess clamped her jaw shut and stared up into his handsome face. Much as she wanted to see each and every one of those people reap the justice they deserved, naming names now would eradicate the only collateral she had should Saint-Aubin come knocking. That list might well be her curse, but it was also the only bargaining tool she had to save her from his wrath. Losing her temper after being caught red-handed was not sensible. Attacking the irksome man who held her was stupid.

She could feel the warmth and strength of his big body through her nightgown and the odd tingling on her lips from being so intimately close to his. If only he didn't smell so wonderfully sinful, she might be able to ignore those things. Now her body hummed with an awareness she did not welcome. Insufferable man!

Although as undeniably irritating as he was, so far, he was the only gaoler who had not chained her up. If she continued to fight him, that state of affairs would swiftly change. She already bitterly knew to her cost, escaping while clapped in irons was nigh on impossible. It had taken a small and unexpected army of gnarly English sailors to liberate her from Cherbourg in the dead of night, a stroke of good fortune she still couldn't quite believe.

A stroke of good fortune that was giving Jess her first real shot at freedom and fresh air in over a year.

She breathed out all her frustration and fury, allowing her muscles to relax in surrender. There would be another time. Another opportunity. She needed to be less opportunistic and more strategic if she was going to escape Lord Flint. 'I don't know their names. I was never privy to that information. I simply know that the organisation is vast.' Because it was worth a try, she offered him one of her mother's smiles and felt her pulse flutter as her eyes dipped to his lips of her own accord. *Mon Dieu!* 'As I have said, I was just the messenger, Monsieur Flint.'

His returning scowl could have curdled milk. 'Define *messenger*?'

'Translations mostly.' As his hold had loosened, Jess gave a dramatic flick of her wrist and shrugged. 'I wrote what I was told to write when I was told to write it.' Largely true. 'I have no

idea what happened to the letters afterwards.'
She did now. They killed people.

'Then why do you claim he wants you dead,
I wonder? Seems like a gross overreaction for
someone so insignificant.'

Jess hated that dismissive tone, the under-
stated English sarcasm he did so well. She
wished he would let go of her. Standing within
the warm, inviting cage of his arms was distracting. Up close, this unusual, irritating aristocrat
looked even more divine and for some reason
her nerve-endings were enjoying the feel of his
hands on her body. 'Saint-Aubin does not like
loose ends, Monsieur Flint. He will not rest until
this loose end is securely tied.'

'Or more likely, he will come to rescue you
if you fail in your own valiant attempts to return to France.'

He thought she wanted to return to that hell
hole? A team of horses would have to drag her
there lashed to a cart. Death would be more welcome. But at least her performance was convincing despite her two failed attempts at grasping
her freedom. Saint-Aubin's spies might vouch for
her outrage and that in turn might make him lenient. And Jess had more chance of harnessing
the power of invisibility than hoping that monster might show her any mercy. If they found
her here, wherever here was… 'I do not want to

hang, Monsieur Flint.' But she would rather hang than suffer Saint-Aubin's punishment.

Caught between the Devil and the deep blue sea. Odd—she had always wondered what that quaint British analogy meant and now, ironically, she understood it fully. Saint-Aubin was the Devil incarnate and Lord Flint the sea. Except Jess never expected she would need to actively resist the urge to dive in.

'I doubt your dear *papa* wants that either.'

'You do not know him as I do. I am better dead than in the hands of the English Crown. He will sacrifice me in a heartbeat.' And he would enjoy it. In her mind she heard his manic laughter at her screams and shuddered.

'A father doesn't—'

'He is *not* my father!' She spat the words with too much venom, making the intuitive Lord Flint tilt his head and eye her in a detached, calculated way which showed him to be every bit the King's man, out to catch a bigger fish and not at all the compassionate and reasonable man he purported to be. Whatever she said would be used against her in a court of law or at the hands of Saint-Aubin's henchmen if they made her answer for her actions. Jess needed to play her pathetic hand of cards very close to her chest and keep her impetuous, errant mouth shut.

'But he brought you up as his daughter, did

he not? You grew up in *his* chateau.' Lord Flint
smiled rather smugly down at her. He had a
nice smile, even smug it did peculiar things to
her pulse, and she hated him for that more. 'In
Valognes. A sprawling estate, by all accounts,
wealthy, too—but then Saint-Aubin is one of
Bonaparte's favourites and continues to support
him despite his exile. We know that Saint-Aubin
is the Boss's supplier of brandy, just as we know
that you ensured that same illegal brandy arrived
safely in Britain. Dates, times, ships. You met
him, didn't you? Old Boney. You were there to
see him pin a medal on your adopted papa's chest
after the Battle of Vittoria. I can assure you, our
intelligence has been most *thorough*, Lady Jessamine. We know all about you. Which is why I
fail to believe you are in any danger from Saint-
Aubin. Your own dear mother is *his* lover and
has been for twelve years.'

His intelligence wasn't that thorough. 'My
mother is dead, Monsieur Flint. She died six
weeks ago.' Although any favour Jess had had
with Saint-Aubin had died long before that. Not
that he had ever showed her any real favour. That
chateau had been a gilded prison which Jess had
been forbidden to leave. He had tolerated his
mistress's daughter when it suited him, then
grossly abused her when his mistress lost interest or was too ill to continue with his dirty work.

That answer seemed to surprise him and for a moment his handsome face clouded and his hold on her body loosened. 'I'm sorry. It is hard to lose a parent.' It was harder to take on the unwelcome mantle of one. 'You have been through quite an ordeal in the last month then, haven't you?' He had no idea. Ordeal didn't quite sum it all up. Jess had languished in a bottomless pit of hell. One she had clawed her way out of only to come face to face with the dreadful consequences. She doubted freedom would ever ease that new pain. 'Her passing, your capture and now...this.'

There it was again. That deep well of compassion swirling in those hypnotic green eyes, more intense in the moonlight for some reason than in broad daylight—then it was gone like a puff of smoke in a gale. 'How can you claim to not remember the names of your fellow traitors when each letter we have intercepted is personally addressed to them in your hand, Jessamine?'

'If you insist on dismissing the proper formalities, my name is Jess! Jessamine was my mother.' The mother she had once loved and now wanted no reminder of. A selfish, self-centred woman who put herself first, last and always. The mother who had willingly participated in despicable things. Forfeited their relationship for Saint-Aubin. Allowed him to treat her daughter abominably in exchange for the easier life he gave her. Flint took her outburst as grief rather than anger.

'I'm sorry. For my inappropriate informality and for your loss.'

She wriggled out of his hold and turned her back. Gazing up at him, seeing his concern, feeling that pull of confusion weakened her resolve.

'Tell me their names.'

'My head hurts… I feel dizzy.'

'How convenient.'

'So dizzy…' She clambered on to the bed and pulled the covers over her tightly like a shield. It did nothing to lessen her awareness of him. Jess could still smell his cologne on her nightgown. Still feel the warmth of his big hands on her skin. The untrustworthy sense of security she had simply knowing he was there.

'We'll save the rest of this enlightening conversation for the journey tomorrow. If you are well enough to attack me in the night, I dare say you are well enough to ride in a carriage.' His booted feet retreated to his pallet by the door. She heard the whisper of the thin blanket as he arranged himself across the door. 'Sleep tight, cunning Jess.' He was smiling again. She could hear it in his voice. Picture the way those green eyes danced. 'And to save any fruitless rummaging later, I've tucked the key to the window safely down my breeches. I *dare* you to come and retrieve it.'

* * *

She sat like an affronted statue next to him, the very picture of wounded martyrdom, staring silently at the scenery through the carriage window. She had been like that for well over an hour. The only chink in that armour had appeared as they had stepped out of the inn and she had seen the single carriage, yet instead of showing relief that she was apparently so poorly guarded, it had been fear that had briefly flitted across her features instead. Fear so visceral, he had to fight hard against the compulsion to tell her not to worry—armed men were hiding all along their route, ready to pounce on any villains fool enough to chance their arm.

That fear bothered Flint, although he was yet to put his finger on exactly why. Fear aside, she was still reassuringly opportunistic. The door on her side was locked and chained with the fattest padlock Gray could find, the key safely sat in his pocket on top of the carriage. The wily Jess had tested the lock with her fingers when she thought Flint hadn't been looking as they had bounced over a rutted part of the road. Since then, she had cast a couple of surreptitious glances towards Flint's door, which to rile her he had settled his back to half-lean against while he pretended to sleep at her side, his long legs stretched and folded on the opposite bench in case she got any ideas.

It was a position which also allowed him to study her unhindered. In sailor's breeches she was stunning, but in the fashionably feminine attire his men had brought across from Plymouth, the seething Lady Jessamine was breathtaking. The beautiful hair had been pinned into a tousled chignon that suited her. Long, curling strands framed her face beneath the wide rim of her bonnet. Thanks to a decent night's sleep, another tonic from the physician when he declared her recovered enough to travel and a couple of hearty meals, the dark shadows had lessened and there was a delightful pink bloom to her cheeks which hinted at her English ancestry beneath the French.

Flint fully intended to shake the hand of whoever had been responsible for selecting that particular coral-striped muslin gown from whichever shop it had been procured. The instructions had been explicit, she needed to stand out, but not that noticeably. He had expected something garish and tawdry, not a confection that oozed class. The garment might have been made expressly for her, so well did it fit. The bodice hugged her curves like a second skin and displayed enough flesh to make a man look twice, but not so much as to make her obscene.

Then it fell to skim her hips in a column that left one in no doubt that the body beneath it was all woman. Above the neckline was a tantalising glimpse of an impressive cleavage, something surprising when one considered her distinct lack of stature and almost painfully thin waist. She looked exactly like any other lady of good breeding, only better.

Damn her.

The sight kept making his mind wander to places it had no business going and the primary reason why he had pretended to sleep. Looking was giving his vivid imagination too many ideas and taking his mind off his mission. But he wouldn't prove old Fennimore right. The near loss of a parent was an excellent incentive to look, but not touch. Or believe a single word she said.

'We need to stop.' Flint felt her finger prod him in the thigh. He cracked open one eye and feigned boredom.

'We'll stop when we reach our destination and not before.'

'When will that be?'

He took out his pocket watch slowly, flicked it open and then clicked it shut. 'Dinner time. Another hour or so.'

'I cannot *wait* an hour.'

'Ah… I see. There's a chamber pot under your seat.'

The anger was instantaneous and, despite his better judgement, the sight of it excited him. He had to close his eyes again to stop the bark of laughter escaping his throat.

'Monster! How dare you even suggest such a thing!' She stood and rapped on the ceiling. 'Stop the carriage! *Immédiatement!*'

'They won't listen to you.'

'Make them stop. I will only be a few moments.'

'During which you will doubtless try to make a dash for it again.' He sighed loudly as if vastly put upon. 'All very tiresome and, if I may say, my fiery Jess, a tad predictable. I expected more imagination from you.' For a man who claimed to loathe female hysterics, he couldn't seem to stop himself from goading her or enjoying her reaction.

'*Ah, seigneur!*' She quickly suppressed the flash of temper. 'Why are you always so suspicious?'

He smiled in response and watched her jaw stiffen. 'Would it be too much trouble to pull in to the next inn? You can stand guard outside the retiring room.'

Flint glanced disbelievingly at her indignant face. 'What part of being a prisoner are you struggling to understand? I have learned, to my peril, that you cannot be left alone for a second. Even if we stopped, which we won't by the way, you will remain in my direct line of sight at all times. You have lost your right to privacy until I cheerfully hand you over. Not only am I in charge, I am now your constant companion. Your trusty shadow. Always there. Glued to your side. For the duration... But because I am a gentleman, I shall close my eyes.' Some devil inside him made Flint reach down and grab the chinaware and present it to her like a gift.

He watched her mouth fall open and her dark eyes swirl with molten fury. She went to shout and he gently pressed his finger to her lips, then momentarily forgot what he wanted to say when an odd heat travelled up the digit and made his own mouth tingle. Annoyed, he snatched the offending hand away and folded it tightly across his chest. 'You may use what has been graciously provided or you will wait till we get to Plymouth.'

'Plymouth!' He probably shouldn't have said that, because her rage burned incandescent. Nor should he have touched her mouth because it apparently had the power to scramble his brains. 'Plymouth is to the west coast, *non*? Why are we travelling west when London is to the east?'

'Because we are expected at Plymouth. That was where the ship was heading before you launched yourself off it.'

'Who is expecting us in Plymouth? My trial is in London!'

'And we will make our way to London from there.'

'That makes no sense! Plymouth is the complete opposite side of the country! It will take days to get to London!' Five to be exact, on the convoluted route they had planned. *'Je n'en crois rien! Imbéciles!* Why did that stinking, floating prison not take me to Dover or Portsmouth or anywhere else sensible? This is complete stupidity...' Her voice trailed off and Flint saw the exact moment that realisation dawned. Her hand fluttered to her face. It instantly paled. 'You are using me? All your talk about fair trials and dignity are lies to appease me. This has all been planned.'

'I think you are allowing your imagination to run away with you.'

'Really?' Proud resignation replaced the temper. Her emotions could swiftly change like the wind—if they were real. 'Now it all makes sense. Now I understand why the navy abducted me in Cherbourg and then sat outside the harbour for days waiting. You wanted Saint-Aubin to know you had me. You wanted to taunt him by flaunting me under his nose! And now you intend to taunt him still by taking me to the capital on the slowest route possible. I am bait.'

There was no point lying, every bit of her theory was correct, so he stared at her levelly. 'You are too valuable to both Saint-Aubin and the Boss for us not to. One or both of them will send minions who will attempt to retrieve you...'

'*Je n'en crois pas mes oreilles!* I am to be sacrificed to catch a bigger traitor!'

'There will be no sacrifice. My men are armed and...' It wasn't wise to tell her all the details. She didn't need to know that during every step of their journey they would be escorted by fifty of Lord Fennimore's finest who had arrived a while ago. Fifty crafty, invisible and highly skilled operatives who would shoot first and ask questions later. Saint-Aubin's motley crew of would-be kidnappers didn't stand a chance. He had blabbed enough by mentioning Plymouth and tipping her off. A stupid mistake when he knew better. A mistake he had only made once before nearly a decade ago in his career as a government agent. A career he had been born and nurtured to follow. Duty and patriotism were in his blood. One mistake didn't erase hundreds of years of service. Two might.

'You *will* arrive safely in London. Your trial will be...' What? Quick. Decisive. Everything you suspect and more? A foregone conclusion from a frightened government baying for your blood. He couldn't say that to her. All at once,

Flint was swamped with guilt for riling her in the first place. 'Your trial will be conducted correctly.'

'I see.' She exhaled and somehow became much smaller. She sat staring sightlessly at the opposite bench. Acceptance of her fate. Painful minutes ticked by, forcing him to see the unshed tears in her dark, frightened eyes and watch the erratic rise and fall of her chest as she struggled to maintain control. No tears of martyrdom. Always so proud. So brave. He wanted to loathe her, yet had to stop himself from comforting her instead. After an age, she turned to him and his gut clenched at the stark despondency in her gaze.

'It is funny. During that long swim, I genuinely feared I might drown or be bludgeoned against those rocks. Now, Monsieur Flint, I am genuinely sorry that I wasn't.'

Beneath the delicate skin of her neck, Flint watched her pulse beat rapidly rather than see the awful terror in her eyes. What had happened to fiery Jess? Why wasn't she shouting and railing at him now? That he could deal with. Instead she slowly turned to stare listlessly out of the window, the healthy bloom on her cheeks gone and her proud shoulders deflated.

Chapter Seven

Jess allowed the weight of guilt and despondency to swallow her for the rest of the journey, finding it almost incomprehensible that the British government thought that she would be safe in one lone carriage accompanied by two drivers and one lying aristocrat as they attempted to draw out Saint-Aubin's evil comrades. Her situation was indeed dire and she was out of ideas to save her skin while her current gaoler refused to leave her side. Knowing that at any point they could be ambushed, that the arrogant Flint and his men would be slaughtered before her eyes and she would be dragged kicking and screaming back to France, filled Jess with more dread than she knew how to deal with.

If they caught her, then her only hope was to plead horror at her initial abduction and reassure Saint-Aubin that every detail of her mother's damning little book was consigned to memory.

Then, if he believed her, Jess would go back to being his slave, forced to continue writing those letters and sending more innocent men to their deaths. For what? All to save her own skin—a weak and worthless skin she would despise occupying for the rest of her days.

Death was a better option.

Next to her, her unwelcome companion was feigning sleep once again. That was fine by Jess. She hated him more now. She had nothing to say to him. Instead, she focused on the blurred bushes and trees at the roadside as the carriage sped past, her heart in her mouth, searching for the men who would hunt her down. Simultaneously praying to God that he'd find a way to save her. Just this once.

By some miracle they arrived in Plymouth without issue and the carriage pulled into a busy inn in the centre of the crowded port town. Lord Flint held her arm tightly as he helped her down, then wrapped hers securely through his to lead her through the inn. She allowed it to go limp in the hope he would relax his grip, but he merely looked knowingly at her and held her tighter.

'Would you like some dinner?' The dining room was filled with curious travellers, any of whom could be her enemy. How dare he attempt to put her on display like a juicy maggot on a hook!

'Go to hell!'

He turned to the amused driver who had followed them in, asked him to organise a tray to be sent to the room, then dragged her up two flights of narrow stairs at pace before depositing her in the sole bedchamber at the top of the building.

'I hope you find the accommodations for tonight satisfactory. The trunk over there should have everything that you need—but if you require anything else I'll send my man to fetch it in the morning before we depart.'

Jess let her eyes wander to the enormous leather trunk before piercing him with her glare. For once, she had no words, yet was content to simply allow her roiling hatred for the man to bubble openly.

'I see you are angry at me again.'

'An understatement, Monsieur Flint.'

'For what it's worth, I prefer the anger to seeing you sad.' He huffed out a breath and raked a hand through his thick hair, the unintentional dishevelment only serving to make him more attractive, the wretch. How dare he say nice things! 'If you need anything, I'll be back soon.' Then he stood awkwardly for a few seconds before clamping his hands behind his back, stiffly inclining his head and leaving her all alone.

As the key clicked decisively in the lock, it didn't take her long to realise why her shadow felt confident enough to disappear. Despite the long drop to the cobbled courtyard below, a drop so reminiscent of the one in Cherbourg that it instantly made her queasy, the two windows were barred on the outside and although she could open the glass and let in the fresh evening air, the gap between those bars was barely enough to slide her hand through, let alone anything else. He had chosen this room on purpose.

Of course he had. Monsieur Flint had a plan, a detailed one, and Jess didn't.

She tossed her new bonnet on the small dressing table and sat listlessly on the bed. *I prefer the anger to seeing you sad.* As if her misery somehow made him miserable, too! Did he think words would make up for him intentionally putting her life in jeopardy? Did he think she was a fool who would fall for such a flowery, insincere statement?

Although he had sounded sincere and his sea-green eyes had been pained.

Idiot! Stop thinking such nonsense! She shouldn't waste her time pathetically attributing substance to a meaningless, throwaway comment when she had an escape to plan… The trouble was she had been starved of affection and friendship for too long and was now seeing flickers of those emotions where none truly existed. Jess sincerely doubted *he* suffered from a similar affliction.

Except… He had come to her aid more than once with the toothless sailor. He'd torn a strip off the crew for debasing her. He had brought her food and seen to her comfort. He had listened to the physician's instructions to allow her to rest instead of pushing on with his plan to deliver her to London. He hadn't as much as harmed a hair on her head. Irritated, Jess took in the room properly. A fresh nightgown had been laid out on the comfortable bed. There was a hairbrush, hairpins and ribbons on the dressing table. A trunk filled with more clothes she imagined were much like the fine garment she was wearing. And despite everything she had done to escape his clutches, her wrists were blessedly free of manacles. She might well be bait—but she was being treated like a lady.

Why was that?

Maybe the compassion she had seen in those compelling green eyes had been real after all? Which meant there was a chance he might have human emotions buried under all that aristocratic indifference?

An Achilles heel?

The polite tap on the door followed by the jangling of keys interrupted her train of thought and her silly pulse fluttered at the prospect of seeing him again. Only it wasn't the arrogant and exasperating Lord Flint who carried the tray in. It was his grinning driver.

He offered her a courtly bow and proffered the tray as if it were the Crown Jewels rather than a plate piled with bread, cheese and ham. 'Your dinner, my lady!'

She glanced past him to the tiny landing where the other coachman, a very burly fellow who looked more suited to bare-knuckle fighting than handling the ribbons, stood guard. '*Où est* Monsieur Flint? Have I scared him away?'

'Flint is made of stern stuff, my lady. As the only brother of five troublesome sisters, there is no one better to deal with your tomfoolery than him. He has the patience of a saint. But alas, even saints need an hour or two to themselves. I'm afraid you are stuck with me until then.' He bowed again and winked. 'Lord Graham Chadwick at your service, *mademoiselle*. But you can call me Gray. Far more handsome and charming than Flint, I'm sure you'll agree.'

Charming, yes. Handsome, too, but not in the league of her golden-haired gaoler.

'Lord Chadwick? And there I was thinking you were naught but a simple coachman.' She peeked up at him from beneath her lashes and was delighted to see that this lord was more than happy to be flirted with. Except flirting with him seemed disloyal, so Jess annoyed herself by changing her expression to one of openness rather than enticement.

'Five sisters? The poor man must indeed have the patience of a saint.' Jess picked up a chunk of bread and nibbled on it, smiling. 'Do they run him ragged?'

'Like you wouldn't believe, my lady.'

'Young ladies will do that. We are all very temperamental. *Non?*'

'These are all older and want him married. The poor chap can't venture home without their aggressive matchmaking. It's hugely entertaining to watch.'

'I should imagine it is.' The image of her gaoler rolling his eyes in exasperation while indulging his sisters' machinations with good humour skittered across her mind. 'Is he a good brother, Monsieur Gray?' Because he was respectful, almost noble, in his manner. As if he understood women and was careful how he treated them. Even when Flint restrained her he was gentle. Jess could honestly say he hadn't physically hurt her once. Even when he had used his body to pin her to the bed. Such an experience should have been unpleasant—but it wasn't. A large part of her, the part she had absolutely no control of, had really rather enjoyed it.

'I suspect so.'

'But a committed bachelor?'

'So many questions and all about Flint.' He grinned and folded his arms. 'Do you miss him already?'

'Merely curious.'

'Understandable. It's good to know your enemy.'

'That is the problem, Monsieur Gray, I am not entirely sure Monsieur Flint is my enemy. I can't quite make him out. I have spent hours in his company and yet know next to nothing about him. I find myself *wanting* to trust him. Perhaps if I understood him better, I might be inclined to entrust him with my confession, but—'

Gray chuckled and held up his hand. 'Let me stop you there. You're good. I'll give you that. Flint was absolutely correct. Just the right combination of beautiful and tragic to lull a man into falling for your lies. Very convincing. It's also a good job I am not a *simple* coachman, else I might do something foolish and satisfy your curiosity. Even better, Flint won't fall for it either—but I'm looking forward to seeing you try. Enjoy your dinner, *mademoiselle*.' He turned and started back towards the door, only to pause, his face the very picture of mischief. 'I shall tell Monsieur Flint you are quite taken with him and miss his presence keenly. I dare say that will give him a laugh.' He closed the door before her chunk of bread hit him in the face.

Flint did a subtle circuit of the inn, but needn't have worried. Gray had two-hirds of the Invisibles stationed around the perimeter, disguised as everything from ostlers to drunkards. A quick glance upwards confirmed there were also two on the roof, as they briefly poked their heads out of their hiding places and nodded in acknowledgement before blending seamlessly back into the chimneys. The rest were already in position on their route or readying the next inn they would stop at. There were eyes and pistols everywhere. If any of the Boss's henchmen came calling tonight, they were more than ready for them. The fools would be rounded up and made to talk. Hired henchmen often spilled their guts to save their own backsides. Especially if there was a King's Pardon on offer. Flint had the papers signed and ready and sat in the same locked box as Jess's arrest warrant. Every detail of this mission had been meticulously planned. Knowing that made him feel more in control again and served to remind him of the purpose of his mission.

Escort the traitor to London slowly. Arrest every cockroach that crawled out of the woodwork along the way. Deposit her in London and then move blithely on to the next mission.

Clear cut.

That simple.

Although getting less simple by the second.

If only he had a clear-cut plan to help him cope with tonight. The inn might well be awash with the King's Elite, men who knew their role in this mission and would behave accordingly, but the dark-haired vixen he had to spend the night guarding was another matter. There was no telling what Jess would do and Flint was mentally preparing for every eventuality from finding the bars on the window removed using twisted hairpins or some other innocuous items she had fashioned into a tool—because she was that resourceful and determined—to wrestling the wench to the ground if she attempted to steal the keys again. Something his needy body was rather looking forward to even while his head violently castigated it for being so weak. Whatever she threw at him, he knew one thing for certain—tonight was not going to be easy. The temptation to post himself outside the door on a chair was overwhelming.

Except he didn't trust her to be left alone too long—even with bars on the window. The two hours he had been absent were quite long enough and, despite Gray listening intently through the door, ears were no substitute for eyes. The only eyes he trusted to watch Jess properly were his own.

That was his story and Flint was sticking to it, even if he didn't fully believe it himself.

He took a moment at the bottom of the narrow staircase to enjoy the peace and then steeled his shoulders ready for the chaos.

Lord save him from troublesome women!

He still wasn't over his forced two months of rustication in Cornwall and his nerves were shot. Flint had spent the better part of the last few hours attempting to calm down, only to find his thoughts constantly turning to her. And what a jumbled mess they were, too. No matter how hard he tried he couldn't shake the image of her frightened and broken. The brave tears and the smart mouth. The fighter and the defeated. The traitor and the woman. All tangled up with a healthy dose of inappropriate lust and his in-grained need to protect the woman he was duty bound to deliver to the courts. Tonight would be pure torture.

Three stairs up and he found himself neatening his cuffs and smoothing down his hair. Damn woman! All this enforced proximity was driving him mad. Gray's cheerful face at the top of the landing did nothing to appease him.

'Is everything to your liking?'

No. There was still *her*. 'Yes. Let's put this inn to bed.'

'Then she's all yours, my friend. Good luck.' Gray tossed him the key and disappeared down the staircase. That was one small consolation at least. Flint's misery would be spared an audience.

He strode to the door with purpose, allowed his lip to curl with distaste, then pulled himself together before he knocked in case his frustrated fist splintered the wood. 'I'm back.'

'Come in.'

Good lord, she sounded positively calm. Something so out of character it immediately raised all his hackles and had him narrowing his eyes. Warily, Flint undid the lock and slowly poked his head around the door, waiting for the projectile that never came.

'*Bon soir*, Monsieur Flint. Back to vex me, I see.' Although she couldn't see because *she* was sat at the dressing table with her back to him, running the hairbrush determinedly through her waist-length hair impatiently. And, damn it all to hell, it shimmered like the polished ebony keys of a pianoforte in the candlelight, a thick, silk curtain falling over just the one shoulder that his fingers ached to touch. That hair needed proper restraining for the sake of his frazzled nerves and wayward body. 'Is your trap set? Does the whole of Plymouth know I am here, waiting to be killed? A veritable lamb to the slaughter?'

The nightgown she wore dipped slightly to expose the creamy expanse of perfect skin covering the nape of her neck. One didn't need to be an expert in women's fashions to know the front of the neckline dipped lower still, or that the fine, soft linen would drape in such a way as to make a statement out of her bosom and allow the silhouette of her figure to be tantalisingly visible when the light caught it. Later, if he survived the night, he was going to tear a strip off the idiot who had purchased all her clothes. What the hell had the fellow been thinking? That wasn't a sensible everyday nightgown at all. That was the sort of confection a woman wore on her wedding night to entice her new husband! And all that lovely hair was down! Torturing him. Why hadn't she plaited it? Because she wanted to seduce him. The witch.

'You are perfectly safe.'

'And you are a fool if you think either one of us is safe. Please remember I said that before they put a bullet or a dagger in your chest. Monsieur Gray has made your bed so you can sleep the restful sleep of the deluded.' She turned, gesturing to the pallet on the floor, and he very nearly groaned aloud. How, exactly, were they all supposed to keep their minds firmly on their mission when confronted with Jess looking like that? If the shops were still open, he'd send the fool out to purchase her staid and sensible garments, with high necks and no shape. A smock, perhaps? Made of thick wool. Or chainmail. And a very unbecoming nightcap which he would personally double knot beneath her chin to prevent it dislodging and releasing that hair. 'I presume you intend to drag it in front of the door again, lest I am foolish enough to attempt to escape with armed guards stood outside.'

She stood and he almost groaned again. That neckline might well be the death of him. The shadowy outline of her waist and hips came a close second. It was hard to ignore the way they undulated as she walked to the bed. Eve tempting Adam—or was she merely the snake? 'Goodnight, Monsieur Flint. Let us both pray it is not our last. I shall leave you to blow out the candles.'

Clearly now intent on being a complete masochist, Flint watched her clamber on to the bed and pull the covers over. They didn't help. Intent on not looking at him, the vixen was lying on her side facing the window. The thin blanket moulded to her curves like a second skin, making her backside resemble a juicy peach ripe for the picking. The unrestrained ebony tresses calling to him. *Touch me...you know you want to.*

Like a man walking to the gallows, Flint wandered to all three of the candles in turn and snuffed them out before dragging his bedding miserably to the door. A pointless task, really, as sleep of any sort was now nigh on impossible. Not that her words had bothered him over much, because he knew there were fifty men close by who had his back, but because she had occupied his head again in a wholly inappropriate way and he knew already nothing would dislodge her. Instead, he removed only his coat, stretched out on the pallet and fixed his gaze firmly on the ceiling, and wondered what he had done to deserve this stint in purgatory with the most beautiful, maddening and, lord help him, most alluring woman he had ever met. Up in heaven he swore he heard his father laughing at him. *Got me shot, lad. That'll teach you.*

Chapter Eight

The soft tap on the door woke him up with a start. 'There's someone outside.'

Gray's whisper suggested that whoever it was, they were not yet aware that his Majesty's finest were all lined up waiting for them. Neither was the wide-eyed temptress who had suddenly shot bolt upright in her bed. All that dark hair an inviting tangle around her head. Flint put his finger to his lips to warn her to keep quiet. For once, she did as she was told.

'How many?'

'Hard to tell. The port is starting to wake to catch the tide, but the same man has certainly wandered past three times now and there is no doubt he's trying to gauge the lay of the land. I've put Trent and Dobbs on standby to follow him in case he comes past again.'

'Keep me posted.' Flint lay back down heavily and rubbed his tired eyes.

'You're going back to bed? Saint-Aubin's assassin is outside and you're going back to bed!' Her hiss was too loud to be a whisper.

'Of course I'm not going back to bed. I am merely trying to wake up and equilibrate before I get up.'

'We don't have time for you to equilibrate! We need to leave! *Tout de suite!*' She was already off the bed and frantically rummaging in the trunk for clothes. 'They are here! *Mon Dieu!*' A half-boot flew out and thudded on the floor, she scooped it up in the hasty bundle in her arms and dashed behind the screen. In moments, the inappropriate nightgown had been torn off and tossed over it, and the knowledge she was now stood quite naked within feet of him, her hair no doubt tumbling down her back, her shoulders, her breasts… Damn and blast, that was unnerving. If the screen toppled over in her haste to dress, then he wasn't entirely sure he would ever recover.

'Calm down, woman! There is no need to panic. The inn is secure. Gray was simply doing his job by reporting his suspicions…'

'Suspicions!' She gave up hissing and shrieked. 'You don't know these men like I do! They are ruthless! Killers!' The screen juddered ominously. 'Get up!' A filmy chemise seemed to float into the air before he watched her arms wriggle into it, closely followed by a gown, then she emerged looking totally scandalous and gloriously wanton. 'Lace me up!'

Damn woman couldn't have looked more gorgeous if she tried. One arm held up the front of the dress to cover her modesty. Unfortunately, with her other hand holding up as much of her tousled hair as possible, Flint's eyes drank in the sight of her bared neck and the graceful curve of her spine beneath the soft fabric of that chemise. Flint found himself rising and walking towards her like a man hypnotised, before his brain caught up and overruled his body with a frigid splash of common sense.

This was all very convincing. The panic and haste. The wide, fear-filled eyes. The need to escape—except this minx wanted nothing better than to escape *him*. What better time to do it than when your comrades were loitering outside, within arm's reach, ready to whisk you back to France?

He eyed the dangling laces like cobras. Jess had to know he was attracted to her. Aside from the fact that she was absolutely stunning and not averse to using her looks to befuddle men, she must have felt the evidence of it when he had pinned her beneath him the previous night. It had been glaringly obvious.

His body might well be responding again,

but he was no fool. The manipulative Jessamine knew exactly what she was doing now, just as she had then. Well, two could play that game.

He allowed his hands to give in to the temptation to touch her hair, gathering up the loose tendrils to move them out of the way, making sure his hands gently brushed the sensitive visible skin at the back of her neck. Her startled intake of breath was its own reward and made up for the fact that his body was now humming from the brief contact and his nose wanted to bury itself in her hair. His palms grazed her bared shoulders, lingered, before he loosely grasped the fabric and took his time arranging the gown properly on her shoulders. Flint was standing so near to her he could hear her soft breathing and knew that she could feel his on her neck, too, because she stopped breathing for a few seconds before her wits returned. 'Hurry up!'

'I am more accustomed to *unlacing* ladies' garments than lacing them.' She shivered at the gravelly sound of his voice so close to her ear. 'You'll have to bear with me...' One hand trailed along the length of her spine through the gossamer fabric of her chemise, making her back arch delightfully. Were those goosebumps on her neck? Surely that was a good sign. Her encouraging reaction made him smile. 'I'm a novice as a lady's maid—but I'm enjoying myself immensely.'

She heard the laughter in his voice and her head whipped around. She had the audacity to look outraged. 'You are making fun of me?'

'No, *my lady*. I'm playing you at your own game. You are not the only one who can use their wiles effectively.' Flint hooked an arm around her waist and drew her back, unceremoniously pulling the two gaping halves of the garment together. 'Did you seriously think I would fall for your obvious seduction, Jess?' His fingers made quick work of the laces while he tried and failed not to be thoroughly seduced by her perfume. Who the hell had bought the vixen perfume as well? Jasmine, too! If ever there was a scent to conjure unwanted images of warm summer nights and clandestine assignations.

'Seduction!' He had to give her credit for the affronted squeak. It was a very convincing touch. 'There are men outside trying to kill me! We need to go now!'

He tied off the laces and pushed her a good foot away for the sake of his sanity. 'No, they aren't. They might try to kill me, but we both know those men out there are here to liberate *you*. They probably have a rowing boat bobbing in readiness in the harbour and a fast ship anchored offshore. And before you argue the toss, it's probably best that you know now I have no intention of leaving until the sun is out and our bellies are full of breakfast. Might I remind you that *you* are bait and we *want* them to come. The fact they have apparently taken the bait so soon cheers me immensely.'

He snatched up his coat and stalked to the door. 'Fix your hair. There is far too much of it! I'll send Gray in with a tray once I've eaten.'

Jess listened to the key turn in the lock and simply stared at the door. Her heart was beating so fast, it drowned out all the other sounds in her spinning head. She felt sick, her legs so unsteady she staggered to the bed and sunk helplessly on the mattress.

They weren't leaving. *Mon Dieu.*

There were murderers outside and they weren't leaving.

It was unbelievable. Unthinkable. And for now she was powerless to do anything about it. She sat numb for several minutes before pacing to one of the windows and gazing out. Her room overlooked the deserted courtyard where the height and the shadows played games with her, hinting at movement and danger which was probably more imagined than real. For the sake of her own sanity, she concentrated on every solid outline and curve, trying to separate fact from her own fevered imaginings and her irrational and crippling fear of heights.

Two carriages, one of them the very carriage she had ridden in yesterday, stood half-bathed in lamplight from the large lantern suspended in the archway. A few yards away, another light illuminated what she presumed was the kitchen. The blurred, distorted shape of a maid carrying something scurried past the leadlight glass. A cat jumped on to that same window ledge and Jess nearly jumped out of her skin, before her eyes contradicted what her hammering heart feared.

Whatever danger lurked outside this bedchamber, she needed to be logical to outwit it. Forcing a calmness she did not feel, Jess gave herself a sound talking to. It couldn't be far off dawn. Soon the sun would chase the darkness away and there would be less opportunity to hide in the shadows. They wouldn't dare strike during daylight in such a central location. Which either meant the clock was ticking or Saint-Aubin's assassins had assessed the lay of the land, just as Gray had stated, and decided this crowded inn in the middle of the busiest thoroughfare in Plymouth was not the ideal location for an abduction. Attacking this close to dawn wasn't worth the risk, or at least she hoped that was the conclusion they had drawn.

Jess opened the window and craned her ears,

but heard nothing out of the ordinary there either. Beyond the archway, the sounds of the town waking up were clear. Carts and the occasional voices. Potential witnesses. Too many to chance it? If only she could see the street, then she might feel safer, but alas, she had no choice but to put her life in the hands of the frustrating Flint and his minions and her own common sense. There was no point in spending her time on tenterhooks. Fear would only serve to create panic, when logical and strategic thinking was needed. This was her current lot in life and would remain so until she found an opportunity to escape.

Over the course of the next hour she watched the sunrise and the inn come alive, yet there was still no sign of Saint-Aubin's henchmen or the uncompromising Lord Flint. As Flint had promised, Gray delivered a tray of food, but refused to be drawn on what was occurring outside. Despite the bright daylight, it was clear they intended to keep her wholly in the dark. Jess picked at the food only because she knew she had to keep her strength up, but each mouthful tasted like dust that was painful to swallow. After that she began to pace and was close to wearing a hole in the carpet when she heard his boots on the stairs. She knew it was Flint because her body sensed him before he spoke, the awareness making her pulse quicken as she un-willingly recalled the feel of his warm breath on her skin. Detestable man!

'Time to go.' He was talking to Gray outside, but the sound of his hushed tones made goose-bumps rise on her neck just as they had when he had touched her this morning. It reminded her of the feel of his warm hands on her skin and, despite the pleasant temperature in her bed-chamber, she shivered at the memory. In those emotionally charged moments, that brief contact had cut through her fear and made her forget ev-erything but him.

Stupid, stupid fool!

Jess made sure her expression was thunderous when he opened the door. 'Your carriage awaits, *my lady.*' He stepped inside, closely followed by Gray and the bare-knuckle fighter. They hoisted her new trunk and carried it out, leaving her with him. His green eyes travelled the length of her body in assessment, then narrowed. 'I thought I told you to do your hair.'

Surely he had better things to consider than the state of her coiffure! 'And I clearly remem-ber telling you yesterday that you can go to hell. That sentiment has not changed today, nor will it.' If he hated the sight of her hair down, all the better. Jess would never pin it up again in his presence. She flounced towards the door and he let her pass, but caught her arm before she reached the stairs. Jess glared at his hand as if it was something offensive, yet felt the peculiar heat of it nevertheless. The contact made her skin tingle.

'I'm your shadow, remember. Joined at the hip.'

'As if I could forget.' If only.

Jess went willingly down the stairs. The more miles she put between the lurking assassin and herself, the better. The inn was no less crowded this morning than it had been last night. So many strange and potentially dangerous faces, she allowed him to wrap his arm around her waist and use his big body to shield her as he led her through the throng, bizarrely grateful for his presence and the extra pair of eyes. And his were everywhere. Against her hip, she felt the reassuring length of his pistol in his coat. He was prepared to defend them should the need arise and that was some comfort.

The courtyard was less busy, but it was obvious the day had long begun. An ostler was polishing a carriage. A married couple stood next to their luggage, waiting for their conveyance. Behind them their two small children were entertaining themselves and laughing. A stable boy lugged fresh straw towards the stalls. Through the archway the street beyond was alive with the normal activity of daily life. The sight of all that normality brought a lump to Jess's throat alongside a wave of longing so strong she almost sighed aloud, momentarily forgetting the need for haste in the wake of the sight of such luxury. How long had it been since she had seen the world like this? Oh, how she wished she could be part of it again. The simple things that people took for granted. Things she never would again…if she was spared.

Gray opened the door of the carriage beyond and Flint led her towards it, just as another conveyance turned into the yard. Instinctively he gently manoeuvred them to one side to allow it to pass. The high-sprung carriage was glossy and obviously expensive, its owner clearly very powerful and probably oblivious to how lucky he was to experience that splendour he was encased in. Jess remembered thinking those things before her heart stopped. Because the aristocratic face watching her with amusement from the window was one she recognised only too well and hated above all others.

Saint-Aubin.

Himself.

Que faire, mon Dieu!

Chapter Nine

⸻⸻⸺∿∿∿⸺⸻⸻

The woman sitting next to him in the carriage
seat was most definitely not the same woman he
had left the inn with. Flint had no idea what had
changed, but something had and it was making
him uneasy. One minute she had been unconsciously smiling wistfully at the hustle and bus-
tle of the courtyard, the next she was scrambling
up the steps to the carriage and eager to be on
their way. Now, his maddening prisoner was as
white as a ghost, her small fists were clenched,
and there was a tension and fragility about her
as she peered out of the window that he had not
seen before. It was worse even than when he had
tracked her down after her dramatic and fearless
escape from the ship—the rapid transformation
bothered him.

In the two minutes since they had left, he had
watched her intently, curious to see if the change
in her character was all part of her act. But as

each second ticked passed, she seemed to become more and more distressed. Shrinking into herself. Or he was an idiot for falling for it? Of course.

'All right, Jess. I'll play along. What's the matter?'

Silence. Almost as if she hadn't heard him. Without thinking, Flint reached out his hand and touched her arm. Her hand came up to grip his.

'I saw him.' Her usually bold voice was very small. Something about it didn't sound right, but as she still had her back to him he couldn't see the truth—or the lies—in her eyes. 'He was there. At the inn.'

'Who was there?'

'Saint-Aubin.'

'Saint-Aubin?' The mere suggestion was laughable. French war criminals didn't dare set foot on British soil. They certainly didn't set foot on British soil when they had a perfectly robust criminal network in place to do their dirty work for them. She was playing him again and that grated. For show he chuckled, shook off her hand and settled back in the seat comfortably. 'The Comte de Saint-Aubin-de-Scellon is here. In Devon. Risking his neck, his entire lucrative smuggling operation and the future freedom of his beloved Emperor Napoleon simply to retrieve the daughter of his mistress, when he could just as easily get the Boss to do it for him? I'm sure he loves you like one of his own, Jessamine...'

'He hates me.' That small voice again. 'He hates me with a vengeance. Because I have given him good reason to hate me.'

Flint was tired of talking to the back of her head. If she wanted to play games and spin yarns, she could do it straight to his face. 'Yes, I'm sure...' His hand reached around to cup her chin to turn it and the words stopped dead in his throat.

She was crying.

Not the preferred, single, stoic tear he had seen before. Not done in a becoming and suitably heart-wrenching fashion designed to manipulate. These were proper tears. Flint had seen enough fake ones to know the real thing when it was presented to him. Her contorted face was awash and more spilled silently over her lashes like a waterfall before she succumbed to them fully and crumpled over her lap.

Numerous years of female histrionics at home had hardened him to tears, or so Flint thought, but these—these were something entirely different. These physically hurt. He had never witnessed utter despair and hopelessness before. It was as if she had given up and he hated it. She didn't deserve that.

He knew that in his heart.

Which had clearly gone quite mad.

Impotently he observed, no knowing what to do or say and not trusting his visceral response any further than he trusted her, until he could stand it no more and hauled her into his arms. Immediately he regretted it. She burrowed into his chest, her small shoulders quaking with the exertion, and all he wanted to do was take away her pain.

'There, there...' Pointless words, but all he had. He couldn't tell her it would all be all right, because it wouldn't. Ultimately, she was destined to be executed and he was tasked with delivering her to the executioner. A mission which was getting harder and harder the more time he spent with her.

Because he wanted to believe her, damn it. Not her words or her practised deceptions. He believed the emotions swirling in her dark eyes. Trusted the nagging instinct which told him she was intrinsically good despite the mountain of evidence to the contrary. Was his usually impeccable judgement now so hopelessly clouded with lust and...whatever else this odd connection he felt for her was, stronger now that he held her than ever before. Whatever it was, it was unwelcome and stupid. Flint was allowing himself to be dragged into her web. She was probably no better than the woman all those years ago who had bewitched him, lain with him, then used Flint's own pistol to shoot his father as she had tried to escape. Thankfully, the bullet sailed straight through, missing all his vital organs. But the subsequent infection…

Flint still hadn't forgiven himself for allowing her to seduce him when he knew, deep down in his gut, he was being played. Although this time, his gut told him differently. Should he trust it? And so soon? The last thing he should be doing was displaying his weakness and comforting her, yet he knew he couldn't stop. Not now that her face was tucked against his heart and her hands were clinging to him like he was the only piece of driftwood after a shipwreck.

It seemed more appropriate to hold her tightly and rock her gently, something he had discovered worked exceptionally well with infants, although this grown woman felt nothing like his assorted nieces and nephews. Just as precious, or indeed more so, and his solemn duty to protect regardless of her crimes. 'Let me help you, Jess.'

'If only you could.'

'I'll do my best.' As he said it, Flint realised he would likely do whatever it took to take away her sadness, because her sadness hurt him, too. 'Trust me to help you.'

Miraculously, the racking sobs turned to less worrying hiccupping as she forced herself to breathe. Her face tilted up and she searched his face. 'I want to believe I have a life to live. I want to trust you.'

'You can.' The pain in his own chest was yet to lessen so he found his nose buried in her riot of loose hair and nuzzled.

Nuzzled!

This had gone far too far. The vixen had bewitched him. He needed to let go!

'I'm s-sorry. I d-don't cry. I n-never let m-myself cry, but...' The rest of the sentence was swallowed by ugly snorting and moaning of the like he had never heard before and prayed never to hear again; the truth of the tears leaking through his waistcoat, shirt and piercing his heart through his ribs like a dagger.

'Better out than in.'

Were any more inane platitudes going to spill from his mouth? More importantly, why was he incapable of letting go? That the latter might have something to do with the icy tentacles of dread which had snaked up his spine and kindled real fear on her behalf was a worry. In his line of work, Flint had learned to trust his instincts. They hadn't truly failed him yet. However, those same instincts were screaming at him to trust her and listen. Properly.

'Why does Saint-Aubin hate you?'

She stilled in his arms. 'Because I did something very bad.'

'Define *bad*?'

'Something catastrophic. I—I...' She lifted her face to meet his and allowed him to search her eyes. 'I t-took something valuable...then I destroyed it. On purpose. He will stop at nothing until he gets it all back.'

She was talking in riddles. 'If you destroyed it, how can he get it back?'

'B-because it is all in here.' She tapped her head. 'Every name. Every contact. Every ship he uses. Now that my mother is dead and her precious notebook is at the bottom of the sea, only I know it all. He will stop at nothing to get it all back. N-nothing...' She crumpled again and buried her head in her hands, rocking herself in the loose cage of his arms while the full extent of her confession sunk in.

Did she really hold that much power? This tiny, unpredictable, maddening woman? 'What are you saying, Jess? I thought you were just the messenger?' They all had. A knowledgeable one who would be eminently useful to their cause, but not the font of all knowledge. The linchpin.

'*Oui*. That is true. But after the war my mother helped Saint-Aubin build his network. He entrusted her with the organisational details he had no patience for.'

'And since your mother's death, that notebook and that task was yours?'

'I helped her. I had no choice. When she passed he forced me to continue. He was cruel. Ruthless. And I was...' Her eyes lifted to lock with his, then immediately dipped as if ashamed suddenly. 'When the navy came and dragged me to the ship, the opportunity presented itself to destroy that book and all it stood for—and foolishly I took it...' She dissolved again, disappearing into her hands, leaving Flint reeling. Was she suggesting that Saint-Aubin was too detached from his business? Too focused on raising Napoleon's new army to concern himself with the details? Surely not—because if she was, then it meant the information she held inside her stubborn and brilliant head was more than damning. It was essential.

'I thought he would hire men to drag me back to France... *Ah, mon Dieu! Je suis perdue—c'est la fin!* Of course he—he has come here himself! It is all too valuable. He doesn't trust another soul to hear it!'

And only she knew it all.

The gravity of the situation made the carriage suddenly oppressive. Jess was the solution. With her testimony, they could crush the entire smuggling ring to dust in one fell swoop.

Her fingers curled into the fabric of his shirt

as she stared up at him beseechingly. 'Promise me—if he finds me—I beg you, Monsieur Flint…kill me! Kill me before Saint-Aubin gets his hands on me!'

In that moment, Flint had an epiphany. She wasn't desperate to escape in order to get back to France. Jess was running away from it.

For her life.

The rag-tag group of opportunist kidnappers the King's Elite had been expecting were more likely to be an organised battalion of criminals fighting for their lives, too. Powerful men with powerful connections and the resources to enact a devastating revenge rather than hang for treason themselves. They needed an entire legion of soldiers armed with cannons, not fifty of Lord Fennimore's finest!

There was so much more he still needed to understand. Gaps in his knowledge that would take hours to fill and get straight. So many moving parts and details he would need to prise out of her, the full extent of her treachery for which she would still need to answer. But if what she was saying was true—and God help him, but he believed her—then the woman they were stupidly using as bait was the miracle they had been waiting for. The weapon to bring down the whole of the Boss's vast and devastating smuggling ring. And they had made her a sitting duck. His first priority now had to be to undo the damage before it was too late. The second they left Plymouth and hit the open road…

His fist pummelled the ceiling of the coach. 'Turn around! Take us back to the inn as quick as you can!'

She flinched, betrayal etched on her lovely features as the carriage instantly veered at speed. 'You said you would help me!'

His finger touched her lips again while his other hand cupped her cheek tenderly, willing her to understand he had meant what he'd said. 'I know. He's there. But so are some of my men. If we stay on the road…' Flint didn't want to think about the awful possibilities. 'Back at the inn you'll be secure in the short term while I figure out a way to get you out safely.' Where he could draft in the Excise Men and every Royal Navy sailor docked in Plymouth to guard her and her valuable secrets.

The next ten minutes were the most fraught of Jess's life. The carriage sped back to the inn, turning sharply to enter the courtyard while Gray bellowed. In response, men came from every direction, pistols raised, though not at them. They surrounded the carriage, looking out, while Gray poked his head in and Flint issued a stream of orders. Jess couldn't help peering out of the window, but the glossy carriage carrying Saint-Aubin was nowhere to be seen.

Using his body as a shield once more, Flint rushed her inside with the small army of armed men ringing them. She was ushered briskly back to the solitary bedchamber at the very top of the inn again, only this time the door remained blessedly open and the small landing and narrow staircase were crammed full of guards.

'I'll be back.' He squeezed her hand reassuringly, then did something incomprehensible. He pressed his own pistol into it. 'Just in case.' And then he was gone, pushing past his men and disappearing back downstairs, leaving her all alone but oddly touched.

He must believe her. He must see something worth saving.

For the first time in for ever Jess wasn't all alone.

Beneath the floor, she heard the disgruntled sounds of the patrons and staff being evacuated as his men commandeered the inn. Doors opened and slammed and furniture moved as every guest room was thoroughly searched. When the all clear was shouted, Jess finally breathed. Then promptly stopped when at least twenty horses galloped into the courtyard. As none of her guards appeared perturbed by this, she went to the window and sagged in relief when she saw Flint directing a stream of reinforcements. He was clearly in charge, yet not one of his men wore a uniform. Farmers, ostlers, the man who swept the bar, the bare-knuckle driver who had sat atop the carriage, even Gray — all of them snapped to attention at the sound of Flint's voice.

The frenzied activity was followed by an eerie calm. When it should have been the busiest part of the day, the inn stood silent. No longer an inn, more a fortress. Despite everything, Jess began to feel safer. Someone brought her tea. She sat on the bed to drink it. As soon as she had finished, she kept her finger on the trigger and simply stared at the open door, waiting.

Chapter Ten

By late afternoon, Jess found herself dressed in rags, her face smeared in soot and her hair pinned tightly to her head and hidden under a boy's peaked cap. Gray had personally issued her the disguise a few minutes before and administered the soot himself, but had yet to explain why she was wearing it. Apparently, the fewer people who saw her transformation, the better. The bedchamber door was now firmly shut.

'Do you not trust your own men?' A worrying thought, especially as she had trustingly lain the pistol down to change and had not seen it since.

'With my life, *mademoiselle*, but if one of them is captured and tortured this is the only way we can all be certain they won't confess what they know.' At her sharp intake of breath, he shook his head, but his normally cheeky smile had vanished. 'Hopefully, I'm being pessimistic, something I am prone to in moments of stress.

The truth is they'll all feel better knowing nothing and it is the usual way we do things.'

'I know nothing and I don't feel particularly good about it.'

'Flint will explain.' He tidied up the cloth he'd been using to dirty her face and stuffed it in the sturdy large box he had brought in with him. 'It's his plan.'

She would have probed more, but it sounded as if an army was marching outside. Many boots thudded in unison and seemed to be headed to the inn. Taking her lead from Gray, Jess tried not to feel disturbed.

'The cavalry's here. Or, in this case, the Royal Marines. A few Excise Men and there might be some navy there, too.' Motioning for her to stay back from the window, Gray looked out and smiled in relief. 'There's at least seventy uniforms down there. Not a bad effort for such short notice, but one of the few benefits of being here in Plymouth. There's barracks aplenty. Flint wanted to put on a show. I dare say they've scared off Saint-Aubin for the moment.'

'Are they to be my escort?'

'No. I am.' Lord Flint strode through the door and closed it behind him. 'They are a decoy.' He pulled at his cravat and shrugged out of his coat, then began to briskly unbutton his waistcoat, while Jess tried to concentrate on the ramifications of his words. Not easy to do when it was obvious he was undressing.

'But there are about a hundred armed men down there. Surely some of them will be accompanying us to London?'

'We're travelling alone.' He gripped the hem of his shirt and pulled it over his head. Instantly her silly pulse fluttered as she drank in the sight of his broad chest. The perfectly formed muscles on his arms and shoulders. The intriguing dusting of dark golden hair that arrowed downwards and disappeared beneath the waistband of his snug breeches. Breeches that hugged a very pleasing behind. *Mon Dieu!* Very nice indeed.

Gray tossed him a dingy garment and he effortlessly caught it in one hand. 'We'll continue to head west out of Plymouth, but with some skilful misdirection, Saint-Aubin and his henchmen will believe you are headed east.'

The magnificent chest disappeared under the tatty, long, grey shirt and to her shame she mourned the loss of it. Why should she feel bad for that? Jess had promised herself to fully enjoy all of life's tiny pleasures going forward and the sight of that handsome man's chest was wholly pleasurable. As long as *he* had no idea that it affected her, what was the harm of looking her fill? 'Are they going to march all the way t-to... London?' *Mon Dieu!* He had dropped his breeches with no warning. Toned, golden legs were clearly visible beneath the irritatingly long shirt which hung to mid-thigh. Where was a gentle breeze when you needed one? The needy woman inside her was desperate to feast her eyes on that derrière. Gray's knowing smirk suggested he suspected she was drooling, so Jess tore her gaze away and forced herself to wander back to the bed to sit in a manner she prayed made her appear nonplussed rather than considerably warmer than she had been five minutes before.

'Too dangerous. Too much chance of them realising that it isn't you in the coach, but a slight and rather surly Scotsman who is not impressed with the prospect of wearing a frock. Poor McBride.' He and Gray shared an amused grin at the thought. Her gaoler's—no, her rescuer's— green eyes danced and that dancing did disconcerting things to her already off-kilter insides. Or perhaps that was the muscles in his thighs? The indelible memory of his naked chest... 'The Marines will escort *your* carriage to a heavily armed warship anchored in the harbour and sail with you, complete with a full naval escort, all the way to Tilbury. Only then will they march to the capital. It should be quite a spectacle. Meanwhile, we escape while nobody is looking.'

Saint-Aubin would be looking. He was no

fool. 'There will be assassins watching every door.'

'Something I am banking on.' Gray passed him the tin of soot and he smeared it liberally over his own face and hair. It was the first time Jess had seen Lord Flint looking anything but dapper. However, the rough-and-ready dishevelled look suited him just as well. Perhaps better. In working men's clothes he certainly seemed more approachable. The soot smudged away most of the aristocratic aloofness and she liked his hair rumpled. 'I want them to be in no doubt *nobody* left surreptitiously.'

There was a soft tap on the door and the bare-knuckle fighter poked his head in. 'Everything is set. McBride is ready, although still fuming. But to his credit he looks quite bonny in a gown.'

'Then let's get on with it.'

Jess found herself propelled from the sanctuary of her temporary bedchamber and taken to the furthest end of the narrow landing, desperate to ask a million questions, but conscious that time appeared to be of the essence. Using Gray's cupped hands to boost his foot, Lord Flint opened the tiny loft hatch in the ceiling. Its position and poor light had rendered it almost invisible beforehand. Using only the power of his arms, he effortlessly levered himself through the hole, then his dirty blond head and one arm poked back down. Gray hoisted her to grasp it and she practically flew through the air into the cramped and airless attic beyond. When a sack and a selection of brushes joined them, she got her first insight into the plan.

'We are posing as chimney sweeps?' Which suggested heights! Of all the plans, he had to choose one involving a drop!

'A perfectly legitimate reason to be on a roof. But only I am the sweep. You are my climbing boy. Every decent sweep has an apprentice to stuff up a chimney.' His charm didn't lessen the way her stomach clenched at the prospect. Drat him. Although despite her irrational fears Jess could see the sense of it, as long as he had another plan to get them safely off the rooftop, too.

He stood, balancing on the joists, and helped her to her feet before the hatch was sealed again. However, instead of being plunged into darkness, a thin shaft of light lit the way and they soon emerged hunched behind an enormous smoking chimney where another man waited for them. Jess gazed around, keeping her gaze forward to combat the inevitable panic and was surprised to see how close all the rooftops were. The different shades of tiles stretched before her like a road.

'There's a fellow keeps wandering up and down the alley. You'll have to be quick.' Crouching low, he took them to the edge of the roof where they silently waited. Her silly eyes drifted downwards and fresh bile rose in her throat. It was a significant drop on to hard cobbles. A fall here wouldn't break bones, it would kill.

Exactly as Flint's man had warned, a fearsome-looking fellow passed below. No sooner had he gone than a plank of wood was used to bridge the frightening gap between the inn and the building across the alleyway. Flint darted across it carrying the brushes, making the passage look easy when it was anything but.

Like a fool, she looked down and dizziness swamped her. The prospect of the sheer drop very nearly cost her the remnants of her last meal. One wrong step and Jess would plummet three storeys. *Ah, bon sang!* Too many feet away, Lord Flint beckoned for her to follow.

She dithered. Then set her jaw stubbornly. It was the only way. Just don't look down. Her foot felt like lead as she planted it on the plank and her legs trembled as she edged out. Jess forced her feet to shuffle along. Forced herself to swallow past the knot of fear lodged in her throat and to remember to breathe. 'Just six more steps, Jess. You're almost there.'

Six steps.

She shuffled again.

Five.

'Take my hand.'

She grabbed it, ridiculously grateful that those muscles in his arms had a purpose beyond the aesthetic, and practically threw herself towards him. He caught her in a hug that she wanted to melt into, offering pathetic thanks for his solid presence. Instead, she arranged her features to disguise her silly fears and hastily put some distance between both him and the perilous edge and the dangerous chasm below.

As Lord Flint's man quietly removed all evidence of their escape and disappeared, Flint took her hand and dragged her behind the cover of the chimney. 'We're going to take the roofs all along the street away from the port.' He pointed across the sea of slate and tile before them. 'I reckon we've got a good couple of hundred yards of rooftop there. When the coast is clear, we'll find somewhere deserted to jump down and then we'll keep walking. As soon as we're out of Plymouth we'll stick to the fields and the coastal paths.' He made it sound simple.

'Just us?' She must focus on the distant future rather than the knot of irrational panic that had appeared at the words *Jump down*.

'Only in the short term. Gray and some of his men will double back and meet us. Even if he suspects he's been duped, Saint-Aubin will be looking for a beautiful woman and her battalion of ferocious body guards on the main roads. Not a vagabond and his son in the country lanes.'

Flint regretted his honesty the moment he saw her eyes soften at the word *beautiful*. 'You think me beautiful?' The tinge of awe and wonder at the compliment, as if she never received such admiration, reminded him that despite the unexpected change in circumstances he still would be foolish to trust her further than he could throw her.

'Compared to most chimney sweeps? Absolutely.' The dewy expression melted, making him see it for what it was. 'Come on. Let's put some distance between us and Saint-Aubin before the carriage leaves.'

Like most commercial towns, Plymouth had grown to meet the demand, which in turn meant that buildings were crammed together as every bit of available space was utilised. Many of the rooftops butted so close to the next that one only had to scramble up a ledge or take a small step or two down. At the end of the row of houses, Flint left his charge sat huddled in a recess while he took himself to the edge, lay down on his stomach and checked the ground below.

As one would expect at two in the afternoon, the main street was still bustling with activity, but there was no sign of the burly henchman and, to Flint's trained eye, nothing and nobody looked amiss. Still, that did't mean he was prepared to take any unnecessary chances. Their desolate elevated world was currently considerably safer than the ground and it would be prudent to stick to the roofs for as long as feasibly possible. He didn't dare attempt to cross the road. From up here that would be suicide, as the opposite building was a good ten feet away. Even with a decent run up, the chances of him making it were slim. Jess's shorter legs didn't stand a chance.

Their only choice was to go left across the rooftops, a route which took them deeper into the town where there was more chance of someone seeing them. That couldn't be helped and the chances of a random pedestrian taking the trouble to scrutinise two filthy sweeps were slight enough to be worth the risk. The gap between this roof and its neighbour was, he estimated, a little more than four feet at its narrowest. He could make that effortlessly and the minx had already proved herself to be of an athletic disposition. Using his elbows, he shuffled towards her.

'There's a bit of a jump, I'm afraid. A few feet, but certainly doable.' Flint pointed at the spot and she craned her neck to stare at it.

'Doable?' Was that fear in her eyes? 'Perhaps for you, Monsieur Flint.'

'If I go first and you take a bit of a run up, I'll catch you.'

'You will catch me?' She kept taking his words and turning them into a question, her disbelief evident in the tone of her voice. 'I don't think so.'

'The alternative is to clamber down to that busy street and draw unwanted attention to ourselves or sit it out here and hope the men after you don't eventually work their way up to the roof. Of course, we might starve in the interim, what with us having few provisions aside from those brushes.'

Her dark eyes narrowed. 'This is not the time for sarcasm.'

'Nor is it the time for indecisiveness or discussion. We have one viable exit and we need to take it now.' Flint couldn't be bothered to argue and hoisted the brushes on to his shoulder. Making sure the coast was clear and nobody was glancing skywards, he paused, then leapt across the gap.

Chapter Eleven

For a full minute she stood a few feet from the edge and wobbled. That was the only way to describe the erratic swaying, blinking and swallowing. 'Come on! We don't have all day!' He held out his arms impatiently and gestured for her to jump with his hands. She ignored it. 'What is the problem?'

Her eyes lifted to lock with his warily. 'Give me a moment.'

'We don't have a moment!' Flint was quickly losing his temper until he noticed she was a bit green around the gills. Surely this fearless creature wasn't scared of a little jump? A woman who had dived off a ship, risked her life swimming close to perilous rocks and who had scaled a small cliff in the not-so-distant past? 'Are you scared of heights?' He couldn't help sounding incredulous. From what he knew of her already, she was reliably formidable. Admirably so.

'Not so much heights as the drops.' Her eyes dipped again and widened as she glanced briefly at the narrow, rubbish-filled passageway below. The wariness and genuine fear brought his damned protective streak to the fore and he felt guilty for putting her through this ordeal and for not noticing her palpable fear before now.

'You won't drop because I will catch you. Go back a few steps to force some momentum and run.'

'How do I know you will catch me?' Her expression was now pained, her eyes beseeching. Unbelievably, this fearless woman needed his reassurance.

'Because that pretty head of yours is stuffed full of valuable information the government needs. And because I said so. You need to trust me, Jess.'

After what seemed to take a great deal of effort, she nodded and took herself back several feet and inhaled. Her trim body taut, she crouched as if about to run, but her feet remained firmly planted on the roof. She couldn't hold his gaze, her eyes kept dropping and he could see the fear was destroying her confidence with each passing second. The same awful terror he had witnessed in the carriage had returned and all because of a little jump. The unexpected vulnerability tugged at his heart and created a well of tenderness within him.

'Don't look down, sweetheart. You can do this. Look at me. I *will* catch you.'

After an age she did, allowing him to see every bit of the stubborn bravery that made her so formidable struggling back to the fore. Damn, but she was spirited and tenacious! Nothing fazed her once she set her mind to it and he liked that about her. Respected her even. She faced every obstacle head on, no matter how much she feared it. He held out his arms again, smiling his encouragement this time, willing her to face her fears and trust him, his feet braced in readiness.

'Jump, Jess. I promise I won't allow you to fall.'

'If you do, Monsieur Flint, and I die, then I promise you I will return as a ghost and haunt you for ever!'

In her customary difficult fashion, no sooner had she issued that warning salvo than she dashed forward and threw herself across the gap with such force she sent them both flying backwards as he grabbed her.

Flint's body absorbed the brunt of the blow. The combination of the unforgiving tiles and the cannonball that was Jess pushed all the air out of his lungs in a whoosh as she landed sprawled on top of him, clearly astounded and delighted to still be alive.

'You caught me!'

'I said I would.'

She was smiling down at him, her face inches from his, her cap listing on her head at an odd, erotically becoming angle. Clearly she was a woman used to being let down by others on a regular basis because his necessary and practical gesture seemed to leave her overwhelmed with more gratitude than it required—and that bothered him and made him feel quite noble at the same time. What crushing disappointments lay in this conundrum of a woman's past? Who had let her down so badly? Was that why she was so tenacious and indomitable? She had had to be.

'Thank you.' Beneath his fingers, her body trembled slightly. 'I shall cancel all plans to haunt you from beyond the grave.'

Although there was no doubt she would continue to haunt him from the land of the living, his fevered dreams and errant thoughts were bound to haunt him and taunt him to distraction.

'I am delighted to hear it.'

Her uncontrived giggle was infectious and Flint found himself grinning up at her. It was a mistake. This close he could see the flecks of copper in her dark eyes. Count every long, black eyelash. The air around them shifted and for a moment the rooftop and the danger disappeared.

One fat tendril of dark hair had escaped its pins and bobbed in time to her rapid breathing. Breathing that made him supremely aware of her full breasts flattened against his chest and certain parts of his anatomy intimately pressed against hers. The realisation simultaneously sent a hot bolt of lust the entire length of his body which settled inappropriately in his groin. Of its own accord, his gaze automatically fixed on her lips and despite valiantly trying to tear it away, he found himself staring at them covetously and seriously considered surrendering to the sultry call of temptation by pressing his mouth to hers.

His hands appeared to have settled themselves very comfortably in the valley where her spine dipped before flaring again at her bottom. One of hers was spread warmly across his heart. He liked it. Rather a lot. When the tip of her tongue moistened those plump lips and her brown eyes darkened as she gazed down at him, Flint almost succumbed and stole a kiss before common sense returned like a hard punch in the gut.

Aside from the insurmountable obstacle of her impending trial for treason and his own sworn duty to King and country to deliver her to that trial, kissing the tempestuous and terminally unpredictable Lady Jessamine Fane at any time would be foolhardy in the extreme. He had done that and knew the cost. Kissing her on a random rooftop while bloodthirsty assassins were desperate to hunt her down was downright stupidity.

Besides, Flint wasn't attracted to tempestuous women prone to emotionally charged outbursts. He certainly wasn't attracted to traitors no matter how vulnerable or admirably tenacious or breathtakingly beautiful he found them. And he would not be seduced by the feel of her body resting upon his no matter how perfectly her petite, rounded softness melted against his and felt so very right.

Right?

What the blazes had got into him? He unceremoniously pushed her off and quickly rolled out of temptation's way.

'We had best get moving.'

Avoiding her eyes while ignoring the pain in his back and the inconvenient bulge in his breeches, Flint jumped to his feet and made a hash of gathering up the blasted brushes. He dropped one of them twice before he was able to continue and found himself moving with considerable speed simply to put some distance between them. What madness had possessed him to plan an escape that left the pair of them all alone with each other for the next twenty-four hours? Perhaps more.

He'd never walked from Plymouth to St Austell before. It was a solid day's ride. He had done it enough that he knew the route backwards and, because he was more inclined to take his horse as the crow flew, Flint also knew how to navigate the miles of fields and moors which stripped an hour or more off the journey time. But walking and this late in the day...good grief! They would probably have to stop for the night, somewhere well off the beaten track in case they were spotted, and then what?

A long night of forbidden temptation loomed, drenched in an unwanted sea of confused emotions, and there was not a single thing he could do about it except resist. It was then that Flint realised he should have listened to Gray, not insisted that his second oversee the elaborate misdirection on board the boat bound for London.

His reasons had been sound enough. If Saint-Aubin's lackeys had been watching them, then they would need to see a familiar face to believe the decoy. Gray had argued in that case it made more sense for *him* to escort the prisoner, freeing Flint to stand all windswept and smug on the deck. Far more convincing, when a simple driver was more forgettable. But Flint hadn't wanted anyone else to guard Jess and perhaps, although it pained him to acknowledge it, he had not wanted to have to share her company either.

He had wanted to protect her—knowing full well he was also extremely attracted to her and had been since he had first seen her in that brig in the Channel. *Two were less conspicuous than three.* He had actually used those exact words to justify being her sole guardian on this leg of the journey and, being the most senior member of the King's Elite involved in the mission, with the legacy of his impeccable service and legendary calm, flawless judgement in his favour, he got his way.

He had let his urges overrule what was best for the good of the mission, something he would never do again, and those same urges would now torture him on the long walk ahead.

Idiot!

Lord save him from troublesome women and his worrying and inappropriate reaction to this one in particular!

Jess did her level best to keep up with Lord Flint's long-legged strides, but the uneven nature of the rutted moorland he was striding across and her own significantly shorter, tired limbs made it virtually impossible. Clearly he was on a mission to put as much distance between them and Saint-Aubin as possible, something she absolutely applauded, but as they had been walking at this blistering pace since they had alighted the ferry at a place called Cremyll over two hours ago—nor had seen anything not resembling a sheep or rocks in the last hour—it felt unnecessary. They were in the middle of nowhere. Just the two of them.

Of course, there was also the chance that he wanted to put some distance between the two of them now that they were out of harm's way. He had been standoffish since the oddly charged moment when she had thanked him for catching her.

Perhaps he had an inkling that she had rather enjoyed being sprawled across him? Jess had lingered unnecessarily much longer than good manners dictated, but it had felt glorious being held by those strong arms and her mind had gone a little woolly almost the second her body had realised it was deliciously intertwined with his. Or perhaps it was simply gratitude at being alive when for the last few days she had felt so guilty and selfish for surviving at all?

A little woolly! *Ah, Seigneur!* At least to herself she should call a spade a spade. All rational thought had evaporated at the precise moment of contact and she had wanted nothing more than to be close to the bothersome man! For a second, she had foolishly thought he might want to kiss her because he was gazing at her lips and beneath her fingers she could feel his heart beating faster, exactly as hers was—then he had scowled in disgust and knocked Jess sideways in his hurry to get away. He had barely said a civil word in the hours since.

Even when they had clambered down from their safe perch on the rooftops, his behaviour had been abrupt. Despite finding the perfect building to ease their descent, an old warehouse that had been added to so many times they were able to use each new addition almost like stairs, there had been the one drop too steep for Jess's legs and nerves to cope with. Lord Flint had reluctantly taken her hands and lowered her, but she had seen the way his fists had clenched the second she had let go and he had scowled as if he found the merest touch offensive.

Which probably meant he knew what her inexperienced and foolish heart had responded to in that fraught moment and was royally offended by the prospect. In turn, his blatant offence offended, because she wasn't a traitor no matter how much the possibility that she might be still nagged and that had soured her mood towards him as well. That would teach her for lowering her guard and mistaking practicality for kindness. *Sweetheart! Trust me!* The conniving, duplicitous wretch had used exactly the right words to get her to comply. He might have saved her life in the short term, but only to preserve it long enough for her trial. Men were intrinsically untrustworthy. Jess kept forgetting that. He would say or do whatever suited him to successfully get his way. Therefore, she would use him, too, for as long as it suited her. Right now, it suited her not to be all alone when she was practically dead on her feet, sad and alone—and to be with a resourceful, capable man who was duty-bound not to want her dead just yet.

They crowned the top of an incline and Lord Flint stopped abruptly, pointing to the ruins of what once had been a cottage. 'It will be dark soon. We can bed down there for a few hours and set off again at dawn. It's not sensible to try to navigate the moors at night.'

Jess didn't argue. All of a sudden she was exhausted as the toll of the last few fraught days seemed to weigh down her limbs and her shoulders. Wearily she traipsed several feet behind him to the building. By the time she got to the derelict single-storey dwelling, he was unpacking the sack he had continued to carry after he had abandoned the sweep's brush as soon as they were out of sight of the ferry.

Apparently, he had come prepared. Blankets and a tied parcel of food were soon unwrapped and laid out on a surprisingly intact yet chilly stone floor. It was a shame the ancient roof hadn't fared as well, but at least there was enough of it to shelter under if the heavens opened. At a push. She stared through the two remaining rotting beams to the waning sky above.

'I've never slept outside before.' Or this close to a man, although Jess kept that to herself. Admitting she was inexperienced with men in general and nervous at the prospect of lying next to one gave him the upper hand.

'Beggars can't be choosers and we certainly resemble beggars and the moor is reassuringly desolate. But even so, we must be pragmatic. We daren't risk an inn.'

The remote ruin was tiny. There was what was left of one room no bigger than eight feet across and six feet deep. She sat down heavily and tugged off her cap.

'I wasn't complaining—merely making an observation.'

Jess began tugging at the multitude of hairpins which had been required to hide all her hair from the world, then sighed in relief as it finally loosened and she massaged her aching scalp briskly with her finger tips. 'But I shall complain about the hairpins. Who knew my head would tire through wearing them?'

Chapter Twelve

Her hair fell to touch the floor beneath her bottom like a black silk cape, making Flint's mouth go dry as he watched her close her eyes, toss her head back and sigh. Instantly, in that seemingly innocent, unconscious gesture she transformed from the androgynous creature he had convinced himself he could blot out of his vivid imaginings for King and country to a seductive siren who tormented his thoughts in seconds. It was hard to remember the mission when his entire body yearned. Intentional. No doubt.

'Should we light a fire?' She hugged her arms, a tiny crease forming between her eyes as she shivered. 'It is surprisingly cold in here.'

Not for Flint. The sight of all that hair had suddenly made his temperature soar. 'The moors can be a bit chilly even in May—but, alas, we daren't light a fire in case it arouses suspicion.' He found himself draping one of the coarse blankets around her shoulders before sitting back and busying himself by breaking off a huge chunk of bread. Bread he was fairly certain he would now struggle to swallow against errant thoughts of snuggling beneath that same blanket with her later.

'Ah well, I have slept in worse. At least the air is fresh and the sky clear.'

She broke her own bread and chewed, seemingly content to allow the companionable silence to hang. However, all that did was make Flint more aware of how intimate it all was. The spring sunset, the confined area of the cottage and her damned hair tormenting him close enough that it wouldn't take much effort to reach out his hand and run his fingers through it as they ached to. He needed to do something to break the cosy mood and remind himself of his mission.

'Define *worse*.'

'That stinking brig for starters. *Mon Dieu*... so filthy it was like a pig sty.' Those little sprinkles of breathy French in her conversation played havoc with his senses. Tingles danced along his spine at the sound, making him yearn more rather than distracting him. 'Mind you, the *pension* in Cherbourg was no better. At night, I could feel the rats scurrying over my bedding.'

She shuddered at the memory. 'This is a palace compared to those.'

'But I thought you lived in Saint-Aubin's chateau?' The run-down hostel the navy had captured her in was surely just the place where the smuggling business was organised?

'Not at the end. Although chateaux can be prisons, too, Monsieur Flint.'

At his sceptical expression she gave a matter-of-fact Gallic shrug. 'I doubt you will believe me, but as much as I loathed him and despaired of my mother's attachment to him, I had no idea what the pair of them were embroiled in. I assumed the suffocating manner in which we lived was symptomatic of the loss of the war and Saint-Aubin's close connection to Bonaparte. I stupidly thought every former officer of the *Grande Armée* had to live ensconced behind high gates with armed guards out of necessity. What a fool I was. So naïve.' A charming wrinkle emerged between her brows as she appeared annoyed at herself. 'As the years went by, our claustrophobic existence became normal. I grew up with that and stupidly never questioned it. But I rebelled. Repeatedly. And soon I was watched and escorted around the very same grounds I was forbidden to leave. It was cloying, but again, I didn't realise it was out of the ordinary. In many respects, I lived a very sheltered life, Monsieur

Flint. Until my mother fell ill and needed assistance with her work, I was ignorant of their involvement with the smugglers. By the time I found out, it was too late to flee.'

'You're right. I don't believe you.' But his gut wanted him to. 'You never overheard anything suspicious? Nothing was ever let slip over a family dinner?'

'Dinner? I am not sure what you imagine my *family* was like, Monsieur Flint, except to tell you my mother and Saint-Aubin had a very exclusive relationship. A relationship which occurred to the *exclusion* of everything and everyone else. He controlled her and she allowed him to do so unquestioningly because he was the sun and moon to her. I always thought it unhealthy, her intense dependency on him alone, yet she couldn't see his cruel and callous nature and refused to hear a bad word against him because he flattered her ego. But he *was* cruel and he *was* callous and I hated him from the outset.'

'Define *cruel* and *callous*?'

'For a man who has murdered so many, I dare say I got off lightly.' That hand flapped again dismissively, although he was sure the question made her uncomfortable. Especially as the fingers of that hand unconsciously settled to soothe the scar around the wrist of the other, making him believe whatever personal truth she had let slip, she was not inclined to confide it fully yet. 'Suffice it to say, my intense dislike of Saint-Aubin—and his of me—drove a wedge between my mother and I long ago. She preferred to be estranged from her only child than believe any criticism of her lover or incur his wrath. We rarely spoke, let alone shared our meals together. I was moved to the furthest wing of the chateau from their apartments at sixteen. Weeks would go by when I never saw either of them or enquired after them. We all preferred it that way.'

An existence which must have been lonely. As much as Flint's family drove him to distraction with their meddling, he had never been lonely. If anything, his house was filled with too much love. Something he should perhaps make more effort to be thankful for going forward. Jess's solitary existence sounded miserable. 'After my mother fell ill, the illusion of my freedom was soon stripped away.' Unconsciously she rubbed her wrists once, making Flint instantly queasy at the unmentioned implications.

'It was Saint-Aubin who chained you.'

'He found me a challenge.' Something that wasn't surprising, but again her eyes refused to meet his. 'Especially after my mother fell ill.'

'You tried to escape?'

'You know me well already, Monsieur Flint. Many times. I am not inclined to be controlled and dictated to.' Her mouth curved into a mischievous smile. 'And, of course, I almost burned his precious chateau to the ground within days of my mother's death, so he had me removed to the hovel in Cherbourg. Despite the rats and the guards, I preferred it there.'

'Why?'

'The guards were…illiterate.' An odd answer.

'And that was a good thing because…?'

Her expression closed. 'Is this a conversation or an interrogation, Monsieur Flint? And if it is the latter, will my answers prevent me from standing trial or am I to be thrown to the wolves regardless as soon as we get to the capital?'

Flint winced inwardly and sat staring at her for ages. Eventually, he dropped his gaze and raked his hand through his hair impatiently. 'I cannot make promises… There will have to be a trial…' He clamped his errant mouth shut to prevent him from making promises he couldn't guarantee and certainly shouldn't be making, then huffed out a long, guilty sigh. 'The truth is, against all of my better judgement and despite the fact that I still don't trust you as far as I can throw you… I am prepared to… What I mean is…' Prudence dictated he didn't reveal his hand or display his softening towards her lest she use it against him; reality prevented him from offering her false hope. Ultimately it didn't matter what his gut told him. Only the courts could decide her fate. 'If viewed pragmatically, assuming you collaborate fully with the investigation and help us to bring down the smuggling ring, then I am hopeful your sentence will be…lenient.'

'Lenient?' Her eyes hardened like the cold granite walls that surrounded them. 'Define *lenient*, Monsieur Flint.'

She had fumed then. The anger had shimmered off her in waves even as she had lain with her back to him and pretended sleep, and really Flint couldn't blame her. In her shoes, he would have been as heartily unimpressed with his lacklustre explanations and clumsy backtracking, but what choice did he have? If he divided his body into fractions, then three-quarters screamed at him to admit he believed she was telling the truth and firmly believed that she wasn't a traitor. His gut told him she was more an outraged victim than wilfully complicit. Why would Saint-Aubin bother chaining a compliant woman? That didn't make sense. Why would he persist in being both *cruel* and *callous*?

However, that was a feeling—not fact. The remaining quarter, the pragmatic and sensible agent of the Crown, knew he needed more proof than merely her word and that he had a proven weakness for attractive damsels in distress. That part had to guide his actions and he had to temper his need to give her assurances he couldn't yet guarantee. She certainly didn't need to know he fully intended to exert all his influence on Lord Fennimore and the lawyer, Lord Hadleigh, to make them properly listen to her. Nor should he mention he was sorely tempted to move heaven and earth to get her acquitted of any wrong-doing based solely on the existence of those damning scars on her wrists. She didn't deserve to spend another day imprisoned. He felt that deep inside. Did he trust that feeling enough to risk his reputation for her?

His head, filled with nearly ten years' experience of dealing with criminals, said no.

By the time Gray and the rest of the King's Elite made it to Cornwall, Flint hoped he would have prised every detail out of the minx lying next to him, uncovered the truth—whatever that might be—and then the focus of the investigation might shift and her fate could be very different. Or not.

If she was telling the truth, which was a very big *if* indeed, and if she complied.

Right now, he didn't dare sleep in case she bolted again. Another thing he wouldn't blame her for. In her shoes he'd be plotting the same, lulling his guard into a false sense of security and biding his time for the right moment to run.

But if Jess was feigning sleep, it was convincing. She was huddled in a tight ball under her blanket with her back to him, the dappled moonlight shimmering off the curtain of hair that covered her face and her breathing deep and steady. Occasionally she murmured something, appearing agitated and afraid, and he ached to comfort her. He had since they had arrived at this ruined, sorry excuse for a cottage and he had seen the fatigue and worry etched in her lovely face. Despite all her stubborn, dogged strength to escape and survive, and despite her giving as good as she got over their meagre dinner, he could see that her reserves were severely depleted. His troublesome charge was exhausted.

She muttered something incoherent again and whimpered and his heart broke for her. He couldn't get the image of her shackled wrists and the rats clambering over her blankets out of his mind. The depth of her suffering horrified him and those recent scars bore testament to the truth of it. What sort of a monster treated a woman like that? Once Flint got his hands on Saint-Aubin…

Was she shivering?

Gently he reached a hand out and touched what he assumed was her arm and felt her trembling beneath his fingers. It was cold here on the moors. Not bitter by any stretch this late in spring, but the temperature had dropped enough that the air was damp with mist and the granite she lay on wouldn't help keep her warm. If one ignored the obvious curves sent to torture him, there was hardly any meat on her. Flint had felt her ribs and the way her tummy had concaved when he had wrestled her in the sea and seen with his own eyes that she had needed to cinch the cord tight around the scruffy boy's trousers she wore to keep them up. He removed his own blanket and draped it over her, then huddled into his ragged coat to watch her, praying that would do the trick.

After what he assumed was a good fifteen minutes, and when he heard her teeth begin to chatter, he knew he couldn't watch her suffer any more—even if that meant he was doomed to suffer in her stead. Clenching his teeth, he shuffled over and curled his body around her back to warm her, mindful of maintaining enough distance that they didn't exactly touch.

She sensed the heat and instinctively pushed her body back against him, sighing something nonsensical, accented in sleepy French. The hair that taunted him tickled his nose, forcing him to brush it away. Typically, it felt like spun silk and his fingers lingered in the ridiculously long strands far longer than was necessary and certainly far longer than a man in his position should.

Scars aside, she still might be a traitor. Flint was a devoted agent of the Crown. He gritted his teeth and focused on what he had been tasked to do. What England expected him to do. *These odd feelings were transient. He'd experienced similar before...although different. Very different... His career was his life.* Focus. *Focus!*

When her delicious peach of a bottom nestled itself comfortably in his lap, Flint almost groaned aloud at his body's instantaneous reaction, but she was cold and she needed him, so like the *imbécile* she accused him of being, he wrapped his arm around her and let her gratefully absorb his heat. As he expected, it was torture. Then he squeezed his eyes closed, tried to banish all carnal thoughts from his mind and replace them with sensible reminders of his sworn duty, praying for strength and the swift onset of dawn.

Chapter Thirteen

Jess woke slowly in a cocoon of warmth feeling more rested and light of heart than she had in a long time, reluctant to spoil that heady sensation any time soon. She cracked open one eye and swiftly shut it because the early morning rays of the weak dawn sun were too much to cope with just yet. She snuggled into her cosy eiderdown, looking forward to stealing a few more minutes of rest, and then stiffened. The comforter was neither quilted nor filled with the softest down feathers, it was male. Against the wall of her back she could feel his heart beating rhythmically through his ribcage, feel the corded muscles of his thighs wedged beneath hers and something long and hard rested intimately against her bottom.

She considered outrage, but couldn't, because his arm was draped possessively around her waist and his deep, even breathing warmed her neck. Lord Flint was snoring softly, his nose apparently buried in her hair. It was a wholly pleasant sensation, a giddy combination of heat, comfort and an overwhelming feeling of security.

Mon Dieu! Had they spent the whole night thus?

Had she snuggled against him in her sleep or he her?

And more importantly, for the sake of her pride, was he aware of it?

Gingerly, she attempted to move, only to have that strong arm tighten and feel his hips press scandalously against her, so that the full extent of his arousal was gloriously obvious. It did peculiar things to her nerve endings in places she rarely thought about and gave her body shameless ideas. More shockingly, she wasn't inclined to move.

'Morning.' His voice was thick with sleep, but she recognised the exact moment he properly came to because the previously relaxed muscles in his abdomen tightened instantly a second before he released her and rolled hastily away.

They both quickly sat and stared at one another, Jess clutching the blanket like a startled virgin on her wedding night, him deliciously rumpled and clearly embarrassed. The overnight golden stubble suited him and brought out the green of his eyes. His shirt was hanging open at the neck, displaying too much of his chest and reminding her of how she had feasted on the sight of it yesterday. He pulled his coat to cover the unmistakable bulge in his breeches, which immediately drew her eyes there at the exact same moment a ferocious blush heated her face and neck. Mortification made her lash out.

'What do you think you are about?'

'You were cold… Last night. Shivering, in fact. I gave you my blanket and when that didn't work, I moved closer to share my body heat.' He scrambled to his feet and crossed to the other side of the cramped building. Jess had never seen him so discomposed, which was just as well, because a flustered Lord Flint was adorable. In his panic, he became delightfully formal.

'Please accept my most humble of apologies, my lady… I…' He huffed out a noise, a cross between a sigh and a groan. Then stared resolutely at his feet. 'I have no excuses. Except to say you were fast asleep and shivering and I was worried about you… I had intended to move away the moment you were warm again, but I must have nodded off.'

His absolute contrition, the evidence of the two blankets currently covering her body and the knowledge that she had been so perfectly content lying in his arms that she had slept a full night for the first time in months meant she didn't have the heart to make him feel worse. By the looks of him, he was in utter turmoil. And he was blushing. The arrogant, normally unreadable aristocrat was blushing.

'Then let us forget it happened.'

As if she could. She could smell his delicious, subtle cologne on her clothes and still feel the comforting imprint of his body against hers.

He didn't look up. 'Yes. Probably for the best. Thank you...um...we should get going.' With more haste than was necessary, he began to pack away all evidence of their occupation while Jess pinned her wayward hair to her head to within an inch of its life before stuffing it back under her cap. A chunk of bread appeared beneath her nose.

'Eat.'

'Not now, maybe later.'

'There's nothing of you, Jess. You need to build up your strength.'

Their eyes met for the first time since waking. Beneath the lurking embarrassment, his were filled with concern. She found herself complying and nibbled on the crust self-consciously, conscious he was watching her and that something intangible yet significant seemed to have changed between them. She couldn't think of anything to say and he said nothing more to fill the void. When she finally choked down the last of the bread, they both stood wordlessly and set off again across the moors.

They walked at a more sedate pace than the previous day, the obvious isolation of the narrow lane negating the need to rush now that there was no sign they had been followed. It was just as well. The toll of the last few fraught days had left her drooping with fatigue to such an extent putting one foot in front of the other was now an effort. Once again, he had not bothered appraising her of their destination or of how many more hours they were to walk today and didn't appear to want to. Initially, he had probed her about the contents of her mother's notebook and the English aristocrats who were involved with the smugglers with his customary officiousness, but when it became clear she had no intention of telling him anything, Lord Flint had walked the last hour alongside her in awkward silence, his gaze fixed ahead and his expression once again inscrutable.

Jess wished she knew what he was thinking. Was he still embarrassed about this morning? What had possessed him to be so solicitous in the first place to feel it necessary to see that she ate, shared his blanket and dropped all the proprieties to keep her warm? And did any of it mean anything at all, or was she foolishly transferring her own confused emotions on to him in the hope that his opinion of her would soften?

The silence was deafening.

She was annoyed with herself at feeling disappointed because he hadn't offered her any new hope last night to cling to or any hint at his believing in the possibility of her innocence. Her heart screamed that he had almost confessed that he knew she was not a traitor and she so wanted to put her faith in him. She wanted to trust him. Wanted to dare to hope that the sense of security she experienced around him was real rather than transient and that he might see past her crimes and understand she had no choice. Maybe then the nagging guilt that kept forming a tight band around her lungs would begin to lessen and Jess would begin to forgive herself, too. Her head cautioned that it made no difference if she thought the exasperating Lord Flint the most dependable man she had ever met, or the most decent and kind, reminding her that she hadn't met many men outside Saint-Aubin's criminal circle other than her indifferent and cold father. She hardly had a wealth of experience, therefore, to trust such a naïve judgement. He had a job to do and that job was to deliver her safely to the authorities.

Last night was proof of that. Just when she had started to open up to him, he had immediately become officious again, then refused to be drawn on her future or expand upon his precise definition of the word *lenient*—other than to say there was at least a chance she wouldn't face execution if her version of events proved to be the truth. But if it meant she lived out her days as a prisoner, then it was merely swapping one intolerable, unjust existence for another. Which put her right back to where she was before she had confided in him—contemplating yet another escape and facing an uncertain and undoubtedly perilous future all alone. As usual. Just thinking that made her more exhausted.

Jess should be contemplating the best way to extricate herself from his presence for ever rather than hoping for him to miraculously become her saviour rather than her gaoler. She should probably do that soon, well before they reached London and the next locked cell that awaited her. Yet just once she wished fortune would favour her and throw her a bone. If only Lord Flint would give her a chance. *Je souhaiterais…*

'What's wrong?'

His voice wrenched her back to the moors. 'Nothing.' The word came out snippily, she couldn't disguise it.

'You've been huffing and puffing for at least twenty minutes.' Childishly, she ignored him. Of course she was huffing and puffing. Not knowing where one stood had a tendency to cause such a reaction. *Crétin!*

'Look—I know you are still angry at me about this morning.'

Insufferable, clueless man! 'I am not bothered about this morning! I am still irritated about last night!' And now she had inadvertently told him she had rather liked waking up in his arms. He must have noticed because his step faltered briefly. Then he was silent again while he contemplated what was no doubt a suitably banal, measured and insipid response. The agent of the Crown's response. Irritatingly officious to the last. Jess let it hang while her anger bubbled. The trickster! She picked up her pace and purposefully looked away from him in case he saw how much he had hurt her. Nestled among the grass and wildflowers on the verge was a milestone: *Penzance 48 miles.*

They had not turned to be on the road to London. They were still headed west!

Very west. Miles away from the marines and the militia who could protect her and probably closer to Saint-Aubin's cut-throats. Jess stopped dead and positively glared at him. There she was feeling selfish for being tempted to escape when he was being so kind, only to discover he wasn't being kind at all. 'How dare you!'

His face remained impassive, apparently

oblivious of the latest evidence of his duplicity. 'I'm sorry I didn't give you the reassurances you wanted last night, genuinely I am. I am in an impossible position. As much as I like you personally—and, believe me, I certainly never expected to—my first duty is and always has been to the Crown and it is my duty to see justice done. Can you at least try to see things from my point of view?'

'Your point of view!' She wanted to slap the sanctimonious piety from his plotting, scheming, dishonest eyes. He was using her as bait again. That could be the only reason he was dragging her across these desolate moors west towards Penzance. A town favoured by Saint-Aubin's network of smugglers—in fact, every smuggler since the dawn of time. 'Why should I care about your point of view?'

His response was the typical withering sigh, as if that was all the emotion the topic required and any more emotion was unseemly. 'Would it help to verbalise your frustrations? It might clear the air and make the next few hours more bearable.'

Clear the air! Crétin! She was livid at her own needy stupidity, frightened, riddled with guilt at her own self-serving inadequacies and apparently had no control over even her own fate despite almost killing herself with the effort to escape. Her temper snapped on a growl and she stalked off, her hands gesticulating wildly as she tried to put into words every turbulent thing she was feeling, but had never verbalised. How did one verbalise the sheer awfulness of the cess pool that was her lot in life?

Clear the air!

Jess was going to give him both barrels.

'Why should I see things from your point of view? You are the one in charge and I have no power! As always! You have no idea what it is like to have no control over your own destiny. To spend every waking moment afraid and incarcerated. No concept of how awful it is to be forced to do things or accept your awful fate blindly. You have choices, Monsieur Flint. I have been given none.' She began to mutter in rapid French, knowing his language skills would struggle to translate it all, but needing to vent her utter disappointment at him in particular out loud. Penzance! Of all the places guaranteed to be most dangerous… *'Salaud!'*

She felt him tug at her arm and swing her around. Clearly he understood that insult very well, because his green eyes were stormy.

'When I said verbalise, I had hoped we might have a proper, reasonable discussion to seek some middle ground. Something that would make our extended time together more bearable.

Something which would help me to understand exactly what is going on and your *exact* part in it. Convince me to trust your further than I can throw you. You ranting and raving in French isn't helping. I want to listen and I want to help. Really I do, but just for once could we converse without all of the histrionics?'

He had the gall to stare down at her reproachfully, as if she were the one in the wrong. The temptation to slap his sanctimonious face was visceral.

'Histrionics! You have a nerve! Do they offend you, Monsieur Flint? Is honest human emotion such an anathema to a cold and unfeeling, *lying* man like yourself? You want to help! Ha!' It felt good to jam her pointed finger into his ribs. 'For the record, I am entitled to some *histrionics*! None of this was of my making and I don't care if you don't believe me! I was taken from my home as a child and dumped in a place that never felt like a home. I've suffered through a war I didn't understand and its awful aftermath—during both of which my freedom was denied to me—and then I am pressganged into the service of smugglers, threatened, blackmailed, abused and chained. Did anyone care?' She shook off his arm and paced back and forth. 'Of course they didn't! For my father I ceased to exist the moment my mother left him, for my mother I became invisible because all she truly cared about was her lover! I had no friends. No family. No life. No choices. I longed to be saved. Prayed for it every night—yet when the British finally came, they arrested me and treated me like a criminal when I never intentionally did anything wrong and my thanks is to stand trial as a traitor!'

Her voice choked, but she bit back the tears. Anger always felt better than despair and they had not broken her yet. Venting it all might be cathartic and might well serve to remind her of how badly she had been treated and give her the strength to continue to fight and continue to believe she was not the awful human being she was coming to fear she might be. Because surely surrendering to Saint-Aubin's vicious admonishments and being seen to do his absolute bidding was counterbalanced by the fact she had still risked her life to send out the truth once her broken mind and body had recovered? But venting certainly wouldn't *clear the air*. At this stage, even pummelling the insufferable Lord Flint to a bloody splodge on the grass wouldn't *clear the air*.

'I tasted my first piece of freedom in a decade and you snatched it away from me.' She prodded him again in the chest with her finger. 'Then used me as bait to serve your own ends. Now I discover that despite your *sincere* and *reassuring* words to the contrary, you are *still* using me as bait! You have the *nerve* to not trust me as far as you can throw me! That is rich! You are the most untrustworthy, silver-tongued fibber I have ever met in my life! That I trusted you, even briefly, makes me sick!' Jess growled and then tilted her head back to growl again at the heavens for good measure. She had stupidly hoped God would send her a saviour for once, not a snake, but He had still sent a snake. A big, lying, scheming viper, albeit one that used manipulative kindness instead of chains, riding crops and heights to get her to comply!

'And now I have bloodthirsty assassins and the man himself on my tail ready to kill me as soon as they are able. Meanwhile, I get dragged across the country with a man who blows hot and cold, is as inscrutable as a plank of wood, officious and feels it is perfectly appropriate to spend the night wrapped around me! Who expects me to be reasonable. To confess all my sins, to trust him with my life when he doesn't even honour me with the slightest detail of my fate or even why he persists in dragging me towards Saint-Aubin's ships and bloodthirsty cronies in Penzance!' She pointed at the milestone with a quaking finger in case he dared to deny it. 'I am constantly exhausted. I am constantly

petrified and I am so sick of feeling unworthy
and all alone. So you will have to forgive me—
for I am way beyond being reasonable or from
seeing things from anyone else's point of view—
for I am thoroughly entitled to my histrionics!
Because I am *not* nor ever have been a traitor
and you *can* go to hell, Monsieur Flint!'

She heard him exhale in the long-suffering
way he did so well and seriously considered
launching herself at him like a crazed banshee
because she was so furious at him, when he surprised her.

'It's Peter.'

'I'm sorry?'

'My name. Seeing as we have, as you have
so rightly pointed out, spent a night cuddled up
together we should probably dispense with the
formalities. And I'm sorry for keeping you in the
dark and for—how did you put it?—blowing hot
and cold. In my defence, I am only trying to do
my job, one you make very difficult. You confuse me and confound me in equal measure, as
I am sure I do you. I will hold my hands up to
being officious at times. It is not intentional—
but the government needs me to be pragmatic
and level-headed, although I find I have to remind myself of that more frequently as I get to
know you. These are unusual, fraught circumstances and therefore difficult for both of us to

adjust to.' He sighed and paused, then gave a tiny shake of his head as if having a silent conversation with himself.

'I also do appreciate that, thanks to this morning, I have made today unnecessarily awkward.' His impressive chest rose and fell on a deep breath and he briefly looked towards his feet. When his eyes raised, he offered her a half-smile. 'And I can assure you I am no longer using you as bait Jess. We are not going to Penzance. Nowhere near. I am neither that cruel nor that stupid and my only mission at this time is to keep you safe. We are going to my house. Penmor. We should get there in a couple of hours at the most.'

'Your house?' He was taking her home? 'You are taking me to *your* house?' That was an intensely personal gesture. Wholly unexpected. It completely knocked the wind out of her sails. 'Is that wise?'

'It is off the beaten track, a good forty miles from Penzance and an unlikely place to hide while my men attempt to round up Saint-Aubin and his associates. Even if they track you down—which I sincerely doubt, by the way— Penmor was built to withstand a siege. Not that I anticipate one. Gray will arrive with plenty of reinforcements in a few days and we'll keep you safe from harm. You have my word. It seemed prudent to go in completely the opposite direction to where Saint-Aubin, the Royal Navy and the whole of Plymouth would think we'd go. My house here in Cornwall seemed like the logical place to bring you when we have no clear idea of exactly who we can trust. I should have told you all that yesterday, but in all the confusion I didn't and for that I am also sorry.'

'As soon as he realises you are not in London, he will put two and two together.'

'To all intents and purposes I *will* be in London. Gossip will be planted into the scandal sheets informing every one of my escapades in town. Reliable witnesses will vouch for my attendance at events or clubs. My name will go down in the House of Lords attendance book and the newspapers will loudly announce your arrival at the Tower. Snippets of your latest confession will be leaked. Remember—Saint-Aubin isn't looking for me, he's hunting you. We do this all the time, Jess. If we can feed the newspapers information that only you could possibly know, he will have no reason to doubt you are safely in the hands of the British government and have no reason to come hunting here.'

'We? Exactly who is *we*?'

Chapter Fourteen

Whether it was wise or not, and conscious of the need to build some bridges, Flint told her about his involvement with the King's Elite and their quest to track down the mysterious Boss as they walked onwards. He sensed she was in dire need of some honesty if she was going to confide in him fully and probably deserved it, too, when all was said and done. The last thing he wanted was her escaping the safety of Penmor because she was afraid and he was honest enough with himself to realise that was more to do with his feelings towards her than for the ultimate good of his mission. Without her, it was true they were unlikely to bring down Saint-Aubin any time soon, which in turn meant that, if she escaped and tried to make a go of things all on her own, Jess would spend her lifetime constantly looking over her shoulder. That monster wouldn't rest until he had silenced her and Flint would never rest knowing she was in danger and he wasn't around to stop it.

That was his story and he was sticking to it.

It was odd how quickly she had crawled under his skin and made a home in his conscience. Something he ruthlessly pushed to the back of his mind, alongside her potential trial and sentence, because it was so worrying. He had spent his whole adult life avoiding meaningful attachments with women for good reason and did not want to have to acknowledge that his relationship with Jess—a wanted traitor—was rapidly starting to mean something. Aside from his body's embarrassing but entirely understandable response to her when he had awoken with her in his arms, he really didn't want to have to reflect upon his strange reaction to her during the night or the deep well of tenderness which had opened up as he had lain next to her. Or the fact he had gladly held her close because she had needed him and perhaps he had needed her, too, then, because holding her simply felt natural. So natural that, despite the blatant lust, the rightness of it all had made him relax, then sleep soundly for hours because she was there.

Another thing best not dwelled on when he had a job to do and fully intended to do it in spite of what his oddly roiling, confused emotions told him. Much like his foolhardy decision to take her home, when he knew full well there were other places she would also have been safe. The garrison at Plymouth and the navy ship bound for London being two.

But at the time, her safety had been paramount and he had listened to his gut again, even though his gut had sounded dangerously like his heart and he had blithely let it overrule his head regardless and was apparently content to allow it to continue to. Penmor would protect her, just as it had countless others in the past. His gut knew that with certainty, too.

After he had told her as much as he dared, Flint reiterated that he could only help her in as much as she helped with the rest of the investigation. She had nodded non-committally, they lapsed back into silence. By her expression, he had clearly given her much food for thought, but he knew it would take more than a few pertinent details to gain her complete trust. Pushing her for information now wouldn't help either of them, yet the tense silence was unnerving him.

'I should probably warn you about my mother.'

Her head turned and that adorable wrinkle appeared again. 'She will be there?'

'She and no doubt a sister or two.' Now that he considered it, the situation was far from ideal. Not that he was worried about the exact circumstances of his bringing Jess home. His meddlesome family had unearthed the truth about his profession many moons ago. Hardly a surprise when he had reliably followed in his father's footsteps into the murky world of espionage. His family had grown up knowing thousands of secrets and never let anything slip outside the walls of Penmor. He trusted them all implicitly. In that at least.

However, in his haste to find a sanctuary for Jess, he hadn't considered the possibility of bringing danger home, too. It was yet another unforeseen complication he would have to deal with and another reminder of why he usually avoided acting with his heart over his head. His mother would not take being shipped out, even for her own safety, lightly. Nor would his sisters.

It couldn't be helped. As soon as Gray arrived, they would evacuate them somewhere and Flint would have to suffer the inevitable fuss knowing that, for once, it was entirely his fault. In the interim—he glanced at the beautiful woman next to him and sighed, suddenly feeling much older than his twenty-seven years—in the interim who knew what nonsensical machinations would occur?

As he had never brought a female home under any circumstances, nor shown interest in any of the women they had dragged in under false pretences, his womenfolk were likely to see

Jess's presence as significant. If he slipped and happened to cast her a heated glance when he dropped his guard or thought nobody was looking, he knew from bitter experience that one of his sisters was *always* looking. Then, like the banes of his life they always were, they would chatter and conspire together like a witch's coven and meddle with impunity.

Flint would have to be very specific from the outset and let them know in no uncertain terms that Lady Jessamine was his prisoner. One who had been arrested on charges of treason. The absolute worst of criminal charges. She was here on sufferance. Under his protection until the Crown took over.

That might do the trick.

And pigs might fly.

'Gray mentioned you had five sisters. Do they all live at home?'

'None of them lives at home, not that you'd think so by the amount of time they spend there.' More complications. More dramatics. More details to deal with. 'To my extreme irritation, they have all set up households locally. Not one of them lives more than ten miles away. I have no idea how my mother does it—perhaps it is some form of sorcery—but she seems to be able to summon them at will. I've never been able to fathom it. I arrive home and abracadabra—suddenly they are all there.' Unthinking, he sighed again, a little too loudly, and couldn't stop his shoulders slumping. As soon as Jess walked over the threshold, they would all appear like a plague of boils. Wild horses wouldn't stop them. And because he was duty bound to protect them, too, they would have to stay until he could arrange their safe evacuation under guard.

A whole house full of troublesome women. Just thinking about it was exhausting.

'He also mentioned they run you ragged.' She smiled at his downtrodden expression and all at once it was as if the sun had come out, even though it was already out and had been all day. 'They are fervent matchmakers, *non*?'

'Gray talks too much, but alas he is right. They are.'

'And you are worried they will attempt to match us?' This seemed to amuse her and a giggle escaped. Flint wanted to catch the infectious sound in his fist and save it for ever, before he stoutly told himself off for such ridiculous and fanciful whimsy when she was probably a traitor after all. Probably? Definitely! Good grief, he was losing the plot. Agents of the Crown should be above such things and his meddling sisters would have a field day if they knew the way his errant thoughts kept turning uncharacteristically poetic. They would see it as a sign because he wasn't poetic. Never had been.

'They might try, but I shall nip it in the bud. If that fails, please try to ignore it. They mean well.'

'They must be very desperate to see you settled if they would consider a traitor a potential wife.'

It was said jokingly, yet her comment instantly rankled despite his thinking much the same seconds before. Almost as if somebody else had said it to insult her. Before he thought better about it, a version of the words which had been on the tip of his tongue since last night spilled out of his mouth.

'I doubt they'll see you as a traitor, Jess.'

As soon as he said them he wished them back. Not because he had told the truth as he saw it or because it might give her false hope, although both reasons were foolhardy in the extreme when he was going by gut rather than evidential proof. But because she suddenly stood as still as a statue and gazed at him with such blatant relief and affection it humbled him.

'Thank you… Peter. That means…so much.'

When her fingers found his, his hand locked around them and squeezed. He didn't dare say another word nor act on the overwhelming impulse to hold her and kiss her and tell her it

would all be all right. He would make it all right.
Instead he stared down at their joined hands,
swiftly withdrew his and nodded curtly. 'We
should be at Penmor within half an hour if we
get a move on.' Which he immediately did, forcing her to scurry along behind in his wake as his
legs tore up the ground. Ground decidedly less
steady than it had been before.

Jess had no idea what to expect of Penmor.
However, the sight of it shocked her nevertheless.
It wasn't so much a house as he had claimed,
more a castle. The tall, central keep stood high
on a sheer clifftop, a solid bastion of stone
against the backdrop of the sea. On one side
it was flanked by a tall round tower, while the
jagged, tilted, precariously wonky remnants of
another similarly ancient round tower to the left
was covered in rich, emerald moss. The unintentional lack of symmetry suited it. The narrow
road that led to it was carved into the rock and
zig-zagged steeply until it met the wooden bridge
that spanned the deep crevasse. Like the building, it looked to have been there for centuries.
Craggy rocks jutted out of the grass haphazardly
before the land tapered out to the smooth daisy-
filled pasture where they were standing. In the
distance, she could hear the waves crashing on
the shore below and nothing else but the gentle,
warm breeze which played with the few strands

of hair poking out of her awful cap. A romantic, atmospheric tableau from a bygone era that Jess loved immediately.

'It's beautiful.'

'I've always thought so—although completely impractical as houses go. When it rains, you cannot get a carriage up the drive. On the rare occasions that we do get snow here on the west coast, expect to be trapped inside for days.'

Just as he had been since his unexpected admission, he was more awkward in his skin than she had ever seen him. Each time he met her eye, his quickly fixed on another spot in the distance. Now they were latched on to his house. 'It creaks, too, for no apparent reason. I thought I should warn you, in case it decides to grumble in the middle of the night and you fear we have been invaded. Although I dare say at six hundred and sixty-five years old, it's earned the right to creak.'

Typical English understatement that belied the pride which shone in his eyes. 'What happened to the other tower?' Jess pointed to the ruin.

'Cromwell. He took issue with an ancestor hiding the King, so that half of the castle was slighted. That same ancestor never bothered knocking it down, although to look at it you'd think a puff of wind would send it tumbling, so it has remained a feature ever since. My mother is a keen gardener and likes to grow roses up it.'

A charming notion. 'Why didn't he mend it?'

'Impossible, I'm afraid. The staircase is the main support in a round tower and Cromwell blew the stairs to smithereens to make sure he couldn't.'

'Yet it still stands?'

'Penmor is reliably sturdy. The keep shores it up. Besides, I like to imagine it served as the Flint badge of honour in defiance of the Republic.'

'Of course he would be another loyal servant of the Crown.' She rolled her eyes for effect. 'Was he as vexing as you are?'

His gaze flicked to hers, features bland but dancing emerald eyes amused. 'According to my mother and my five harridan sisters, *nobody* is as vexing as I am. Whatever trait I inherited from that ancestor has apparently been condensed into the pure essence of vexatious, however I can assure you it is far more concentrated in the female descendants. You should probably brace yourself and gird your loins for what is to come.'

He had already started up the path, which afforded her the opportunity of admiring him from behind. He cut a fine figure even in sweep's clothing. Tall. Broad. Impossible to hate. 'I'm sure they are all lovely.'

'Oh, poor Jess. You really are naïve if you believe that. They are devious termagants. Scheming, manipulative hoydens. Eye-wateringly exasperating and terminally interfering harpies. Keep your wits about you, my lady, and remember I warned you. Until I can get rid of them, which I fully intend to do with all haste, don't drop your guard for a second.'

They were halfway up the steep path when a servant spotted them. To his credit, the man's mouth gaped for a split second at the sight of his lord and master dressed like a vagrant, before he covered it and bowed. Then he dashed away, no doubt to inform the rest of the house of their arrival. Less than a minute later, a handsome, plump woman with a friendly open smile barrelled down the path towards them with her arms outstretched.

'Peter! My darling! What a wonderful surprise!' She enveloped him in a bear hug which he happily returned. That surprised Jess. The staid and reserved man who always seemed to find emotions so unseemly clearly felt a great deal of affection for his mother and was not afraid to display it. 'Look at the state of you! Why, you are filthy, Peter! What nonsense have you been up to this time?'

'Nothing a good bath won't fix.'

His mother fussed, brushing the last vestiges of the soot from his cheek and attempting to fix his hair. Tiny gestures of love which Jess had always yearned for, but couldn't remember ever

receiving from either of her parents. From anyone at all really. Something that caused a wave
of sadness to wash over her and kindled a forlorn
hope in her heart that perhaps one day someone
might truly care for her and welcome her with
the same beautiful enthusiasm as in this spontaneous, loving greeting.

Watching it became awkward, so she tried
to hide herself behind him and stare at nothing.
The movement brought his mother's matching
green eyes to rest on her quizzically, making
Jess more self-conscious. She should have insisted they stop by a stream to allow her to re-
pair her face and remove the ugly cap from her
dirty head. This was not the right sort of first
impression. Not that she really was in any position to worry about first impressions. She was a
prisoner. Possibly a traitor... 'And who is this?'

'Mother, this is Lady Jessamine Fane. Jess,
my mother, Baroness Flint of Penmor.'

From somewhere in her past, Jess instinctively
remembered her English manners and curtsied,
dropping her eyes in deference and trying not to
appear mortally offended that the older woman
was clearly shocked to learn she wasn't a boy.
'My lady.'

'*Lady* Jessamine Fane?' She smiled, then
turned to her son with her eyebrows raised. 'Of
the Suffolk Fanes? How positively lovely.'

'Mother—before you proceed with that inevitable yet wholly misguided thought, allow me to give you some background as to why we have suddenly turned up looking like...'

'Don't be silly, Peter! Where are your manners? Background indeed. Look at your *pretty* companion! Why, she needs a hot bath and a decent meal and plenty of rest more than you do. She's clearly been through the wars.' The woman's arm slipped through Jess's possessively while she blithely ignored her son's scowl as if he was conveniently invisible and she had suddenly gone quite deaf in the ear closest to him. 'Come, my dear, let's get you settled, then my dour son can crush all my hopes once again under his clumsy, big boots. Have you noticed the ridiculous size of his feet? I have no idea where they came from. His father was perfectly proportioned...'

Surrounded by a cloud of expensive perfume, Jess could only blink and listen. Lady Flint barely paused for breath. In a flash, she found herself marched across the ancient drawbridge, inside the castle and practically trotting up the sweeping staircase trying to take it all in, all the while his mother was giving her a potted history of the castle, the family and the exponential early growth of her son's massive feet. It was surreal.

Chapter Fifteen

〜〜〜

There was no denying that he was rich. Very rich. Penmor was as stunning inside as it was out. Thick Persian rugs, silver candlesticks and heavy, obviously expensive fabrics draped the windows and the beds. Jess's bed was a fairy-tale Renaissance four-poster, its mattress so soft you sank into it and were encased in the crispest, whitest sheets she had ever seen. The bathtub she was currently neck-deep in was decorated with brightly coloured enamel inlays and glass beads. Achingly feminine in its beauty like the room which surrounded it. The soap was of the finest quality, oozing with the soothing scent of lavender, the rich, creamy lather feeling sinful on her skin.

Peter's mother was like a whirlwind who skil-fully didn't take no for an answer. Before Jess had been able to argue otherwise, the bath had been carried in, a maid was unpinning her hair while the older woman went hunting for one of her daughter's old gowns. A pretty, sprigged muslin was then held against her while Lady Flint issued rapid instructions to a maid who was pinning the hem and sleeves to accommodate Jess's lack of height. Only once all that was done did she shoo out the servants and insist on helping Jess undress.

That had been awkward. Lady Flint refused to allow her to be missish, stating matter-of-factly that she had raised five daughters and had seen it all. But, of course, she hadn't seen it all because her eyes had widened when she saw Jess's back and then clouded with sympathy. 'Oh, my dear! You really have been through the wars, haven't you?'

Thankfully she didn't probe as to where the marks had come from. Jess supposed it must be patently obvious they had come by way of a lash, although she hated what they now signified. Her own weakness and cowardice. Saint-Aubin had become relentless until she agreed to his demands. As much as Jess had tried to be steadfastly rebellious, he had broken her more than once and made her beg for mercy. Something she wasn't proud of, less so now that she knew her weakness had led to the deaths of innocent men, and which she certainly had no intention of ever talking about. Not when Jess couldn't bring herself to look at the scars in the mirror. Like Cain, they now marked her for her crimes and likely would for eternity. She hated them just as much as she hated herself for her weakness and Saint-Aubin for making her beg for her life.

Fortunately, Lady Flint simply shook her head, patted Jess's hand affectionately and declared that hot tea was most definitely required this instant and that she should soak in the bath and relax.

For once, she was happy to do exactly as she was told, sinking into the water gratefully and covering those damning scars in bubbles. There hadn't been a sign or sniff of Saint-Aubin since she had seen him in Plymouth yesterday and, thanks to her rescuer's convoluted route across farmers' fields and what she now knew was Bodmin Moor, they had managed to avoid all people save some distant peasants working the land and the ferryman who had taken them across the river between Devon and Cornwall. That small vessel had only just managed to disembark, crammed as it was with the flotsam and jetsam of life who spilled on to the jetty, all of them as ragged and dirty as the two of them, and the haggard ferryman hadn't bothered raising his head when the coins had been pressed into his outstretched hand or as they had silently stepped off the boat on the other side. Thanks to their disguises, they had been hiding in plain sight and remained reassuringly anonymous. Even if Saint-Aubin did come hunting for Lord Flint from London—or even Plymouth—it stood to reason he was at least a good day away. Probably more.

Which gave Jess some time to think carefully about her next move.

Did she put all her eggs in Lord Peter Flint's basket and tell him everything she knew, risking his censure and the subsequent and very real potential of a trial, or did she slip away again unseen and take her chances all alone?

Her head and her heart were torn.

Her heart was more than a little bit taken with her handsome captor. Being with him, sharing this ordeal with him by her side, had given her a sense of security and well-being she could not remember experiencing in the recent past. Two sets of eyes and ears, his resourceful mind and access to government resources made him a good ally. If one put aside his often inscrutable nature, arrogant stubbornness and aristocratic bearing, she rather liked the man. When he wasn't being the conundrum. The real Peter and the agent of the Crown Flint were two sides of the same coin—she trusted one, but not entirely the other. Not fully. Her head still had significant doubts.

A man who, by his own account, spied for a

living would be skilled in twisting situations to suit his purpose. If his purpose was unchanged from what it had been when she had first encountered him on that frigate, then there was every chance he was actively seeking to gain her trust now because it made his job easier. The eternal pragmatist, he wanted all the information she held in her head as much as Saint-Aubin did and would do everything in his power to get it. Once it was shared, she was of no further use to Saint-Aubin and her time in this mortal coil was limited.

On the other hand, sharing everything she knew could well result in the end of Saint-Aubin. If the King's Elite could catch him on English soil—and Jess had a fairly good idea which English aristocrats would hide him—she might perhaps begin to atone for the sins she had been bullied into carrying out. That might also mean she could live without the constant fear of his retribution.

If she lived.

Which was the real crux of the matter.

Until all charges were dropped, she still had an appointment with the hangman.

Qu'est-ce que je vais faire?

Flint was just tying his cravat when his mother barged into his bedchamber without knocking. 'What's going on?'

'Lord Fennimore tasked me with escorting Lady Jessamine to London when an unforeseen complication arose and I had to think on my feet.'

'Such shoddy explanations never worked in all the years I lived with your father and they won't wash now. Why were you escorting her to London? Who is she, Peter? And why has the poor girl got whip marks all over her back?'

His jaw dropped as the bile rose in his throat. 'She's been whipped?' Good grief, how many other horrors had Saint-Aubin subjected her to?

'Repeatedly and recently, if I'm any judge. Some of the scars are older. Then there are the abrasions on her wrists…' Typically it was concern, not fear, that he saw in his mother's face and Flint realised that it might not be such a bad thing she was here after all. Lord only knew Jess deserved some serious mothering after all she had been through, a job his mother excelled in. Whipped? His head was still reeling. When he got his hands on that bastard! 'I can count every rib, too, so it doesn't take a genius to work out she has been grossly abused. She's in trouble, isn't she?'

There was no point denying it. 'Perhaps you'd better sit down.' She lowered herself to perch on his mattress and he sat next to her and took her hand, wondering if he should soften the words or just say them straight out. Straight out won. Sugar-coating it wouldn't wash with the canny woman who had birthed him.

'Jess has been arrested and charged with treason, Mother, for her part in aiding and abetting an attempt to free Napoleon. To make matters worse, she has had a hand in raising the necessary funds to do this through an enormous smuggling operation. An operation so toxic and far reaching it has infiltrated the highest echelons of English society and now threatens the stability of the British economy—so the charges are serious. Very serious. She was seized on Lord Fennimore's instructions by the Royal Navy during a night-time raid in Cherbourg. However, the leader of the French smugglers has crossed the Channel and wants her back. It would seem Lady Jessamine holds vital information the smugglers need. As it is the same information our government also needs to finally destroy them, and fearing an ambush on the road to London, I set up a decoy in Plymouth to fool them she was on route to the capital to await trial and brought her here instead.'

Her fingers went lax in his as she digested this. 'I see.' As the former wife of a spy as well as the mother of one, and well versed in the peculiarities and dangers of espionage, she absorbed this bombshell with admirable calm. 'Were you followed?'

'I'm fairly certain we weren't. We crossed the moors on foot and didn't pass within spitting distance of a soul. As they appear to have taken the bait, we have at least twenty-four hours' grace. Possibly forty-eight. I'll know for sure just how well hidden we are when Gray arrives in a day or so.'

'When do we expect the reinforcements? And how many?' Typically, her thoughts went to the practicalities. Penmor had hosted fugitives, soldiers and seekers of sanctuary before—not for many years and not since his father's death, in fact—but she knew they would require extensive supplies before they battened down the hatches and isolated themselves from the world.

'At least fifty Invisibles and probably the same again in militia should arrive in the coming days. The rest will patrol the shore in Excise boats. You won't need to worry about those.'

'A full-scale occupation, then—which suggests you expect trouble.'

'I hope not, but there is a distinct possibility in the coming days. This particular band of smugglers have an extensive and powerful network here in the south and no shortage of informers in town. If they get one sniff that Jess is not where we claim she is, they will backtrack and leave no stone unturned until they find her—which is why I've already summoned the girls. If somebody does come hunting, they and their families are vulnerable outside these walls until I can figure out a way of keeping them safe elsewhere. I've sent servants to watch their houses tonight as I don't want them travelling *en masse* this late. People notice such things. Their visiting on the morrow will not seem out of the ordinary, because they are always here. Then we'll pull up the drawbridge.' A bridge Flint was suddenly exceedingly thankful he had.

Thinking out loud, he began to pace. 'Once Gray is here, I will work out a way to evacuate you all. Perhaps a boat or...'

'You cannot mean to include me in this plan!'

'You need to go with the girls. I don't want any of you embroiled in this.'

His mother's arms folded across her chest and she stared at him as if he was mad. 'That will not be happening. The girls, I agree with. There is no need to put them in harm's way unnecessarily. But I am staying put.'

'Now, Mother, I know this is your home, but...' One pointed finger prodded him in the ribs in the same spot Jess had stabbed earlier. Clearly it was a day for rib jabbing.

'I will not leave that girl at the mercy of a house full of men. She will need to be properly

chaperoned, the poor dear. To avoid tomfoolery.'
His mother stood, self-righteous, and walked towards the door with her nose in the air as if her
word was final.

'Aside from the fact my men are disciplined
and would never take advantage of a lone woman
with *tomfoolery* as you so politely put it, I will
be here, too. Close by at all times.'

'Which is what worries me the most.' Her
fingers closed around the door knob before she
turned to glare. 'I have eyes, young man! I saw
the way you looked at the girl and she you. The
pair of you are quite besotted. Without proper
supervision, *tomfoolery* is inevitable!'

Flint's jaw dropped—he was affronted. No
matter how accurate his mother's assessment
was of his lustful feelings, or how his blood
fizzed at the idea that Jess might have similar
feelings towards him, his mother's irrational
line of thinking needed to be nipped in the bud.
Besotted! He most certainly was not. Besotted
suggested there was more between them than
mutual attraction and lust. The lust was natural. Like an itch that needed scratching. He was
a respected and disciplined agent of the Crown,
a man who was staunchly wedded to his bachelor status and allergic to the sort of manipulative
emotional theatrics a woman like his prisoner

was capable of. And fully in command of his urges, damn it. 'She is a traitor!'

'Of course she isn't.' It was his mother's irritatingly patronising voice. The one that grated the most. 'I know you too well, Peter. So like your dear father. Your actions speak much louder than your words.'

'My actions? Have you conveniently forgotten that she is to stand trial or that she is likely complicit in the raising of a foreign army? We have a slew of evidence. Witnesses. A trail of letters that lead right back to her. Facts that cannot be glossed over, Mother, and a significant deterrent to any *tomfoolery* or romantic attachments between her and me, I can assure you.'

His mother smiled and shook her head. 'Tell yourself that if it makes you feel better. I know the truth, my dear. And it is simple. You would never dream of bringing a traitor home and, just like your father, I trust your instincts implicitly. You would never willingly bring a woman here either—unless she meant something to you. Her presence here is significant, my darling. Aside from the obvious lust I see burning in your eyes, I also know besotted when I see it.'

Chapter Sixteen

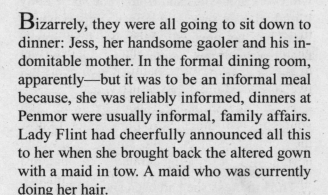

Bizarrely, they were all going to sit down to dinner: Jess, her handsome gaoler and his indomitable mother. In the formal dining room, apparently—but it was to be an informal meal because, she was reliably informed, dinners at Penmor were usually informal, family affairs. Lady Flint had cheerfully announced all this to her when she brought back the altered gown with a maid in tow. A maid who was currently doing her hair.

As if she were an honoured guest rather than a captive.

Jess still couldn't quite believe it.

She had pushed back, stating that it wouldn't be proper in view of the circumstances and probably wouldn't be welcomed by her son, but Lady Flint would hear none of it and insisted regardless. Cook was making dinner for three and it would be served promptly at six. Then she had breezed out of the door with the same sense of purpose as she had arrived, leaving a bewildered Jess being laced into the gown and beautified by the equally as indomitable maid.

The young woman gazing back at her in the mirror looked like an English lady with her hair piled fashionably on her head. The pretty muslin long-sleeved dress covered an equally pretty chemise and half-corset. Her legs were encased in white-silk stockings and from somewhere Lady Flint had even procured dainty slippers which fitted her feet perfectly. More hand me downs from her daughters' youth, but unexpected and welcome nevertheless. The style had also been thoughtful, almost as if the older woman realised her scars were a private matter and not for public display. The sleeves had been hemmed, then trimmed in lace which covered her ugly, damaged wrists completely.

The kindness she had been shown was overwhelming, when technically she was a prisoner charged with treason. Something his lordship's mother made plain she knew when Jess had protested and then swatted away like a fly.

She might technically still be a prisoner, although thus far her bedchamber door was yet to be locked and nobody had forbidden her from wandering around. That he had granted her that small freedom warmed her. Neither had he interrupted her pleasant afternoon of relaxation. She hadn't seen him since they had arrived, had spent a good hour in the bath pondering what to do, then a few more catching up on sleep on the decadent four-poster. To her great surprise, she had gone out like a light the moment her head had hit the pillow. Only stirring from deep slumber when awakened with more hot, fortifying tea and the arrival of Peter's mother, the dress and the realisation that she had dreamt in English for the first time in a long while.

Perhaps because she had been speaking it exclusively for the first time in years? Her mother tongue had been banned in the chateau, her mother happily lapsing into her first language in all communications because her lover loathed all things English and the pair of them were French. Over time, Jess, too, became more French, only resurrecting the lamented English side when she had been strong-armed into assisting her ailing mother with the damning letters. Although even then she had not spoken it. She had never dared. Saint-Aubin flew into a rage at the merest English syllable, but it was all flooding back now. The nuances and musical patterns of the language of her youth. The language of home or, at least, of the home she had hoped, secretly schemed and longed for.

The maid stepped back and admired her work. 'You look lovely, my lady.'

Jess smiled, oddly moved at the sight of her own reflection. She did look lovely and couldn't help hoping he would think so, too, before dismissing the silly thought out of hand. What difference did it make what he thought of her frock? He was her gaoler and ultimately still determined to hand her over to the courts regardless of how pretty her attire. Deflated, she promptly considered finding any excuse to procrastinate. An impossible task when everything had been done for her. If Lady Flint's blithe instruction to head down the staircase and turn right at the bottom was any indication, Jess was free to make her own way down to dinner, too, as soon as she was decent.

A casual family dinner. With him and his mother.

An imminent prospect which was making her uncharacteristically nervous.

Stupidly, she was attaching more significance to the occasion than it warranted.

She took her time descending the staircase, taking in the sheer beauty of the place as well as consigning it to memory in case she needed it. As one would expect in a household of such grandeur, there were servants dotted around, but all seemed to be engrossed in their work rather than guarding Jess. All of them looked up, curtsied or bowed their acknowledgement and called her 'my lady'. Only the burly footman posted at the front door had the look of a sentry, yet he, too, inclined his head politely as she sailed past.

As promised, she found them both in the dining room where dinner had been laid out in chafing dishes on the sideboard. Lady Flint smiled in welcome. Her gaoler rose and for a second appeared to be lost for words.

'Good evening, Jess.'

'Good evening…' Her voice trailed off and she covered her disquiet with a brittle smile. Despite his early assertion to the contrary, she didn't feel right about calling him Peter. Not when he was all starched and formal, rather than rumpled and smudged with soot and his mother was present. Baron Flint of Penmor was still sinfully handsome, though. Jess would have to be blind not to notice that and looking every inch the wealthy peer she now knew him to be in his perfectly tailored coat, sedate yet expensive silk waistcoat and snowy-white austere cravat. He was not out of place in this castle. It suited him. She felt exactly like a fish out of water. Floundering. Pride made her hold her regal posture despite the strange jitters in her tummy.

After a prolonged hesitation when his eyes slowly raked the entire length of her body, he eventually inclined his head, then helped her into the chair solicitously, his fingers leaving a trail of tingles where they had briefly touched her forearm. Only once he was back in his own seat again did he talk. The tone, unlike the satisfying admiration in his eyes, distinctly businesslike. 'I've instructed the servants to leave us to talk privately and uninterrupted. There is much to discuss.'

That sounded ominous. 'I suppose there is.' Especially as Jess was now resigned to her fate. In short, and after much soul-searching, she had come to the conclusion it was better to be here in this ancient castle with this unflappable and resourceful man than outside on her own. She would tell him everything and hope that in doing so she hadn't just signed her death warrant. 'Where would you like to start?'

She braced herself for a barrage of accusatory questions. As if he sensed her disquiet, his golden head tilted to one side and his expression softened. 'Well, firstly, I should appraise you of the castle's security to put your mind at ease.' His hand closed around hers on the tablecloth, warm and comforting. 'I don't want you worrying about Saint-Aubin.'

As if he had only just noticed it, his eyes flicked to where his hand lay on top of hers and he briskly removed it, his voice becoming officious once again. 'As you might have seen when we arrived, Penmor was built with siege in mind. The architect put this castle on a single rock stack that is separated from the main cliffs by a wide gully. Once the drawbridge is raised—which it is now—it is nigh on impossible to reach. To climb the stack would mean approaching from the sea. With the rocks below and the enormous crashing waves, only a fool would be mad enough to attempt it. Even if intruders did get past the sea, the rock they would need to climb is a sheer forty-foot wall of solid granite. The only obvious way in or out is via the drawbridge and up the steep path we climbed. A route which is perfectly visible from inside and is now being watched constantly. There are no other visible entrances.'

Lady Flint grinned. 'There is a *secret* entrance. One that only the family and a few trusted servants have ever been privy to over the centuries. A passageway chiselled into the stone with narrow stairs leading downwards. It must have taken years to complete, but whoever made it took it out on to the moor beyond and disguised its entrance within an old bothy that sits out of sight from Penmor. Nobody would ever know it was there.'

'Should it become necessary, one of us will lead you through it to safety.' His brisk interruption suggested he was not impressed with his mother's openness and did not trust Jess enough to share the location. 'Once my men arrive, some will also be posted out on the moor for additional protection—however, until they arrive we are completely secure. By tomorrow, we will have enough supplies to survive a good month cut off from the rest of the world.'

'The handy thing about having so many daughters with families of their own is the local merchants are used to fulfilling large orders from Penmor and we've always stockpiled food anyway and have done since my hus—'

'Jess doesn't need a history lesson, Mother.' But Jess saw the cautionary glare in his eyes at the same time Lady Flint's jaws clamped shut. More evidence he distrusted her. Justified, she supposed, but his lack of faith still stung. 'I should warn you that there will be visitors aside from my men, so things might be a little cramped in here in the coming days.'

'Visitors?'

'Yes!' Lady Flint clapped her hands in excitement. 'All of the family will be here in the morning. My dear girls, their husbands and all my darling grandchildren. We shall have a houseful. Peter insisted.'

More people to feel self-conscious and gauche

around, as if the guilt and her own selfish desire to survive weren't unsettling enough.

'It isn't a party, Mother. I summoned them for their own safety.'

'Of course you did—but once they are here and as long as nobody comes searching for Jess, I see no reason why we cannot enjoy one another's company to the fullest. The children will need entertaining and we ladies can enjoy gossip and tea. I do so love a noisy house.' She jumped up and bustled over to the sideboard. 'You stay put, Jess. I shall make you up a plate while my son does his best to make everyone's arrival sound like a dreadful chore, when it will be nothing of the sort. You'll see. We'll all have a lovely time. I know the girls will be curious to meet you.'

'And so it begins.' Jess watched him roll his eyes at his mother's obvious exuberance before they settled on hers and locked, all the previous formality instantly gone. The message was clear. His mother was a law unto herself and nothing he said or did would change her. 'Remember—gird your loins, Jess.'

'Why would she need to gird her loins, Peter? My, you are such a curmudgeon sometimes. Do you want poor Jess to think badly of us? When I said the girls would be curious to meet you, Jess, I meant merely that. There is nothing to fear. They are all sociable and friendly young women. You will adore them all.'

'I am sure I will.'

While his mother busied herself at the sideboard with her back to them, he raised his palms up and mouthed *Gird your loins*. Then he winked at her and it did odd things to her insides. His family exasperated him and amused him in equal measure. And an informal, flirty Lord Peter Flint was devastating. 'Know that I am sorry for putting you through this ordeal and try to find it in your heart to forgive me for exposing you to my boisterous and annoying family.'

Those kind, hypnotic green eyes were dancing with mischief at her answering smile, the air in the room suddenly shifting so that there was just the two of them. Jess's pulse quickened as she lost herself in the unexpected but powerful moment. His gaze held hers transfixed, unwavering while the ghost of a smile played on his lips. Then his eyes dropped to her mouth and she watched them darken while the intimate atmosphere about them seemed to crackle with something potent and unspoken. Was she imagining it or did he feel it, too?

Jess was so immersed in him she nearly jumped out of her skin when a loaded plate landed in front of her. 'I shan't rest until you've eaten it all, young lady. Lord only knows what awful things you've had to live through, but you are here now and I shall look after you. So will Peter, won't you, Peter?'

He grunted some response from where he now stood helping himself to food at the sideboard and Jess realised she had probably imagined the peculiar, heated tension because he now seemed decidedly nonplussed and more focused on piling up his plate.

Lady Flint came closer and patted her hand. 'Tell me how you came to be left to the mercy of a gang of cut-throat smugglers?'

He kept forgetting his higher purpose and dropping his guard. No wonder she accused him of blowing hot and cold. He flipped from hot to frozen in a heartbeat when his duty to King and country doused the frequent flames with a bucket of ice water, reminding him of his mission, the weight of the responsibility the government had placed on his shoulders and the dreadful consequences of the last time he had allowed carnal lust to cloud his judgement with a prisoner. With each passing day, it seemed he had to fight harder to avoid falling under this particular prisoner's spell. The rapid about face wasn't intentional, but entirely necessary. As much as his gut wanted to believe her—and,

God help him, he was nearly fully convinced—
Flint still needed tangible evidence of her claims
before he as much as considered giving her some
benefit of the doubt. That was his job, damn it.
One he lived and breathed like his father before him.

It was all well and good Jess telling his mother
over dinner her version of events, a story that had
been difficult to hear despite sensing she was sa-
nitising it, yet it still made him hate Saint-Aubin
with every fibre of his being, but his sympathy
had to be founded on fact. Facts more conclusive than her scars and his niggling belief she
was as much of a victim as the loyal servants of
the Crown who had been murdered by the Boss.

His head, gut and heart had to be aligned.
Whatever his gut and heart said, Lord Fennimore would only listen to Flint's level, pragmatic, thorough and reasoned head. And rightly
so. Too many men had died searching for the
Boss and he couldn't allow the best suspect and
lead they had slip away because she had a beautiful and convincing face and his body was more
than a little tempted.

The inappropriate lust he constantly suffered
around her could well be clouding his judgement. As much as he was coming to like and
even respect her, he was damned if he would
allow those complicated and unwelcome feel-

ings to destroy his reputation and perhaps his future within the King's Elite, an organisation his father had helped to set up and shape. One that stood for integrity and justice. One that always did what was intrinsically right no matter how hard that was to do.

It was Jess who needed to prove herself worthy. He couldn't and wouldn't stick his neck out for her otherwise. Not on the strength of a dose of unwelcome and inappropriate lust and the natural sympathy he felt at the wounds inflicted by Saint-Aubin. Emotional reactions would not help him find the truth.

He stood, quashing the peculiar sympathy and desperate desire to avenge her with a decisive toss of his napkin. 'Now that dinner is over and you are safe, it is time to stop playing games. If you want to remain safe, you need to tell me everything you know.' A tad officious, but necessary. Flint didn't want to ache inside thinking about how she had been chained and beaten. How her mother's medication had been held to ransom by Saint-Aubin to blackmail her into assisting with his villainy. Didn't need to picture her alone in a rat-infested cell being whipped into submission to write unspeakable things. Knowing she had been in fear of her life or imagining how lost and alone she had been for half of her life—and probably still was. Frightened, vulnerable. Imprisoned. Didn't want his impeccable judgement clouded with the human emotion which clogged his throat and made doing what he needed to so very hard.

'I want names, Jess. Names, times, places. Every detail you have stored inside your head.' The abrupt change in tone had her face turning sharply to his, her expression pained. 'I can't help you if you won't help yourself.'

'Surely that can all wait until tomorrow? Poor Jess has had a terrible few days and a short nap and one dinner is hardly going to restore her fully.'

'I don't have time for that. I need to send something back to London to stop Saint-Aubin coming here. Something damning and unique. Something only Jess could have leaked. I need something that will convince him irrevocably that she is in the Tower where we say she is and that she is slowly but surely revealing all his secrets.' And he didn't need his mother watering down the gravity of his words with her well-meaning interruptions. It was hard enough to focus on his mission as it was. 'We'll talk in my study, Jess.' He glared at his mother. 'Alone.'

Chapter Seventeen

She looked nervous. Jittery and more like a young lady burdened and in trouble than the manipulative vixen he knew she could be when she set her clever mind to it. Where had that vixen gone? He knew where he stood with that incarnation of Jess. Her hands were clasped in front of her, but her fingers could not remain still as she followed him solemnly into the study and waited for him to close the door. Flint could have led her to the two comfortable wingbacks near the window, but he needed the desk between them as both a prop and a barrier, so he gestured to the upright chair in front of it and took his seat behind. 'Before we get into specific details, what can you tell me right now that would panic Saint-Aubin.'

For a moment she sat hunched and defeated in the chair, then her head snapped up and he watched with admiration the steel she forced into the proud set of her spine. 'Define *lenient*.'

'I can't make promises nor will I, but you have my word that I will do everything in my power to see that proper justice is done. If you are an innocent victim of a vile set of circumstances, co-operate fully and help us destroy Saint-Aubin and the Boss, then I will move heaven and earth to prove it. I hold some sway over my superiors and my reputation speaks for itself. I will be listened to. If you do not co-operate, lie to me, conveniently twist the truth to suit your own ends, fudge the details or persist in being silent, then I will throw you to the wolves.' He tried not to wince as he said that, staring back at her with the same stubborn resolve that mirrored hers.

'There is a ship anchored at Folkestone for repairs. An armed Indiaman called the *Grubbenvorst*. It sails under the flag of the Dutch East India Company, but is in reality one of Saint-Aubin's biggest and fastest ships. It ran aground in rough seas delivering brandy to the Marquis of Deal in Kent and tore off its rudder. Two of the masts are hollow and there is a secret compartment in the hold which disguises a second hold below. Aside from brandy, it is used to smuggle English guns into France. You will find the latest shipment of guns in that hold and perhaps in those masts. The Marquis of Deal always pays in guns. The captain of the vessel is a man called Boucher. He fought alongside Saint-Aubin during the war. Are those enough *details*, Monsieur Flint?'

More than he could have hoped for. Flint picked up his quill and began to scratch them all down. 'One seized ship, one arrested English traitor, one high-ranking smuggler clapped in irons and a hold full of guns.' He grinned at the prospect. The smile slid off his face when he gazed back at hers and saw she was hugging herself. 'You are doing the right thing, Jess.'

'Am I? If your plan fails or the evidence stacked against me in court outweighs what I say, then I die either way. At least an execution will be quick, I suppose. Saint-Aubin will drag the event out for his pleasure.' He saw the hurt and fear swirling in her eyes before she resolutely turned away and walked with her arms still wrapped around herself towards the window. She gazed out at the night sky and shivered.

'What did he do to you?' A foolhardy question, because he didn't need to know. Knowing would eat away at him and make the inconvenient need to protect her more acute.

'It doesn't matter.'

'It matters to me.'

'I've told you before, he found me a challenge and beat me until I wasn't.' Once again her expression became closed and he realised whatever violence she had been subjected to was too raw to discuss. Her tone became flippant. Dismissive. 'Will you have an arrest warrant drawn up based solely on my accusation or will the government require conclusive proof before they arrest a peer of the realm?'

He wished she would confide in him. Wished she would trust him with whatever burden haunted her and made her shrink into herself so completely. Of their own accord, his legs lifted him from his chair and took him to her. His errant hands placed themselves on her arms and gently rubbed some warmth into them through the thin sleeves. 'It will be all right, Jess. I promise.'

'Of course. This coming from a man who cannot make any promises or even confide in me what his own opinion is.'

'I'm not sure I follow.'

She turned to face him, her eyes locking with his and imprisoning them. 'You have never said, but I have to know. Do you think I am a traitor?'

'What I think hardly matters in the grand scheme of things.'

'It matters to me.' He schooled his features at her well-aimed dart, promising himself he would be professional if it killed him, then shrugged, nonplussed. He wouldn't allow her to know he was having serious doubts. 'I see.' He watched the unshed tears of disappointment gather in her dark eyes before she turned away again and hated himself for hurting her with his lacklustre, insincere and officious answer.

'My head and my gut are torn.' Where had those damning words come from? 'My head needs evidence. The government, my superiors, even the King himself will require tangible proof that you are telling us the truth that go beyond those scars.' She made to stalk away and he grabbed her arm and spun her to look at him. Needing her to understand his reticence and hope that in so doing she would stop being so miserably disappointed in him. 'Please try to see things from my point of view. I have to weigh all of the evidence through a detached and pragmatic lens.' She was holding back the tears valiantly, but even so one got away. It trickled down her cheek and Flint couldn't stop himself from brushing it away with his thumb. 'Don't cry, Jess. I beg you. I can't bear it.' His palm cupped her cheek and more unchecked, unwise words spilled out. 'I brought you home so I could protect you, for pity's sake.'

'That doesn't answer my question.'

'I can't answer your question!'

'Always the pragmatist. Hedging his bets and talking in riddles! Blowing hot and cold again.

Even now!' She snatched her head away, so he caught her around the waist instead, needing to make her understand the awful dilemma he was in. Needing also to remind himself, knowing he was wavering because she was sad.

'In my line of work I have to be pragmatic. I am an agent of the Crown. That means I don't have the luxury of indulging my emotions. I have to listen to my head above all else!'

Her dark eyes held him mesmerised. They were so expressive. So distraught. So betrayed. He was drowning in them. All at sea. Nothing solid or familiar to cling to. Losing control. 'I don't want to hear pragmatic! I don't want to know what the agent of the Crown thinks. I hate him! I want to hear what you think. The real man. The one I see flashes of when you forget yourself. The kind but irritating one who seems to care about me. Forget your head.' She pressed her hand flat against his chest, her expression so wretched and beseeching his throat constricted at the sight. 'What does your heart say, Peter?'

'That you might be innocent, damn it!' His thumb brushed away another tear as he tried and failed to remain detached.

'Might?'

'It's the best I can do.'

And he hated himself for it. Hated the betrayal and despair he saw swirling in her dark eyes. Hated the way it made him want to take back every word. He hadn't meant to kiss her, but once he did it was like a dam burst inside him. Flint gathered her close and poured every bit of the tangled, confused emotions he was feeling into a soft kiss that was a little too heartfelt—but he didn't have the willpower to care. Soft changed to passionate in a heartbeat. She clung to him, her fingers curling into the front of his waistcoat while her mouth moved with the same urgency and unsuppressed passion as his, her petite body melting against his perfectly.

He had no concept of time. He didn't remember edging them both towards the wall or lifting her off the floor so that her face was level with his—it felt too good feeling her hands in his hair and her legs hooked about his waist while his own hands went exploring. Rational thought disappeared the second her untutored tongue first brushed against his and all that mattered were the overwhelming but intoxicating new sensations their unleashed, forbidden passion created.

Like a starving man at a banquet he became greedy, tearing his mouth from hers and feasting on her neck. Tasting every inch of it before his lips found her collarbone and then the top of her breast. She moaned as he touched it through the fabric of her dress and he groaned when her nipple hardened in response against his palm.

The garment now an inconvenient layer when he wanted to feel all of her and his breeches were now so tight they physically hurt as his ready body strained against them. She arched when he tugged down the neckline, pushing her breasts towards him, but the dratted dress was too fitted to expose her fully to his mouth and forced him to wrestle clumsily with the laces at the back instead.

The insistent knock at the door followed by his mother's voice brought him crashing back down to earth with a bang.

'There's tea and port in the drawing room. Shall I bring it in?'

Flint wanted to shout at her to go away. Whether she was protecting Jess or him, her convenient interruption was as unwelcome as it was timely. She had predicted tomfoolery and clearly her outlandish suspicions were now founded because they were both breathing hard, but still clinging to each other.

That he had lost his head so thoroughly was a worry—because he never lost his head any more and certainly not from a mere kiss—but he would happily do it all again in a heartbeat because that kiss was everything. Unforgettable and addictive, yet encased in the overwhelming feeling of rightness he kept experiencing around her. If she was attempting to manipulate him with her allure, she was succeeding and that possibility made him furious at both of them.

But judging from Jess's equally stunned and wide-eyed expression, she was as shocked by what they had just succumbed to as he was. Thanks to the rude interruption, she had stiffened in his arms, although was still held suspended from the floor, her hair in glorious disarray, her mouth damningly swollen from his kisses. Her eyes darkened with desire. She looked thoroughly ravished and more beautiful than he had ever seen her.

'We will be there presently!' Had his voice ever sounded so guilty or so gravelly? Probably not. His partner in crime hastily unhooked her legs from his waist and he gently lowered her to the floor. As soon as her feet touched the ground she put a good six feet of distance between them, stuffing the delightful mounds of her full breasts back into her dress and then frantically fussing with her hair, all the while refusing to meet his gaze. It was just as well. Flint didn't have the wherewithal to disguise the awe, frustration and confusion he was feeling. Not when his body was on fire for her alone and would likely burn for her all night, and the Persian carpet beneath his feet felt unsteady.

Something primeval within stopped him from apologising simply because he wasn't sorry.

Kissing Jess might well have been stupidity incarnate, a dangerous misjudgement and totally at odds with his mission, but it had felt right and—God help him—he wanted to do it again and would if his mother wasn't likely to storm in at any second. Instead, inane words presented themselves and he grabbed them like a drowning man, hoping they might anchor him until his normal, pragmatic mind took over the carnal, possessive and unfamiliar, uncontrollable emotions that now possessed him.

'Well—that's enough confession for one night.'

Then the same errant legs that had got him in trouble in the first place marched to the door and then headed down the ancient hallway towards the sanctuary of the drawing room at breakneck speed.

Like the biggest of cowards, Jess had jumped at the chance to take her breakfast on a tray in her bedchamber rather than venture downstairs. She had hardly slept all night and the creaking timbers of the old castle, the unfamiliar surroundings and the nagging kernel of guilt which made her continue to doubt herself were only marginally to blame. That kiss held the lion's share and still haunted her as the maid insisted on dressing her hair before she ventured downstairs to face him.

She had nothing whatsoever to compare it to—the overall effect of it both last night and now was unsettling to say the least. *Mon Dieu!* Why had her mother never warned her kissing felt like that? One minute she had been staring up at him petrified for her future, the next all those fears evaporated when his lips had touched hers and she was pawing at his chest and back shamelessly, thoroughly enjoying the feel of those big hands on her waist. Her bottom. Her breasts! When his thumbs had grazed her nipples… *Ah, bon sang...* She had wanted more even though she wasn't entirely sure what more was.

Thankfully, Lady Flint's timely knock had prevented Jess from being a complete and shameless wanton and her hot, passionate almost-lover—because she was honest enough with herself to say she would have allowed him all of her and more—transformed into her uptight and stand-offish gaoler instantly. Blowing hot and cold once again. Confusing her. Was that on purpose? He'd spent less than five minutes in the drawing room before excusing himself to ostensibly plan the next steps of his mission—or rather reminding her that *she* was indeed his mission—leaving Jess floundering with his mother, who kept watching her every movement with undisguised interest while she casually sipped her tea.

Jess had fled shortly after, pleading tiredness, and then spent hours flat on her back on the bed in bemusement while willing her suddenly heavy and insistent breasts to stop yearning for his touch. Or for her silly, naïve heart to stop worrying at the meaning behind his words. If he thought she might be innocent, then there was hope. Did she dare grasp it and trust him completely? She wanted to. Flint was all she had and…and she was coming to care deeply for him. That kiss had proved that. Beyond the passion, her heart rejoiced. Yearned. Dared to want more than just passion.

She had precious little experience of men. Aside from the smitten guard in Cherbourg who had made it plain he wanted more, yet still jumped at Saint-Aubin's orders even if those orders led directly to her physical punishment. She had flirted with the guard to get him to post the *corrections* she had made to her letters after Saint-Aubin left with the originals, citing her newest injury as the reason why they couldn't indulge their passions and convincing him the new letter would ensure she didn't receive another beating before the last wounds had healed. Because he couldn't read and because he wanted her, he had complied. Despite the obvious welts across her back and bruises to her face, his patience had been wearing thin in the three weeks she had strung him along. Jess was in no doubt he would have taken what he wanted within days had the navy not unexpectedly come for her. Like Saint-Aubin, the guard had done what he needed to do to get what he wanted.

Was Peter like that? Were all men? Jess had no dealings with males outside of servants. Even with that guard, she hadn't really known what she was doing. It had all been bravado, all copied out of sheer desperation from her mother down to the last nuance, and all talk. The guard had thankfully never touched her beyond the occasional stroke of her face while she flirted through the bars of her cell and the thought that he might had made her feel sick from the outset.

She had no such qualms with her handsome Englishman, as her passionate, physical reaction could testify. He had kissed her. Of that she was sure. Jess hadn't fought it, she'd shamelessly welcomed it, but he had been the instigator. Did that mean anything? Had he only done it as a ruse to make her confide more in him? Had it been a mistake born in the heat of the moment? Did he regret it now? Was that why he had turned immediately cold and detached—or was he torn? She didn't know and wasn't anywhere near brave enough to ask him. There was no doubt kissing a suspected traitor put him in a difficult predicament and pragmatically—oh, how she now loathed that word!—he would probably have to distance himself from it whatever he truly felt. If he felt anything. And perhaps that was for the best. For him at least. Jess had no idea any more what was best for her. It was hard to be rational when her entire existence seemed to involve varying levels of turmoil, none of which she apparently had any control over.

Perhaps her intense attraction to Peter was because he was the only solid and constant thing in her life right now? She didn't need any more heartache and disappointment. One more would break her. Deep down she knew the words he had uttered before the searing kiss had been the truth. A man in his position did not have the luxury of indulging his emotions. Whether his heart believed her or not, such a pragmatic man as he would never allow that fickle organ to overrule his thick head. Alongside that thought festered the other. That kiss might well have been a deliberate ploy to lower her defences. Which was why she must never lose her head around him again. Lord Flint had the power to break her heart.

At the tap on the door her maid pushed the final hairpin into her creation and went to answer it. Another maid entered and bobbed her a curtsy. 'The ladies are downstairs waiting for you, my lady. Lady Flint says they have left the men to talk business and have adjourned to the morning room for tea. When can I tell them you will be joining them?'

'She is ready now,' said her assigned maid helpfully, blissfully ignorant of the fact Jess was hiding and happy to do so for the rest of the day. Not only were Peter and his mother downstairs, when she hadn't steeled herself to face either, but after hearing carriage after carriage arrive, she could only conclude that all his sisters and their assorted families were downstairs as well. On top of everything, she was now expected to socialise.

Like a woman about to face her own execution, an irony that was not lost on her, Jess stood and followed the maid out, not daring to scrutinise her reflection one last time in the mirror. Last night, a quick glance had confirmed what she had suspected. Her lips had been red and swollen, her eyes overbright and her wayward hair a damning tangle. No doubt Lady Flint had swiftly worked out she had just been kissed— and thoroughly. While her hair might now be presentable, the incessant tingling in her lips probably meant they still looked swollen and the peculiar yet wholly improper ache between her thighs was guaranteed to ensure her eyes remained overbright. As soon as she saw *him*, then inevitably recalled exactly how she had wrapped her legs around his waist and where she had encouraged him to put his hands, the ensuing blush would be ferocious and visible for miles. Like a beacon for all to see.

Good grief!

Chapter Eighteen

'Jess! You found us! Do come in.' Lady Flint was sat holding a teacup on a large sofa, flanked on either side by two pretty blonde women who made no attempt to hide their curiosity. Opposite on another matching sofa were three more. All clutching teacups and all staring at her with smiles on their faces.

Then her step faltered and it took every last ounce of stubborn pride not to run away with her hands over her face. Looking decidedly put upon and sat alone on a huge wingback chair was the only male. He smiled a little sheepishly and rose politely, his hands clamping behind his back in a manner that told her he felt as awkward about what had happened between them as she did. But he was here, in a roomful of inquisitive strangers, and for that she was grateful. 'I couldn't leave you to face them all alone, Jess.' Then his eyes flicked to his sisters and back and he sighed. 'As you can see, the ravens were dispatched with urgency to summon the coven and they have all flown in on their broomsticks. Lucky us.'

'Oh, for goodness sake, Peter! What a dreadful impression you are giving Jess of your family. Your sisters are a delight and you know it.' Lady Flint turned to Jess. 'My dear girls have always been much more doting than my only son—whom I rarely see enough of and yet is always so sour when he graces us with his presence. I tried to convince him to leave us alone, but he flatly refused and now threatens to spoil our visit. We shall ignore him and still have a lovely visit over luncheon regardless. Just us girls.' She stood and took Jess's hand. 'Allow me to introduce you.'

'A visit? Is that what you are calling this spontaneous gathering? How charming—when we all know this is a shoddy excuse to poke your noses into government matters that do not concern you.'

All five of his sisters ignored him and smiled at Jess as she was paraded in front of them. 'My oldest—Ophelia. Then this is Rosalind and Portia. They popped out in that order.' Jess nodded, more than a little intimidated at so many sisters all in one go and unsettled because *he* was only a few feet away, and only just remembered to curtsy before being guided firmly to the sofa Lady Flint had just vacated. 'And finally, this is Hermia and Desdemona, my twins. Although as you can see, they are not identical.'

Perhaps not, but the likeness of all six of the siblings was uncanny. She could see bits of Peter in all of them. The same green eyes. The same golden wheatsheaf hair. The dancing amusement lurking beneath their polite masks. 'What lovely names. All from Shakespeare, *non*?'

'Indeed they are.' Lady Flint clutched her hands to her bosom. 'I've always adored the theatre!'

'Theatrics more like,' Peter muttered from his pew by the fireplace. Only Jess turned her head to acknowledge he had spoken. To the rest he might as well have been invisible.

'I wanted Pericles or Petruchio, but his father wouldn't hear of it,' Lady Flint continued undaunted. 'He said I could only have a Shakespearean name if he chose it. He went through the complete works, ignored all my suggestions, and found Peter—a minor character at best in *A Midsummer Night's Dream*—and then dug his heels in, refusing to budge.'

'Thank goodness. Ridiculous names, both of them. Lord Pericles Flint! And the least said about blasted Petruchio the better. My father was a very sensible man. I thank my lucky stars daily that at least one of my parents was.'

'So he became stuck with Peter,' said Lady Flint with a shrug, obviously choosing selective deafness rather than acknowledgement, 'which I've always thought is one of the dullest Shake-spearean names ever. *But* as the Bard himself remarked, all's well that ends well because Peter can be very *dull* and serious when he sets his mind to it. Have you noticed what a horrid spoil-sport he is, Jess?'

'Sensible and level headed, you mean, in a sea of unnecessary, overly theatrical drama. And you don't have to answer that question, Jess. Or any other. Remember what I told you—*gird* your loins.' He looked directly at her and her silly pulse quickened. His family exasperated him and amused him in equal measure. And like a fool, she hoped that speaking look meant that last night had meant something to him, too. 'I hope you are ready for the Inquisition.'

'He means luncheon,' said Ophelia, helpfully standing. 'It is ready and has been for ten min-utes, but he *insisted* we wait for you here. Appar-ently, this room is less daunting than the dining room and secretly I believe he hoped we might all suddenly have a change of heart and eat with-out you.'

'Which is a positively splendid idea! Why

don't you all go and eat with your horrid families instead and leave us in peace? We have work to do and surely it is obvious that poor Jess is not up to you lot after her ordeal?'

'You see,' said Ophelia, threading her arm through Jess's, 'so very dull and so very serious. And rude, too. As if we would eat without you after Mother has gone to so much trouble in your honour.'

Mon Dieu! 'There really was no need to go to any trouble. I am inconveniencing you enough already…'

'Nonsense. It's more high tea than a formal luncheon,' interrupted Lady Flint, taking Jess's other arm. 'Lots of delicious finger food so we can concentrate on the conversation. My sourpuss son has another think coming if he believes I would allow you to spend the day *working* without some proper food in your belly. Do you like salmon? Cook does the loveliest poached salmon glazed in aspic.'

'Er…yes.' Although Jess had no clue as to what aspic was.

'Splendid!' That appeared to be the cue everyone was waiting for and, as one, the rest also stood and Jess found herself enclosed in a sea of perfume and muslin as she was shepherded next door, hoping that despite being blatantly excluded from the invitation, Peter was trailing behind.

* * *

Flint was going to kill his mother. Then he would take great pleasure in strangling each and every one of his sisters. Between the six of them, they made the meal interminable. It had started well enough—if being broadsided and bludgeoned could be described as pleasant—then deteriorated rapidly into the debacle he had fully expected it would become. Despite his insisted presence, his womenfolk were incorrigible.

Was Jess married?

Engaged?

What sort of gentlemen usually took her fancy?

What were her first impressions of Peter?

Had they known each other long?

Spent much time together?

Poor Jess answered with surprising diplomacy considering the onslaught, although her eyes had kept darting to his for support despite the unresolved veil of awkwardness between them, and he rewarded her with a resigned shake of the head, knowing he should have put his foot down and stopped this stupid luncheon before it had started and suffered the petulant and noisy sulking from his meddling womenfolk. He needed to talk to Jess. Desperately, and not just about Saint-Aubin.

After a sleepless night he knew he needed to apologise and then declare their explosive passion a huge mistake. How could he properly do his duty when all his waking thoughts were consumed with her? And, more importantly, how could he protect her to the best of his ability if he was the slightest bit distracted with lust? One heated kiss had already rendered him dumbstruck. Any more would...and that train of thought was definitely best not considered when each time he looked her way his body responded instantly.

She was a delicious distraction and one neither of them could afford. Her safety depended on his sanity. It was that simple and that dreadful.

Flint sensed someone was watching him and quickly tore his gaze from the object of his torment, only to find his eldest sister Ophelia openly staring at him in amusement. 'We despair of Peter ever settling down. Thus far, he hasn't shown more than a passing interest in any young lady. Although I am hopeful that will change soon.' She cast him an innocent smile, then went in for the kill. 'Perhaps sooner rather than later in view of current events.'

He shot her a withering look and choked down a fork full of salmon. Damn! He needed to keep his inappropriate urges in check, else throw more fuel to the fire. At this rate, they would all decide he was besotted, as his mother had already no doubt erroneously informed them, and then all hell would break loose.

'We live in hope that one day Cupid's arrow will spear him.' This from his mother, who was thankfully unaware he had just been openly yearning for his prisoner.

'Surely by now you realise I am arrow proof, Mother? Poor Cupid would be foolish to waste them on me.'

His mother smiled and shook her head pityingly. 'Your dear father was just the same. He was staunchly against it until he was shot and fiercely besotted afterwards. He adored me. It all happened very fast. One minute we were arguing in Berkeley Square because he accused me of daydreaming—which of course I was—and causing him to crash his landau and the next we were skipping up the aisle just a month later. It was all *very* scandalous at the time and *very* romantic.' She smiled wistfully at the memory. 'As a baron he was expected to marry well, not set his cap at a draper's daughter, and he did try to fight the attraction, poor thing. But he confessed later that he wanted only me from that first moment in the street.' A worrying detail she had never shared before, worrying because it resonated. He found his eyes surreptitiously wander to Jess. Felt his blood heat instantly.

'And it's true! Opposites do attract. We were

devoted to one another.' His mother sighed, her eyes a little glassy at the bitter sweetness. 'The Flint men are famously devoted to the women they adore, Peter, and fall in love with lightning speed. It is not something you have a choice in, my darling. One day, love will creep up and catch you unawares. It is as inevitable as summer following spring. It has happened to all of us in exactly the same way.' Five blonde heads nodded. 'And we would all like nothing more than to see such a love enrich your life, my darling.' Her eyes flicked to Jess innocently. 'But alas, what brave and fearless woman would take on such a sour and pessimistic young man?'

Then the topic properly turned to him, which was marginally better, although Jess was bombarded with the succession of embarrassing stories the harpies wheeled out when they wanted to properly torment him. How he had not been clever enough to walk before he was one, preferring to shuffle everywhere on his bottom instead. That time, during a long, hot summer when he was eighteen and had thought it appropriate to go swimming in the stream, but had been caught stark naked by the parson and his wife—neither of whom had ever been able to look him in the eye since. Or his personal favourite, an anecdote guaranteed to make his toes curl inside his boots, the regaling of his one and only love poem, written at the tender age of fifteen to one of Portia's friends in which he declared his intention to marry her despite the substantial difference in their ages and the unfortunate existence of her devoted fiancé. A poem Portia had consigned to memory to be wheeled out on special occasions when it was guaranteed to cause the most cringing.

Flint endured every sibling reminiscence stoically, letting his expression show he was heartily unimpressed with the lot of them and flatly refusing to dignify anything with a response. Besides, the horrendous stories were making Jess laugh and he couldn't bring himself to deny her that. Not now he knew she had whip marks all over her back and her lips tasted of ripe summer strawberries.

Things marginally improved over tea because he purposely directed the conversation back to his mission to remind them all Jess wasn't visiting and of the grave set of circumstances they found themselves in. During the necessary lecture and subsequent recollection of the horrors of the last few days as they had escaped Saint-Aubin, his meddlesome womenfolk remained blessedly silent, only interrupting with questions about the exact series of events.

They had been genuinely horrified by most of it and were hugely sympathetic towards Jess.

Beneath their meddlesome exteriors, his sisters had hearts of pure gold. They asked her many questions, probing in that concerned, open way that females did and inadvertently giving Flint a deeper understanding of the awfulness of her plight and the lead up to her capture. Intrigued at the additional details, no matter how difficult it all was to hear, he simply sat back and allowed the ladies to draw her into their confidence. Too late, Flint realised he had walked into another trap and chaos ensued once more.

Ooh! A whole night alone on the moors unchaperoned! How scandalous?

There had been many smiles and knowing looks after that glorious set of questions from Ophelia, which had finished with a loaded and mortifying sentence. *'If you weren't his prisoner, Jess, I would insist my brother do the decent thing and marry you! The scoundrel.'*

Fearing everything was about to get out of hand yet again, Flint slapped his palm on the table decisively. 'Right! You've all had quite enough fun at my expense, go reclaim your families and make the most of your *short* stay here at Penmor.'

He had already outlined his plan to them in the drawing room before Jess had arrived, stipulating in no uncertain terms it was non-negotiable. His sisters, all twelve of their children and their long-suffering and frankly sainted husbands were going to sit out the duration of this mission under the protection for Lord Fennimore in London as soon as his men arrived. An evacuation he was keener than ever to see happen. When the time came, he intended to dispatch his mother, too—although that was still a work in progress. After her stubborn refusal to leave she had dug her heels in. He was simply waiting for the right moment to tell her she, too, was leaving soon.

'Do you think sending us to Lord Fennimore is entirely necessary, Peter?' Desdemona, the most reasonable of the gaggle, looked pained. 'It seems like a lot of disruption and I would rather stay here.'

'Eighteen men have been murdered in cold blood by the smugglers in less than six months.' All the colour drained from Jess's face and she stared at her hands again, making him feel dreadful for frightening her. 'With Saint-Aubin here in the south searching for Jess, I do not want that number to rise. I would rather it was none of you and I can't guarantee your safety here. Our resources will be stretched to capacity. Once all the reinforcements arrive, and with my official hat on, I would rather know you were miles away and safe. Penmor must temporarily become a fortress once again, not a home, and my men have an important job to do that is completely separate from my family. If they come—and we have to accept they might—I don't want to be distracted by having to worry about you all, too.' Not when he already knew he would be at his wits' end worrying about Jess. 'I doubt you will be inconvenienced for more than a week.'

The ensuing silence was audible as they all digested his words. Flint wasn't trying to scare them, merely alert them to the reality. In a perfect world, once Jess spilled all her secrets the King's Elite could take decisive action and destroy the rotten, festering smuggling ring once and for all. They would swarm like locusts and leave nothing remaining. Swift, decisive and righteous justice for the men they had murdered and the woman they had beaten. Saint-Aubin and the Boss wouldn't know what had hit them. But he knew the world wasn't perfect and these were not your run-of-the-mill smugglers. These were an organised army of mercenaries with everything they held dear at stake. The siege would not be pretty.

It was Ophelia who spoke first. 'If you believe we need to go, we will go.' Four blonde heads nodded in agreement.

'I do. Try to think of it as a little holiday. You'll all be staying in Berkeley Square.' Where they could drive Lord Fennimore mad, but where he could also guarantee security would be tightest. His enormous house was necessarily under constant guard and had been for decades. He doubted even the King was as secure as Sixty-Three Berkeley Square. And as his father and Lord Fennimore had worked together for years, his curmudgeonly superior would feel duty bound to have them. Warts and all. He would protect them with the same fervour as Flint would himself. 'Mother—I really think you should go, too.'

'Over my dead body.'

Flint glared and her mouth set in a flat, stubborn line as she glared back. 'It will only be for a week, not for ever.'

'This is my home and I refuse to leave it.' Her eyes flicked to Jess, then back, the implication clear. Tomfoolery. He held her glare and sent a message back of his own. There would be no more tomfoolery. He was a professional. An agent of the Crown. A man who was fully capable of rising above his urges. A man who was most definitely not by any definition besotted.

'Don't look at me like that, young man! I am staying put!'

From the recesses of his mind he remembered a similar occasion over twenty years ago: his father evacuating the entire family from the castle during a particularly dangerous mission here on the Cornish coast and his mother's stalwart refusal to leave. Then, his father had dealt with the situation calmly. He had been so commanding Masterful. So masterful, his mother had bowed down and agreed immediately. Those words came to him now as if his father had gifted them.

'Need I remind you that I am the head of this family and, if I *decree* it, you will go.'

His mother blinked. His five sisters blinked. Then the lot of them burst out laughing.

Chapter Nineteen

The bizarre luncheon was brought to a decisive end with the arrival of Monsieur Gray and another man Jess did not recognise. They disappeared with Peter into his study and didn't re-emerge for over an hour. She was sat in the drawing room with his family when she was summoned. There was no sign of the smiling Lord Gray now. Only Peter and the unsmiling stranger.

'Jess, this is Hadleigh…he's a barrister.'

As Peter appeared uncomfortable announcing this, she asked the obvious question. 'Prosecution or defence?'

The tall, blond stranger met her gaze unflinchingly. 'I work with the Attorney General. Whether or not it is prosecution or defence in your case remains to be seen, my lady.'

She wouldn't flinch or display how petrified that cold statement or the lawyer's presence made her. Nor would she dwell on the fact Peter had failed to warn her that with the promised re-inforcements would come the enemy. Hadleigh wasn't here to protect her, nor would he leave here without her.

'Flint tells me you are prepared to co-operate.'

'Do I have a choice?' Because her knees were now unsteady, she lowered herself into the chair Peter had pulled out for her with as much poise and grace as she could muster, while he deftly averted his lying eyes. No outright lies, perhaps, but certainly by omission. What else had he neglected to tell her while he had been skilfully chipping away at her defences and making her care about him?

'One always has a choice, my lady—although your options are now quite limited. In case you are in any doubt, allow me to outline them for you. You can keep your secrets and guarantee a short walk to the gallows or you can divulge them fully and allow the cards to fall where they may.'

'I believe I will need more clarity on "fall where they may", *monsieur*.' Words less reassuring than the feeble *lenient* which had been dangled previously. She shot Peter a disgusted look for his duplicity. One he returned blandly, but which still had the power to wound.

'Flint has indicated that you might be a vic-

tim in all this.' There was that word again—
might. The dangling carrot at the end of a very
hard stick. Giving her just enough hope to make
her comply, but easily withdrawn whenever they
wanted. 'And if that proves to be correct, then
the charges will be adjusted accordingly.'

'Might? Prove? Such *comforting* words. Do all
the King's men avoid giving a straight answer?'
She had the satisfaction of watching the man
who had kissed her, then cruelly dismissed her,
glance awkwardly at the floor, leaving Hadleigh to answer.

'Let us be clear—we have letters written in
your hand, sent to English peers and smugglers
alike, which state plain as day the exact dates,
times and by which vessel they are to expect
or deliver illegal shipments of smuggled goods.
Those same letters instruct those traitors how
much to pay for those cargoes and whether the
price is to be paid in gold or guns. Payments
which went back to your stepfather Saint-
Aubin, to be used against England. Irrefutable
facts which cannot be denied, Lady Jessamine.'

'Then here are some more facts for you, *monsieur*. Saint-Aubin is not my father—step or otherwise. He was my foolish mother's childhood
sweetheart and later her lover. Her name was
also Jessamine and until a few months ago it
was her hand who wrote those letters. When she

became ill, Saint-Aubin needed someone fluent in both languages he could use to quickly and seamlessly fill her shoes.'

'So he trusted you?'

'He trusted I would not be callous enough to decline when he held my mother's medication to ransom and refused to allow physicians to urgently attend her.' Her eyes drifted of their own accord back to Peter against her will, only to see he had wandered back to the window. His entire body turned away while she suffered. 'Tell me, Monsieur Hadleigh—would you refuse, too, if you could hear your mother screaming in agony in the next room?' Peter's broad shoulders suddenly stiffened, but once again he remained mute.

'Flint tells me you weren't close to your mother.' Clearly, he had happily shared everything she had confided in him. Perhaps even their kiss. Something she should have anticipated, but which still hurt immensely. For her it had been special. For him a means to an end. She tore her eyes away from him and tried to ignore he was there.

'We were different people, but I never wished her ill. She was still my mother and the only relative I had.'

'You had your father. He is still very much alive and resides where he always has in Suffolk.'

Immediately, she felt the cruel slice of that cold betrayal again as if it were fresh and raw. 'Perhaps if I had been born male, he might have cared. Unfortunately for me, my mother's abandonment as war broke out between her country and his worked in my father's favour. He was able to start afresh and forget I existed. I wrote to him. Multiple letters. Begging to come back home to Suffolk. He ignored all bar one, then he callously told me to desist.'

Those damning words were engraved on her battered heart. *'As far as the law and my conscience are concerned, I have no daughter. You cannot be dead to me because you never were alive.'*

'I sincerely doubt he would welcome me back there now.' And even if he did relent, she would never forgive him for abandoning her, too. 'It is hard to ask for help when one is all alone in the world.'

Her eyes did flick back to Peter then, wondering why every person she dared to form an attachment with always let her down. He met her gaze head on, his green eyes stormy, his expression suddenly intense, both fists clenched tightly at his sides. For a moment, she thought he would stride towards her until he turned his back once again.

'Let's get back to the letters, shall we.' The

lawyer slowly paced to the desk and picked up a bundle which he held out to her. 'Which of these are in your mother's hand?' She knew the answer already, because none would be. Her mother's missives had been handed directly to Saint-Aubin's trusted lieutenants. Not an illiterate guard who wanted to bed her, who had been so blinded by the promise of sating his lust he delivered them to whichever England-bound packet happened to be in the harbour.

Jess rifled through them to count how many of the five she had convinced the guard to send for her had made it to their intended destination. They had four. Three sent to the now imprisoned and soon-to-hang Viscount Penhurst and one to the newly exiled Earl of Cambourne. She would allow herself that one celebration. All that pitiful flirting and pleading had done its job no matter how much self-respect it had cost her. Not that she had had much left after Saint-Aubin had tortured her.

'None. These are all in my hand.'

'And isn't that interesting? Some would say damning.'

'Surely the more interesting question is why, after years of failing to get even one sniff of the hundreds of communications, the British suddenly began intercepting those letters in just the last few weeks and were easily able to decipher them?' Jess tossed them back on to the desk, watching them fan out haphazardly across the surface, and folded her arms defiantly. 'Or how you came to know the exact location they all came from in Cherbourg? Or the names and exact addresses of Saint-Aubin's contacts they were addressed to here in England?'

'The French are not the only nation skilled in code.'

'Code? A monkey could have deciphered those letters. Was that you, Monsieur Hadleigh?'

His eyebrows raised. Other than that, he was as unreadable as rock. She disliked him immensely.

'Tell him about the *Grubbenvorst*, Jess.'

She sensed Peter staring at her. Every hair on her head, every nerve under her skin felt his eyes. So she did. Because he had asked her to and because she had nothing else left but the truth and because she knew her heart would bleed if she dared look at him and not see he cared.

The lawyer listened intently, interjecting with a myriad of questions which seemed to take the story around and around in ever-decreasing circles that dragged the telling on interminably. When she finished the inscrutable Hadleigh sighed. Part of her sympathised as she was now so tied up in knots she hardly believed what she had said herself.

* * *

After two hours of solid and intense questioning, Jess's head hurt. Hadleigh had a way of backtracking and querying every detail that had her second-guessing herself. When he declared it time for a break, it took all her strength not to slump in the chair and demonstrate to the horrid man that he was putting her through her paces. Her brain felt as though it had been wrung out in a mangle. 'We shall reconvene in an hour.'

'We shall reconvene tomorrow. Jess is still exhausted from her ordeal and needs a decent meal and a good night's sleep.' It was the first sentence Peter had uttered during the entire interrogation and, despite her anger at his betrayal and at herself for giving him the power to hurt her with it, she was grateful for his interference.

The lawyer's eyebrows raised again, the only emotion he showed with any regularity. 'I see. Well—if you are sure, Flint?' The implication was clear. He wasn't.

'I'm sure. And as I am the ranking agent on this mission, that is the end of it.'

With nothing registering on his unreadable features, Hadleigh gathered up her letters and stood, looking as cool and as rigid as an icicle. 'Then we will reconvene at eight sharp.'

Jess listened to the sound of his retreating feet, sensing Peter's stare again and wondering where she would find the energy to deal with the next challenge this bizarre day would throw at her. He didn't make her wait long.

'We need to talk.'

She allowed her eyes to slowly travel to his face with visible hostility. 'By that you mean you have things to say and because you are in charge of everything and everyone here, I am expected to listen. I suppose that is an improvement on what I just had to sit through. You might have warned me I was to be interrogated immediately after being so thoroughly scrutinised by your sisters over luncheon.'

'I knew about neither. My sisters and my mother are a law unto themselves, my control over them is tenuous to say the least, and Hadleigh is…well…for want of a better analogy, Hadleigh is the law. As the Crown-appointed prosecutor, he took it upon himself to accompany Gray back here and now that he is here… Oh, Jess. I'm sorry.' He huffed out a long sigh and raked his hand through his thick hair in agitation. 'One inquisition I could have prevented—the other I had no control over. Neither were necessary today.'

'I would have preferred hours with your matchmaking family over Monsieur Hadleigh. He is…' She struggled for the words to properly convey what had just occurred and settled for an expression of absolute bewilderment.

'He is famously thorough and excellent at what he does. His reputation as a brilliant barrister precedes him—canny, sharp and scrupulously fair. His sole purpose, as far as he is concerned, is to get to the truth regardless of who that truth benefits. He's personable enough when you get to know him.'

'Personable! *Je ne crois pas mes oreilles!*'

'Yes, I'll grant you, watching him work was an experience. He is unrelenting. But you did well. I'm glad you have decided to co-operate.'

She hadn't. Not fully. Until she was sure about Hadleigh's true purpose she would keep the rest of the names of the turncoat peers in her back pocket in case Saint-Aubin did find her and made her beg for mercy like a coward. Surely that was sensible collateral? Or perhaps that merely cemented her status as the worst of cowards? Selfishly concerned with only her own future. But she knew Saint-Aubin better than anyone and knew what he was capable of. As a last resort, she had to hold something back— unless it was too late. Which it undoubtedly was.

'What choice do I have? Thanks to you, I am a powerless prisoner in a remote castle with a price on my head.' She should have escaped on the moors when she had the chance instead of sleeping in his arms and falling for his charm. *'Un assassin ou un procès.* The archetypal Hobson's choice, *non?'*

'The simple codes you embedded in those letters certainly suggest you were actively trying to alert the British to what was going on. That fact Hadleigh took them with him means he will check each and every one with a fine-tooth comb. He may well come to the conclusion you were trying to assist the government.'

She had merely been trying to get Saint-Aubin arrested and in turn gain her freedom. It had all been about her and an end to her suffering. Jess hadn't considered how desperately the Crown had needed the information. But she didn't bother correcting him. It was difficult to know how it all affected England when she had been denied all knowledge of the outside world for years. It was a hollow justification and, once again, she was irritated by his lacklustre support. All those letters, letters she had risked her life writing, apparently merely suggested she wasn't a traitor. Her gaoler resolutely always avoided the clear-cut implications of a simple yes or no.

'Gray has been dispatched to arrange the boarding of your Dutch ship, the arrest warrant for the Marquis of Deal and the safe evacuation of my family. All things considered, we are making good progress…' He appeared to steel himself then, pulling himself up to his full height and clamping his hands firmly behind his back. Something he did when he wanted her to see he was the one in control. 'Which brings me to what happened last night…'

Chapter Twenty

There was no point in beating around the bush. As awkward as the next few minutes were bound to be, Flint needed to lay down some boundaries for the sake of his own sanity as well as his career. 'There is no denying there is an attraction between us.' He found himself rocking on his heels like an admiral inspecting the fleet and couldn't seem to stop. Her usually expressive face was suddenly unreadable and she stared back at him blankly, making him more nervous and feel ridiculously foolish. But one of them had to tackle the subject head on.

'We are both adults and, under usual circumstances, pursuing that intense mutual attraction would be a perfectly normal thing to do.' He was certainly inclined to pursue it, but he had to do what was right for the Crown, not the seemingly permanent bulge in his breeches. 'Unfortunately, our circumstances are as far from normal as it is possible to be, therefore it would be prudent to have matters out in the open in case that unfortunate attraction rears its ugly head again and catches us unawares.'

Not the exact words he had been rehearsing since the middle of the night, clumsier and annoyingly more officious, but close enough. Whatever his body wanted, his inappropriate attraction to Jess shouldn't be something he was prepared to risk either her life or his reputation on—no matter how much it hurt to say it all aloud.

'The fact is, neither one of us is in a position to pursue the attraction. As an operative of the government, I have an important job still to do and I have to remain impartial, detached and wholly focused. Something I catastrophically failed in last night.' If Saint-Aubin had stormed the castle while he had been kissing Jess, Flint would have missed it. The kiss had been that potent. That all-consuming. That dangerous. 'Giving in to our passions then was foolhardy, as I am sure you will agree, and going forward, I believe it is best that we try to forget yesterday's kiss ever happened.' A kiss which he was still reeling from and would likely never forget until he took his dying breath.

'Very wise. It was a mistake.'

'Don't get me wrong, it was a wonderful kiss

and all, spectacular even, and I'm not denying I might want to do it again—once this blasted trial is over we might even consider...' At the last moment he was able to clamp his teeth together and not say *picking up where we left off.* What the hell was he thinking? 'What I mean is...'

The rest of that potentially damning sentence died in his throat as her hasty agreement finally permeated his brain. He found himself blinking, stunned and more than a bit offended that she hadn't made any attempt to contradict him. It had been an epic kiss. Earth-shattering and, God help him, meaningful. *Very wise* sounded uninspired. Wholly uninspired when women usually fell over themselves to gain his favour, Along with his title, fortune and what he had been assured by countless females was a reasonably handsome face. It was supposed to be him letting her down gently, not holding out the flimsy hand of hope by admitting things he had promised himself he didn't truly feel—yet clearly did—or almost confessing he was seriously pondering some sort of future! He, who had never ever considered such a travesty, was wounded by her abundant lack of enthusiasm for one. Flint wanted to pause things; she wanted to halt them. Being on the receiving end of a letdown was unsettling.

'Well...splendid. I'm glad we are aligned on

that.' Although they weren't. The peculiar military rocking was getting out of hand thanks to her turning the tables on him and his heart's erratic beating of a woeful tattoo against his ribs, so Flint began to pace. 'As I said, I should like to renew my *assertion* that once this is over then perhaps we can indulge our passions and...' Good grief! What was the matter with him? Why did he keep pushing for more when he should be rejoicing in her pragmatic and logical acceptance of his suggestion? He did not want a more. More with her would inevitably lead to other things. Things he resolutely refused to think about and certainly had never wanted.

'I do not think that would be wise, Monsieur Flint.' What had happened to Peter? And why was she looking at him as if she pitied him? Women never pitied him. Never! He found himself frowning at the outrage.

'You don't?' He'd meant to nod and kill the cringing conversation stone dead. That he hadn't mortified him. But then again, being the one being let down gently was an entirely new experience and not one he was comfortable with. The balance of power between them seemed to have shifted and he didn't like her categoric *no*. It hurt. Why was that?

'Of course it wouldn't be wise.' She smiled

sympathetically like a mother to a child. 'Surely you don't think any of it was real?'

'No. *No.* None of it.' He had. Still did, truth be told, and by her concerned, almost bemused expression she probably knew it. That rankled. His cravat immediately felt tighter and there was the very distinct possibility of a blush escaping his constricting collar and creeping up his neck. He fought it by clenching his jaw and willing it away. A grown man of the world, a man considered quite the catch by most women in society, a man perfectly delighted with his bachelor status who was a cunning and resourceful spy of twenty-seven to boot shouldn't blush. Not when he was getting the result common sense told him he wanted and the one he had come here intent on receiving. He forced himself to meet her amused eyes blandly, fearing that bland in fact looked annoyed. Or worse—wounded. 'I simply wanted to clarify, in case you had interpreted things differently from me.'

'Monsieur Flint—yesterday was a very trying day for me. As were the days before. I was upset, tired, overly emotional and vulnerable and you were being so kind. When *you* kissed me… well, at the time I was so pathetically grateful you offered some hope and that I was safe here in your beautiful fortress, I allowed it to cloud my judgement. I never should have let it happen.

It was a mistake. *Don't get me wrong...*' she had an irritating talent for skewering him with his own words ' ..it was a perfectly pleasant kiss as kisses go—but it meant nothing. I *like* you. You are a very nice man when you are not being staid and terminally vexing, however, in regard to your suggestion that we can pursue the attraction when this is over is, frankly, preposterous.'

'It is?' His neck heated unhindered then and he wished the floor would open before it became visible above his collar. She was making a fool out of him and he was rapidly losing the upper hand. Perhaps he had already lost it if the word future was hovering menacingly in the recesses of his mind? He was now so confused and inexplicably hurt. 'What I mean is... Of course, you are quite correct...' Whatever he had wanted to say to regain some of his dignity fizzled out when she rose and undulated towards him. For a second, the emotionally bewitched new side to his usually level-headed character hoped her seductive smile and knowing dipped lashes signalled she was lying about her lack of reciprocal feelings towards him and, unacceptably, his silly heart soared against his will.

'I am so glad we have cleared the air.' She cupped his cheek, her thumb moving in gentle circles which ricocheted down all his nerve endings and set his body on fire all over again. His lips tingled and his eyes dropped to hers hungrily. *'Tu es très gentil parfois...'* She benevolently gave him a moment to translate those words—*You are a very sweet man sometimes.* Words that he couldn't deny made him hope. Then ruthlessly bludgeoned him with the next before he had the wherewithal to control his outrageous thoughts. 'And despite my horrendous lapse in judgement yesterday, you *are* sweet. I meant that *assertion* most sincerely. Let us not muddy the waters with anything else.'

Flint stood immobile like a statue, until she sailed out of the room, then collapsed into the nearest chair.

Winded.

That was the best way to describe how he felt. Winded, offended and embarrassed. Winded because he had genuinely thought the magnificent passion they had shared last night was mutual and all consuming. How had he got that wrong? Yes—he had kissed her first. But she had kissed him back with equal enthusiasm, or so he had stupidly thought. Offended because she clearly hadn't. While he was still reeling from the after-effects of their passion, Jess was remarkably nonplussed about it today. Which was evidential proof it had been a totally forgettable experience as far as she was concerned.

What had she disliked about it? It had been

a damn fine kiss. One of his best. Hell, who was he fooling, it had been *the* best. He doubted he was capable of better—which was worrying food for thought when hers had blown him sideways but clearly left her indifferent. And he was beyond galled—bordering on the mortified—because she now knew irrefutably he was not just attracted to her, but willing to pursue that attraction as soon as he was able. Flint had never been so humiliated in his life, yet he had nobody to blame for that state but himself. In trying to regain the upper hand in their confusing relationship, he had handed it to Jess on a plate. *'You are a very sweet man sometimes.'* What an insipid and insulting compliment that had been. A little pat on the head to soften the succession of body blows she had deftly dealt him.

Rejection hurt. Almost as much as his carnal yearning for her did. Unconsciously he rubbed the heel of his hand against the part of his chest that ached the most until he realised he was actually rubbing his heart and the pain in it was increasing rather than lessening.

That stopped him dead in his tracks.

Surely that couldn't be right? It was well known that humiliation left a bitter taste in the mouth, fear churned the guts and embarrassment caused the toes to curl. Aches in hearts—painful, clawing, incessant painful aches in hearts—

suggested he was either having an apoplexy or… Dizziness swamped him. Good grief! He was heartbroken?

No…it couldn't be. His feelings were mired in the carnal. They were desire, lust. An itch that needed to be scratched. Transient. Not a lasting emotion involving his heart.

Or could it?

Flint had never allowed his feelings to become romantically engaged before so had little concept of how such things felt. Was this more than lust and sexual frustration? Had his mother been right and he was besotted? It couldn't be.

His mind began to whir back through the last few days to clarify, replaying every interaction and his emotional reaction to them. The repeated and visceral need to protect her from harm. The panic he experienced if he considered, even momentarily, she might be taken from him. The need to chase away all her sadness and fear and save her from both Saint-Aubin and the hangman. The way he had held her in his arms as she slept, when behind all the lust lurked an overwhelming sense of rightness. The admiration he held her in that transcended the physical. Her bravery. Her tenacity. Her noble stoicism. The way his heart ached when he thought about all she had suffered and ached more simply by looking at her or being with her. The perfect sense of completeness when he had finally succumbed and touched his lips to hers. The pain now clawing his chest because she had dashed all his hopes.

Flint had brought her home.

That in itself was damning proof, because his mother was right. Not only would he never bring a traitor home, he would never bring a woman home either and willingly suffer all the meddlesome speculation of his family.

Unless she meant something.

There was no denying she now meant something. Something that jumbled up everything inside and left the ground unsteady. Something that made his heart hurt at her rejection and soar when she smiled. Something that had nothing to do with his head or his gut, yet everything to do with them at the same time. Something all-consuming and all-encompassing and wholly unpalatable. Yet oddly not unpalatable at the same time.

Maybe a little love *had* crept up on him while he least expected it? Inappropriate, not at all what he wanted, blatantly unrequited and it would seem, ultimately, doomed. How fittingly typical when he never should have looked in the first place and undoubtedly no less than he deserved for the weakness.

* * *

Jess didn't see him for the rest of the day or most of the next. She couldn't face a family dinner and he deftly avoided both breakfast, luncheon and the interminable and lengthy second interrogation with the Crown Prosecutor in between. She kept telling herself it was just as well, because she was still hurt and angry at the sanctimonious way he had retracted the kiss they had shared and all it had meant, reminding her he had a job to do—one he was more than happy to put before her. While a huge part of her had been expecting it—because she was still his prisoner and very much still headed to the gallows if today's proceedings with the lawyer were anything to go by—hearing him denounce what was between them as nothing but a foolhardy, carnal attraction that should never have reared its ugly head stung.

Pride made her lash out rather when he had tabled the offer of possibly pursuing that attraction in the future—if she proved not to be the traitor he clearly still believed her to be. If he thought it that abhorrent now, and blatantly still did not believe her despite his wholly lukewarm assertion the night before that he might, then she would go to hell in a handbasket before she allowed him to see how much those offensive words had wounded. They merely justified her original plan. To escape and leave it all behind her. Why should she care about the plight of the British government, or one of their irritatingly handsome minions, when they didn't care about her? She owed them—him—nothing. Nothing! If only she could convince her newly awakened conscience and bruised heart of that fact, she would sleep better.

After a concerted effort at searching for the secret passageway out of the castle failed, Jess had spent the rest of the night tossing and turning and second-guessing her decision to put her faith in him when he clearly had none in her. Three more hours in the company of Hadleigh made her question it further. She had only come here because of her misguided faith in Peter. Now she didn't quite know what to think.

It was Lady Flint who rescued her for dinner after several more hours of circular questioning where he probed and she played her cards close to her chest. Despite the lawyer's presence at dinner, the lack of Peter altered the dynamic, yet Jess was glad he wasn't there. If she never saw him again it would be too soon.

The servants were on the cusp of clearing away the plates when the master of the house deigned to show his sanctimonious face. He strode in looking gorgeously windswept and purposeful with Gray in tow, although his handsome comrade paled into the background against Peter's irritating golden perfection. Her silly pulse's fluttering had her stiffening in defiance. She would not care about him, dratted man, nor continue to be offended by his hurtful words and obsession with his duty above all else. He meant nothing. If not right now, then he would mean nothing very soon. She would leave and forget him the second she was free. If it killed her, she would never remember that glorious, manipulative kiss again.

As if he knew she was thinking about him, his eyes flicked to hers briefly, then settled swiftly on his mother. Whatever intense emotion was swirling in those unfathomable green depths, she wouldn't allow herself to attempt to decipher it, even if it did look a great deal like turmoil. She hoped it was. He deserved to suffer.

'Excuse us for the interruption, but we need to speak to Hadleigh.'

The lawyer excused himself and the three men disappeared. Hadleigh returned five minutes later and summoned her back to the study.

Gray was sat. The man himself stood with his back to her, gazing out of the window at the waning evening sky, his hands clamped tightly behind his back. Nobody said a word until she was seated.

'I believe you know Gray,' Hadleigh said taking the chair behind the desk and clearly assuming command, 'He brings interesting news from London.'

Please God let it be good. 'Interesting for me or for you, Monsieur Hadleigh?'

'The Excise Men found two hundred and forty-five guns on the *Grubbenvorst* in the secret hold you told us about. Both the Captain of that ship and the Marquis of Deal have been arrested. Captain Boucher is very tight-lipped. The Marquis of Deal is currently pondering his actions in a damp cell in Newgate, but has indicated he is very eager to talk.'

'I dare say the threat of swinging from the Tyburn tree has loosened his lips.' It had certainly loosened hers.

'I confess, my lady, I am equally keen to hear his testimony. I wonder what light he will be able to shed on you and the true depth of your involvement in the Boss's vast smuggling ring?'

She didn't like the turn this conversation was taking. 'Doubtless he will tell you exactly what he knows. That it is my name he sees on the bottom of the messages informing him of shipments and Saint-Aubin's fee. Although Saint-Aubin was very specific about not having his name mentioned. If I hadn't leaked it to you in a coded letter, you would still be none the wiser.'

'Perhaps…'

'Stop it, Hadleigh!' Flint spoke for the first time since the accusatory conversation started and stalked towards her chair, ignoring the lawyer. 'What he means to say is we are grateful for your information, Jess.' He leaned both hands to rest on the arms, smelling sinfully of fresh air and all the things she couldn't have, and stared directly into her eyes. His looked pained. 'But the *government* requires much more before any consideration can be given to dropping the charges against you.' His green gaze was imploring. Frustrated, although Jess got the distinct impression those frustrations were aimed at Hadleigh, not her. 'Trust us with all you know. I beg of you. Help *us* to help you.'

He stepped back, his movements jerky, taking himself to lean on the fireplace impatiently, those beseeching eyes still locked on hers. Willing her to talk. For several long moments Jess went to war with herself, yet it was those stormy green eyes she wanted to hate but couldn't which overruled all her doubts. Even if she didn't trust Hadleigh one bit and despite her anger at his shoddy behaviour, she still wanted to believe Peter was sympathetic to her plight. It was all she had until she could escape. Holding his gaze for as long as she could, searching for the truth, some elusive glimmer of hope that he was the man her battered, needy heart told her he was and seeing nothing tangible which either confirmed or denied that, Jess finally addressed the lawyer. *Let the cards fall where they may.* She could do nothing else.

'What do you want? People or ships.'

'People,' Hadleigh said without hesitation, 'I want the name of the Boss and the names of every English man complicit in his endeavour.'

'I don't know his name. He could be one of eleven nobles I had to write to.'

'Then let's have the eleven.'

'You already had Crispin Rowley and Viscount Penhurst.' Saint-Aubin had had a massive temper tantrum on hearing of both the death of the former and arrest of the latter. 'Rowley co-ordinated distribution in London and Penhurst controlled Sussex. The Marquis of Deal ran things out of Kent. Camborne ran Cornwall until the Crown got close and he escaped to France. Saint-Aubin put him up for a few days until he found somewhere else for him to hide.'

'So that's where he went.' Peter gave her an encouraging half-smile. 'His estate is close to Penmor. I spent the whole of May trying to link him to the Boss—then he disappeared. I assumed he fled after Penhurst's arrest.' That intense green gaze flickered with something that called to her foolish heart, so she staunchly looked away to avoid it, hating the way she yearned for it to be more than his professional excitement at edging ever closer to his prey.

'Saint-Aubin tipped him off. He couldn't risk another supply chain being destroyed. Those shipments now go to the Crooked Billet Inn just outside Penzance.' Their eyes locked at that admission, both remembering the argument on the road. She saw his immediate understanding and the subsequent apology in his expression. 'The inn is owned by a particularly rough smuggler by the name of Seaton. Few dare cross him as he is famously ruthless.'

'He'll be less ruthless in a cell in Newgate.'

True enough. And so would Saint-Aubin—which might set her free. Jess took a deep breath. If there was a chance he was telling the truth, she had to comply. It was not as if Saint-Aubin was ever likely to spare her. Especially not now that his precious *Grubbenvorst* was lost and both Deal and Penhurst were already in the hands of the authorities. He would know implicitly that information had come directly from her. Spilling all his secrets would at least guarantee that monster was done for if nothing else. 'For obvious reasons, all of the men are in the south of the country with estates near the sea or rivers that run inland.' She ran off another list of names. Every name she knew.

All three men stared at her, incredulous at the mention of so many high-ranking members of the House of Lords, all traitors to the Crown, until Hadleigh broke the stunned silence. 'But which is the Boss?'

'The truth is, any one of them—or none of them—could be the Boss. As I said, I was never privy to his name.' But Jess had her suspicions. 'If I had to hazard a guess, I would say that the Boss was close to my mother while she lived in England. That would make the most sense as she had to have helped Saint-Aubin get his claws into the first British peers. In the early years of their marriage she and my father mostly resided in London, where doubtless she would have met all of them. After I was born, they lived largely separate lives. My father remained in Mayfair while she felt abandoned and ignored in Suffolk, pining for the life she once had in France. But she did have two regular visitors whose estates were not a million miles away. The Earl of Winterton and Viscount Gislingham. I believe the Boss has to be one of them.'

Chapter Twenty-One

Flint didn't bother going to bed. Sleep tonight would be impossible with so much on his mind, both professional and personal. He still couldn't quite believe the depth, scale and breadth of the information Jess had given them. A corrupt peer for every coastal county in the south, sympathetic officials who turned a blind eye to the free traders' movements, lists of inns, ships and hauliers who aided the distribution of the smuggled brandy and the exact locations where those cargoes were offloaded. For two hours she had dispassionately rattled off detail after detail, all information completely new to them and all stored in her impressive head.

No wonder Saint-Aubin wanted her dead.

However, he was not the only one gunning for Jess. Hadleigh was not convinced she was as innocent as Flint was increasingly convinced she was. He needed more proof. Evidence that she had indeed been coerced, even though he conceded that the coded letters were a step in the right direction and her confession blew the case wide open.

Hadleigh wanted Jess moved to London as soon as possible. Something Flint had resisted vehemently, even going as far as digging his heels in and flatly refusing to let them take her by boat to the capital overnight. Regardless of her lack of romantic interest in him and the inappropriate nature of his unwanted romantic interest in her, he couldn't stomach the idea of sending her off to the Crown without him beside her to keep a watchful eye. Here, Flint had some control over how she was treated. There he had none. Once the Home Office, Foreign Office and every other government office got involved then they would demand quick justice and a hasty trial.

That was all assuming she got there safely.

Something none of them could guarantee when both Gray and the Invisibles had had the devil of a job getting back to Penmor unnoticed because the Boss's henchmen were everywhere. They both deemed it impossible to evacuate his family without arousing suspicion. The word was out that she had a price on her head, an eye-wateringly high price, and every ne'er-do-well and snitch was actively looking for a raven-haired temptress just in case she wasn't the woman the British government claimed to be holding in the Tower. As Jess had repeatedly said, Saint-Aubin was no fool and, with his entire life's work now at stake, he was making sure he covered every eventuality. With Deal now in chains, too, the remaining traitorous nobles would also be fighting for their lives. Each one must have their own loyal network at their disposal, networks which criss-crossed the entire south coast and nudged painfully close to Penmor.

Her situation was precarious.

Only yesterday, the innkeeper who had put them up that first night after Jess had jumped ship had been found near death. Brutally beaten in his own bedchamber in that tiny fishing village just a day's ride from Portsmouth. A frightening development which he had insisted was kept from all the ladies to save them from worrying, but Flint's gut told him the net was closing. Saint-Aubin was out there. His gut, his head and his heart knew it.

For now, the moors were deathly quiet beyond the walls, the full moon helpfully illuminating both land and sea. On the horizon he could see the dark outline of the fishing boat which watched the water. A boat fully armed and stuffed full of Excise Men. More men were hidden on the moors and others were watching the entire area closely from the vantage point of these battlements, not to mention the highly trained men who blended into the furnishings downstairs. The castle might well be quiet and dark, but more than he was wide awake guarding it. If anyone came hunting tonight they were partially ready, enough to hold off an invasion until the rest of the reinforcements arrived. Despite Penmor's impenetrable walls, Flint would feel better with another hundred muskets on his battlements. Perhaps two hundred. All these uncomfortable new emotions were clearly making him jumpy.

He bade goodnight to the officer in charge and took the winding staircase down, intending to head to his study to while away the hours of sleeplessness ahead of him, but his feet took him towards her room instead. He needed to check she was safe and sound before he took himself off to mull. If she was awake, then he needed to tell her how much danger lurked beyond the safety of this castle. If she attempted to escape, which she was fully capable of attempting and perhaps achieving, she deserved to know the risks. He should have told her earlier about the huge price on her head and the attack at the inn, but he had been too busy licking his wounds in private and hiding behind his work with the excuse that Gray and the Invisibles had the defence of Penmor well in hand. But Jess was his responsibility and he had been avoiding her. The uncharacteristic cowardice shamed him.

Instead of the darkness he had expected, light bled around the frame of her door. Flint hesitated outside, listening. Trying to convince himself she must have fallen asleep with the lamps burning. When he heard none of the tell-tale sounds of slumber he risked a gentle tap on the door. Not loud enough to wake a sleeping person, but just enough for someone wide awake to hear. She didn't answer and he began to walk away, only to stop dead. After Hadleigh's interrogation he wouldn't blame her for trying to escape.

'Jess?'

He turned the knob and cracked the door open an inch, and oddly wasn't the least bit surprised to find she wasn't there. Who could blame her? He'd been informed she had gone rummaging last night, no doubt still searching for the elusive secret passageway. He had his mother's big mouth to thank for that. With a sigh, he took the stairs down and found the sentry who was hid in the shadows. 'Where is she?'

The Invisible responded to Flint's whisper by pointing to the morning room. 'She's already been through the drawing room. I expect the dining room is next, sir.'

There were no lights on in the morning room and he wasn't in the mood to pretend, not when he could smell her faint perfume and sense her presence, so he simply strode in and closed the door behind him, planting his feet stubbornly in the centre of his mother's favourite Persian rug. 'It's not here, Jess. Any more than it is in the bedchambers or linen closets you searched yesterday.'

There was a beat of silence, then she emerged from behind the curtains. 'I might have known you would have someone spying on me.'

The moonlight cast her in an ethereal light. The long, billowing nightdress almost silver in the darkness. Typically, all her glorious hair was unbound and hung to her waist to tempt him, while her eyes somehow seemed larger as the night time blurred her features. 'Not someone. Many. Although technically, they are not watching you specifically. They are watching everything.'

'I never saw a soul.' She sounded resigned, a little petulant, but looked beautiful. 'And I was looking. I suppose that should reassure me I am in safe hands, *non*?'

'They do this for a living.'

'Ah, but of course. This is their *job*.' The hint of petulance he had noticed before increased. 'All *loyal* agents of the Crown. Like *you*.'

'You're angry at me again.'

'When am I not?' She moved, her hands, gesticulating in the Gallic fashion which suited her so well, but in moving he saw more than those hands move. Beneath the proper nightgown, pert, female flesh shifted enticingly, letting his suddenly rampant body know in no uncertain terms she was completely naked beneath that single layer of fine linen. So much for manfully resisting the attraction. 'Tonight, in case you are in any doubt, I am livid.'

'Because I have thwarted another escape?' Bizarrely, despite his usual allergy to feminine histrionics, he was coming to enjoy Jess's. When she was in a temper she crackled. She was exciting and challenging and he much preferred her like this to the frightened and terrified woman she had been in the darkest moments of the last few days. Days which might well get darker before the sun shone again.

'If you must know, I wasn't trying to escape. I was merely trying to find the route out in case I needed it. There is a difference.' Her hand was on the door handle, ready to flounce out. 'Although after today and yesterday, why I have put my trust in you is beyond me!'

'Hadleigh did give you a particularly hard time.' One they had had several heated words about.

'A hard time? What a quaint, English way of saying the man was a beast.'

'I did step in to help.'

She whipped around to glare at him. 'Yesterday! When you deigned to grace me with your presence! For a man who claimed he would be my shadow for the duration, you left me to suffer him for hours today all alone.'

'I didn't think you'd want me there.' Those words slipped out before he could haul them back.

'Liar! You couldn't face me. You kissed me, then regretted it, so avoided me like the plague.' She looked hurt.

'You regretted it, too.' She had been decidedly underwhelmed. Vocally so. But then he had lied when he told her he'd regretted it. 'Or so you said.' Did the proud set of her slim shoulders and her angrily clenched fists mean something else or was he wishing she shared his forlorn hope? The kiss had changed things and confused him more than ever. This thing between them was not just physical, not for him at least and that scared the hell out of him. 'I don't want to argue, Jess.' Or get into painful discussions about things he didn't want to be feeling. 'But I would like to talk to you now that we are alone.' He walked towards her and couldn't stop himself taking her hand, wishing it didn't feel quite so perfect in his. 'Please—sit. It's important.'

She sat in a chair while he lit a lamp and pulled another chair over to sit opposite her. He then regaled her with everything he knew as fully yet reassuringly as possible. When she learned about the innkeeper her face paled. 'Will he survive?'

'They found him in the nick of time. The physician is hopeful he will make a full recovery.'

'*Mon Dieu*…this is all my fault. I never meant for anyone to get hurt because of me.' Her fingers were worrying the fabric of her nightgown, her eyes immediately full of sadness. Once again, Flint couldn't stop his hand taking hers and lacing his fingers around it possessively.

'None of this is your fault, Jess. All the blame lies with Saint-Aubin. You just need to convince Hadleigh.' But not himself any longer. No matter how much he tried to ignore it, excuse it or contradict it, Flint believed her.

She missed the significant confession in his words. 'I swear to you, Peter I have told him everything I know.' She stared mournfully at their interlocked hands and his eyes followed. The ghostly light made her skin seem white. The ugly abrasions made by her manacles stood out in stark contrast, causing the bile to rise in his throat.

Flint couldn't lift his eyes from the scar. Everything it stood for made his blood boil. A visible and damning reminder of her awful life. Without thinking, the index finger of his other hand went to the spot and gently traced the mark. 'My mother says you have whip marks all over your back, too.'

She stiffened and pulled her hand out of his, almost as if she was ashamed that he knew. 'If Hadleigh does not believe me, I'm not sure what else I can tell him to make him believe the truth.' The swift change of subject was deliberate. She did not want to talk about those scars. Why?

'Have you told Hadleigh how you were beaten?' Had he informed Hadleigh of her injuries? If he had, he couldn't recall it. The last few days had gone by in a blur of fevered activity and his first priority had been ensuring her safety, not talking about her. The man had only ever seen Jess immaculately dressed in the altered gowns his mother had put her in. Gowns which she had ensured covered her wrists and back to maintain her dignity. 'Perhaps he needs to see the truth for himself?'

Her face paled. 'Absolutely not!' Her eyes were darting around like those of a cornered fox. 'I have been humiliated enough—now you want me to strip naked in front of that man? In front of you?'

'Of course not. But a few inches of bare skin will prove to him that you are a victim in all this as well, Jess.' He took her hand again, needing the contact as much as he needed to comfort her. 'Trust me.'

'I am hardly a victim. While I live, innocent men are dead.' Behind the instinctive proud set of her shoulders, she felt guilty. Unworthy. And his heart ached for her. None of this was her fault. In that moment he realised that Jess was two people. The wounded, frightened, sad woman she was most of the time, burdened by misplaced guilt and constant disappointment, and the tenacious, brave, indomitable woman she wanted the world to see. Perhaps that Jess was the one she desperately wanted to be, too—a better version who had not been ground down and stamped all over. Yet to him she was. It took tremendous strength of character to keep coming back fighting when life threw that many terrible obstacles in your way. Somewhere along the line, her own self-worth had become confused. Something as tragic as it was ludicrous.

'You blame yourself.' It was a statement rather than a question because he could see the turmoil in her eyes.

'Of course I blame myself! I cannot seem to stop going over every incident in my mind and wondering what I could have done differently. I was so preoccupied with my own misery...'

'You didn't kill them. The Boss, Saint-Aubin and their hired cut-throats did all the killing. You wrote his letters. Under extreme duress. Once I appraise Hadleigh of your wounds he will demand to see them. This is as much a part of your testimony as naming those corrupt peers— except this is solely about you. Your suffering. Your story. Irrefutable proof of your innocence.' And absolution for Flint's belief in it.

'Innocent? I keep thinking I could have resisted. I could have refused. Instead... *Ah, je souhaiterais...*'

'Stop torturing yourself. If you had refused, then you'd be dead, too. Instead, you are here, helping us prevent more deaths. Those scars prove how much you tried to refuse. The King's lawyer needs to see that.'

When he had first met him, Flint had thought Hadleigh a decent sort. Beneath the determined barrister, he hoped that initial impression was true, because no decent person could look upon the evidence of Jess's abuse with cold, indifferent eyes. Those scars proved she had done everything through force—although plainly she did not see that as he now did. He would cross that bridge later. 'Let's get it over with and perhaps Hadleigh will see things quite differently in the morning. In fact, if he is half the man I think he is, I am certain he will. Trust Hadleigh with the awful truth.'

Still holding her hand and ignoring the expression of dread on her paled face, he tugged her to follow him, leading her up a staircase to the bedchamber Hadleigh shared with Gray. He didn't care that it was well past midnight and happily hammered on the door a split second before he barged in. Only Hadleigh was there, sat bolt upright in bed blinking, clearly rudely awoken from a very deep sleep.

'What's happened?'

'You need to see something. Something too important to leave till the morning.' Because once the lawyer saw it, Flint wanted the image of those whip marks to haunt the fellow till daybreak. He turned to Jess to see her face contorted in a cross between shame and fear. He squeezed her hand and hoped she would forgive him. 'Show him your back, Jess. He needs to see what Saint-Aubin is capable of.' His thumbs found her wrist again and soothed them tenderly, dreading the sight of the whip marks his mother had described, knowing they would thoroughly break his already severely damaged heart. 'You know me enough to realise I wouldn't ask you unless I thought it critical—and neither of us will judge you for them either.'

They didn't need to judge her. Her weakness and submissiveness in front of Saint-Aubin that had led to them disgusted Jess. That painful truth was significantly worse now than it had ever been. Ever since she had learned the fate of those poor Englishmen, the weight of her many failures weighed heavy on her shoulders. No matter how many times she lectured herself, reminding herself that she had done what she had had to do to survive, yet still risked that safety to alert the British, her conscience still wondered if her weakness had been selfish and if things might have been different if she had been strong enough to refuse.

Even in the darkness Jess could see the tenderness shining out of Peter's eyes, the heartfelt concern and the anguish. For her. Almost as if the marks she wore were as painful for him to talk about as they were for her to carry. Hadleigh lit the lamp on his nightstand, his face intrigued rather than inscrutable for once. Peter stood next to him, his jaw suddenly tight, but his expression flooded with sympathy. Because she couldn't bear to look at either of them and see their disgust or catch a glimpse of her back by accident in the large vanity mirror, she turned to face the wall. With shaking fingers, she undid the ribbons at the neck of the nightrail, then allowed just a few inches of the loosened fabric to fall off her shoulders.

She heard Peter's sharp intake of breath before she felt him move up behind her. As she clutched the front of the fabric tightly to her chest, he gently exposed her whole back.

'Oh, Jess…' Peter's voice sounded choked. 'I'm going to kill him.'

'How long have you suffered this?' Hadleigh's voice was deathly quiet.

'Since I was imprisoned in Cherbourg.'

'He had the guards beat you?'

'He preferred to do it himself.' Saint-Aubin had enjoyed defeating her. Revelled in it. 'He likes to be in control.' And she had let him. These scars proved it.

No reply.

After what seemed like an eternity of strained, palpable silence, she hastily pulled her clothing back in place, not turning till the neck was tied tight and she was certain she wouldn't cry the heavy tears of shame that threatened to fall. Peter had stalked to the window. By the set of his shoulders and the whitened knuckles gripping the sill she could see he was angry and hoped it was at Saint-Aubin rather than at her, even though she was angry at herself for her cowering and pleading for mercy each time she had been threatened. Angry and ashamed. Wishing she could have done more, been more, than the petrified creature her mother's callous lover had created.

Hadleigh blinked at her, uncharacteristically subdued.

'I didn't want to write those letters.' But she had. 'I'm sorry. I know that doesn't make what I did right—but I hate that I did it...' And her bottom lip was quivering. For a moment she tried to control it, tried to stand there proudly to explain why she had given in so quickly in the hope they might understand, but when her eyes began to sting she fled. Running along the dimly lit landing to the safety of her own bedchamber and then crumpling to a puddle on the floor in front of the door in case anyone followed her in. Needing to regroup and lick her wounds in private before she inevitably had to confess how her irrational fear of heights and the merest threat of them had allowed Saint-Aubin to control her like a marionette.

But he followed her anyway, damn him, and dared to try the door handle.

'Jess—let me in.'

'Please go away. I will talk about it tomorrow. I promise.'

'You don't have to talk about it. I simply want to see you.' After she failed to respond, the door shifted, her nightgown sliding several inches on the highly polished floor as he pushed it from the other side. 'You might as well let me in because I'm not going away.'

Chapter Twenty-Two

When she stalwartly refused to budge, Flint used his strength sparingly to gradually nudge the door open, needing to be with her and not caring that he didn't feel even slightly in control of his own emotions. They were so close to the surface, hiding them or fighting them would be impossible.

By the time he stepped into the room she had shuffled to sit hunched a few feet away, her dark head pressed against her raised knees. Purposely avoiding his gaze. He closed the door and lowered himself to sit next to her, unsure what to say or do, but haunted by the horrendous evidence of her ordeal. With no helpful words of wisdom and the real and distinct possibility he might weep and howl at the moon or smash his fist into a wall, he wrapped his arm around her and simply pulled her close.

'Are the scars ugly?'

She hadn't looked at them? 'Not ugly. Tragic. But they will heal, as will you. In time you will realise you did all that you could and much more than most would have dared.'

'I hope so. I'm so tired of hating myself.'

'Channel all that hate towards Saint-Aubin, for it is he who deserves it all.'

She burrowed her head against his chest. They sat there together in silence for several minutes, the only evidence of her distress the tears that soaked through his waistcoat and shirt and washed the last of his doubts away. After an age, her voice came out so small he had to strain his ears to hear it.

'When I was younger, I had an accident. I fell out of a tree. I broke a few ribs which healed quickly but the fear that I experienced while falling put me off heights for good. My bedchamber in the chateau was four storeys above the ground. I began to have nightmares. Silly ones in which I was falling towards the earth at speed. One day, back when we still shared the occasional meals together, I asked Saint-Aubin and my mother if I could have a different bedchamber—there was no shortage of them. When I explained my reasons why, they both laughed at me and my request was denied. Irrational fears, according to him, couldn't be pandered to.

'A few months later, I spoke to Saint-Aubin

out of turn one time when I heard him shouting at my mother. She was crying. Upset. I told him to leave her alone. He did not react well to my interference. He always thought me too wilful. Young ladies should be meek and compliant. Respectful of their betters. Stupidly I answered back again.' Of course she had. Because she was a fighter. Someone who stood up to bullies—not that she could see that now. 'He decided to teach me a lesson.'

She paused to suck in a deep breath, almost as if talking about it was an ordeal, too. Flint didn't dare interrupt, knowing the telling would be cathartic and begin to exorcise some of the demons which haunted her.

'He dragged me out of the room and up to the roof, pushing me closer and closer to the edge until only my toes held on and I was forced to lean out and see the ground so far below.'

Horrified, sensing there was more to come, but knowing if he risked outrage on her behalf she might clam up, Flint buried his nose in her hair and held her tighter.

'I was so terrified I apologised and promised to never defy him again—but, alas, I continued to disappoint him and my punishments were always a variation on the same theme. By the time I was sixteen, I had learned it was easier to keep out of his way and for many years we had little to do with one another. My mother, of course, would not believe he was capable of such cruelty, so she never listened me when I attempted to tell her. As a result, our relationship deteriorated, too, and we became quite distanced. Strangers living under the same enormous roof. I genuinely had no concept of what they were involved in until my mother's illness necessitated another translator. Most of the smugglers Saint-Aubin uses are French and the Boss is English—risking communications in French might have drawn attention from the authorities. Those messages were the glue that held the operation together, but he was—is—deeply suspicious in nature and fiercely protective of his contacts. He didn't trust the task to anyone outside his immediate circle.

'To begin with, he used my mother as leverage. Using her pain and medication as ransom. After she died, he lost that power. I tried to escape the chateau, so he had guards carry me to the roof and dangle me over the side until I agreed to continue. A few days later, I dodged the guards and set a fire. I wanted to burn the whole place to the ground with him inside, but failed. That's when he moved me to the building in Cherbourg and put me in chains. Every day he would bring me the smugglers' messages to translate and pass on to his peers and corrupt officials listed in my mother's ledger. The first time I refused, so I was whipped, then taken to the roof. Four guards held me in the air by my arms and legs and swung me repeatedly over the edge as Saint-Aubin laughed. The *pension* was ringed by metal railings. I could see them as I swung over them. Falling would mean certain death—and he knew it. Knew he could control me with my fears. They pretended to drop me twice until I caved in. With hindsight, I know I was too important for him to truly carry out his threats. But then...well, the fear made me weak and he kindled that fear. Used it to make me do his bidding and tell him how much I feared him. He enjoyed that part most of all. From that day on, I endured the beatings, but always surrendered before I was dragged to the roof. But I didn't know men were dying—I swear. Had I done...'

'Stop it!' Flint couldn't bear it. 'You didn't kill those men, Jess. They would have still died without you, can't you see that? Except if you had been tortured to the bitter end you would have died for nothing.' And it had been torture, he now realised. Mental as well as physical and she had endured it and rebelled against it in equal measure. Her continued courage and fortitude staggered him. 'Saint-Aubin would have found someone else to translate all those messages and we would still be none the wiser. Scrambling for clues while those smugglers continued to run rings around us. Thanks to your bravery, and dogged determination to live, we now know exactly who and what we are dealing with. You are a fighter, Jess. Always remember that. You fought him even when you knew it was futile. You fought him every step of the way until you had no fight left. And then you found other ways to fight. Not every fight needs to be physical. You outwitted them. You managed to send those letters to us—knowing they would be intercepted. Because you risked your life, their days are numbered.'

'Perhaps they could already be over if only I'd had the courage to defy him sooner? I wish with all my heart I had. But I was too frightened for myself. I could have told you everything on that ship in the Channel and spared you and your family all this trouble—but I didn't. Just in case he dragged me back. I wish...' He placed his finger over her lips to silence her. She stared up at him her miserable, her dark eyes fathomless.

'If wishes were horses, beggars would ride.' Flint stroked his hand down her hair, winding his fingers in one fat tendril as he kissed the top of her head again. 'Why second-guess yourself? There is no point to what ifs. There are too many variables and combinations, none of which you will ever truly know the outcome to.'

'I *was* selfish. I was only ever thinking about myself!'

'Not selfish. You held back. Understandable. So did I. We didn't know each other and neither of us trusts easily. Under the circumstances, it's a miracle you've come to trust me as much as you have now when every other person in your life seems to have disappointed you or mistreated you abominably. You've been all alone in the world. I cannot imagine how awful that feels.' He tipped up her chin so she could witness his sincerity for herself. 'Your guilt is misplaced, Jess. All that truly matters is the here and now. Forget the past and deal with the future as it happens.'

'You don't understand. I would have happily escaped and disappeared and left you all with the problem. Have you already forgotten you found me searching for a way out again tonight? If I had found it, I am not certain I wouldn't have taken it—despite everything you have done to help me. I am starting to worry that I am more like my mother than I would like to acknowledge. What if I always put myself above others? What if I am incapable of a wholly selfless gesture?'

'Again, after everything you've been through, that is completely understandable—not selfish. Who could blame you for wanting an easier life when you have been denied one for so long? And why would you put others above yourself when you've been on your own in the world for most of your adult life? If you want me to tell you that I think you should take some of the blame for what has happened or I hold you even partially accountable, I'm afraid I cannot. I am just thankful that you are here now, that you are no longer all on your own and I can protect you. I wish I had brought you here sooner. Believed you sooner.'

She was silent and still for several moments before she exhaled, the tension suddenly leaving her arms as he held her. 'Ah, Monsieur Flint, if only wishes were horses, then we would both have a stableful—*non*?' The half-smile told him his stubborn, indomitable Jess was crawling her way back out of the abyss. The Jess who quoted his own words back at him with artful precision. The one who never let anything hold her down for too long. The one he admired and desired and loved.

Loved.

Flint allowed the word to marinade in his mind for a moment as he gazed at her. Certainly not something he had ever searched for or expected, the onset unbelievably quick, decisive and inevitable as his mother had warned. Lightning speed, yes, but not at all abhorrent as he had always assumed. Was she tenacious, spirited and prone to histrionic outbursts? Yes. Were they opposites? Completely. But sat here with her in his arms, those particular quirks of her character were the same ones which called to his heart the most. A heart that now urged him to do what was right.

'Come—I need to show you something.' He helped her to stand, deciding not to listen to his head for once. His stupid head would only over-rule what his gut and heart urged him to do and tonight he was not inclined to listen. The past was the past and Jess needed this.

'If you are dragging me to see Hadleigh again, I shall warn you now I will not take it lightly.' But she followed him down the hallway to the narrow spiral staircase in the west wing, her small hand perfectly linked with his, her trust in him humbling yet joyous at the same time.

Flint paused at the only door and sighed. Hadleigh would hit the roof if this backfired. Lord Fennimore would skin him alive. His career would be over. So be it. She was worth what-ever repercussions came his way. He pushed the door to swing open wide. The giant four-poster bed in the centre of the cavernous room was already turned down by a servant. A light left burning in readiness. She eyed the scene suspi-ciously, hesitating to go in. 'Whose room is this?'

'Mine. And my father's before me.' Trying to ignore the bed and the beautiful woman in her nightgown who would undoubtedly be perfect in it, he went in and tugged her to follow. 'And before him another ancestor, a loyal servant of the Crown. This chamber traditionally passes to the master of the house for one very important reason.' He stopped at the doors of the ancient wardrobe built into the oak panelling. 'This third door is the one you want.' He flung it open, pushing aside the rows of shelves which only one who knew would know they could move and disappear into the wall. He then stepped over the neat line of boots and shoes decorating the bottom, ducking his head slightly as his fingers found the hidden latch. The corridor beyond the secret door glowed golden and he enjoyed the slack-jawed look of wonder on her face as he ushered her inside, making a great show of sliding the shelves complete with their contents back in place behind them before he closed the door.

'In view of the current situation, I had everything prepared as soon as we arrived.' Stacked along the wall of the capacious anteroom was everything from guns and ammunition to a variety of clothes and disguises. 'If you walk dead straight, this passageway takes you to the stairs that lead out to the moors. It's quite a walk, so wear comfortable shoes. When you reach the stairs, don't go right. With your fear of heights, definitely don't go right. That passage leads only to the top of the tower Cromwell ruined. Obviously in days of yore they were able to escape from both sides of the castle. Alas, now that passageway is solely responsible for nought but a hell of a draught in the winter time. Its only purpose—apart from training roses, of course—is as a sanctuary for bats—and I'm afraid they've not been good tenants these last two hundred years.'

He walked her to the top of the impossibly narrow stairs that spiralled downwards steeply and pointed to a waiting torch on the wall near a lit candle. 'Light this, as it is as black as pitch down there, but just in case you dare not risk a light or if the thing goes out, know that there are two hundred and thirty-seven steps. The tunnel beyond is head height but narrow. Keep walking forward using the walls as a guide and when you notice the floor begin to incline upwards and the ceiling get lower you are there. The tunnel emerges through a hatch in the bothy floor.

'Why have you shown me this now?'

'Because I want you to know I trust you and because I will feel better knowing you can leave safely if there is a need. Which I can assure you there won't be.'

'But what if I use it for my own ends? What

if I decide to save myself the inconvenience of a trial? What if—?' He silenced her with a kiss. It was brief, heartfelt and wonderful because she kissed him back, her eyes fluttering closed as her mouth sighed against his.

'I thought we had agreed there is no point in what ifs. I trust you Jess. Implicitly. Let that be enough for now. Now is all that truly matters, after all, and we will deal with whatever the future holds when the time comes.' Because one kiss wasn't enough, he dipped his head again and she melded against him. Flint tried to resist the urge to deepen it and must have given up without much of a fight, because within moments he was lost in her, his greedy palms roaming all over her shapely body, filling his hands with her curves and enjoying all those complicated feelings for the very first time.

Jess had never felt so special. So needed or adored by another person. Yet this kiss was different from the first one they had shared in his study. No less passionate or exciting, but somehow so much more meaningful. Every time his lips brushed over hers, the emotion was real, intense, almost overwhelming. There was an honesty to it that had been missing before, something intangible and untouchable which could only occur because neither of them was holding anything back. He trusted her and she trusted him. In giving her the means to escape he had freed her. They were no longer gaoler and prisoner. No longer enemies or strangers or convenient companions while it suited them. They were one man and one woman. Living entirely in the moment. He wanted her and she wanted him. It was that pure and that all-encompassing.

His mouth left hers to trail hot kisses down her neck, so she arched it to give him better access. She felt his hands slide upwards from her bottom and moaned when he filled them with her breasts. Shamelessly, and of their own accord, her fingers went to the ribbon at her neck again and undid the bow so that the suddenly unwanted linen barrier could be easily removed with the journey of his lips. But he stepped back, his hands caressing the sensitive skin of her neck, gazing at her reverently, seemingly content to leave the rest of her body covered. With deliberate slowness, Jess undid every button of his waistcoat and pushed it from his shoulders.

He let it fall before he allowed himself to do the same, staring intently at her while his hands smoothed the fabric down her arms, the unmistakable desire for her alone like molten emeralds in his eyes.

His breath hitched when first saw her bare breasts, and despite his obviously laboured, deeper breathing, he touched her with such restraint, allowing only the pad of his index finger to gently trace their shape. 'I didn't bring you here to seduce you.'

'I know that.'

'We should stop.'

Because her body demanded it and that single gentle caress was nowhere near enough, Jess brazenly used her hand to press his to cup her aching breast fully. 'I don't want to stop. I want to enjoy the here and now.' Her teeth nipped his ear. 'With you.'

For a moment she thought he might deny her, he stood so still, his eyes so serious. Clearly at war with himself and his own cast-iron sense of responsibility. The eternal pragmatist attempting to do what he believed was right. But then she felt his thumb graze her nipple in glorious rhythmic circles and she knew that his sensible head was losing the battle. To make sure, she kissed him, tangling her fingers in his hair and pressing herself to him. He wanted her. She could feel the unmistakable evidence against her belly.

Like a cat she arched against it, leaving him in no doubt as to her own desire, her hands tugging his hips closer still and curling possessively around his buttocks.

That proved his undoing and the guttural moan in the base of his throat thrilled her. A split second later and he replaced his thumb with his tongue on her nipple, sucking it into his mouth and making her knees buckle from the magnificent ripple of pleasure from the intimacy. She felt her nightgown drop to her hips and didn't care she was naked from the waist up. Why would she when he couldn't see her scars and his clever mouth was now worshipping her other breast quite thoroughly and her hands had found their way inside his shirt and were now happily learning the feel and shape of his chest. His back. Those beautiful broad, golden shoulders.

Because it annoyed him, he dragged the shirt over his head and tossed it aside, finally bringing her against him properly. Skin against skin. Heart against heart. And seared her mouth with a kiss so thorough, so heated, she had to cling to him to stay upright. Jess shivered as the cold stone of the wall touched her naked back and he terminated the kiss abruptly, putting unwelcome distance between them. His eyes scanned the narrow passageway as if seeing it for the first time and he frowned. 'We can't do this here.' Then his gaze rested on her again, raking the entire length of her body with blatant admiration. 'Not when there is a perfectly good bed waiting.' He took her hand, lacing his fingers through hers. 'Will you come with me, Jess?'

'Yes.'

'You don't have to. You can go back to your own bedchamber or you can head down the stairs to your freedom. I want you to know that you have the choice. Go wherever you want. I will not argue with either decision.'

Her heart stuttered and she cupped his cheek. Nobody had ever given her a choice in anything before. The right to make her own decision was empowering. 'Take me to your bed, Peter. Right now, I don't want to go anywhere else.' She wanted to be loved. Needed to know what true love and genuine affection felt like.

After solicitously putting her clothing back to rights, he led her slowly back to his bedchamber and she watched him reset the wardrobe before he stood before her a little awkwardly. Shirtless, his skin glowed from the flickering light of the candle, the flames picking out the golden tones in the dusting of hair that covered his chest and narrowed down his abdomen. 'You can change your mind at any time.'

'If I do, you will be the first to know.' But she was shyly smiling up at him in invitation, the real Jess this time rather than the mirror of her mother she had hidden behind for other men. He looked unsure, too, which made her less self-conscious about her own nervousness, but he reached out his hand to take hers and once she grasped it he led her to the bed. Then he kissed her so tenderly it brought tears to her eyes.

Only when his hands began to slide her night-gown back down her shoulders did she panic. 'Shouldn't we blow out the light first?'

'I want to see you.'

'At least until the scars are gone…' In one seamless, swift motion he sent the gauzy linen to fall to a puddle at her feet, catching her hands in his before she used them to cover herself.

'You're beautiful. That hit me the first time I saw you.' His hand came up to stroke her face, then plunged into her hair, running his fingers from her scalp, across her sensitive breasts to end at her waist. 'This has tormented me. I've imagined what it would look like spread across my pillow so many times…' He gathered it all together and lovingly twisted it to sit over just one shoulder. 'Imagined you in my bed.' His lips found the exact place were her pulse was beating rapidly at the exposed base of her neck at the same moment his hand came up to claim her breast, causing ripples of pleasure to shimmer through her that wiped everything else from her mind.

The flickering candle suddenly forgotten, she gloried in the feel of his mouth on her skin, his gentle hands exploring her arms and ribcage. Her aching breasts flattened against the hard wall of his chest, her back braced against one of the bedposts while he adored her. It was only when she felt his hands carefully turn her that she came to. Too late to stop him looking at her scars. She felt his fingertips trace one on her shoulder and, embarrassed, Jess tried to turn around, but his strong arms had formed a loose cage around her and his lips now trailed where his fingertips had just been.

'What are you doing?'

'Kissing them better.'

'I would rather you didn't.' But as his big hands were now massaging her breasts while his tongue and teeth were exquisitely torturing her shoulder, her admonishment sounded needy and she felt him smile against her skin.

'Are you sure?' As his thumb teased her nipple, the flat of one palm was smoothing down her stomach with purpose. Of its own accord her body arched to meet it and she found her head thrown back and resting on his shoulder as one gentle finger dipped between her legs.

The world tilted and blurred as she totally lost herself in the wonderful new sensations he was creating, supremely aware of nothing except her needy, greedy body, his hard one and the bedpost she was gripping for dear life.

Chapter Twenty-Three

Flint had always believed himself a considerate lover, always mindful of his partner's pleasure as well as his own, but with Jess he had surpassed himself without consciously trying. Something inside told him that she deserved thorough and dedicated loving after a severe lack of any affection all her life—and that was exactly what he gave her. Heart and soul. Dedicating himself to giving her nothing but pleasure and in return he most definitely enjoyed the most splendid night of passion of his life. He had loved her most thoroughly with his hands and then his mouth before he dared to remove his breeches, by which time she was sprawled across his bed, glorious black hair and limbs strewn with abandon and a slightly dazed but totally wanton expression on her beautiful face. He had put that there.

He had known she would be passionate. Everything about her temperament had suggested she was a woman who was incapable of being passive—although she had been deliciously pliant and boldly adventurous once he allowed her free rein to have her wicked revenge on him. And, by God, did she.

The first time he had slowly entered her tight virginal body she had been understandably hesitant at first—stoically determined to endure it for him—until that sensual, earthy passionate nature of hers had fired again and she had clung to him, whispering delightful, breathy endearments in both French and English as they plunged towards insanity together. The second time, she had happily taken charge, riding him with her hands splayed across his chest, head flung back and her perfect, wonderfully responsive breasts jutting out through her tangle of raven hair as she took her own pleasure with the same determined, fiery tenacity as she tackled everything else.

If he remembered it correctly, and he was pretty certain he would treasure that particular memory for ever, he'd told her he loved her then and had meant it. He had never felt such overwhelming emotion before, never given himself solely over to his heart before either, and still couldn't find the will to panic over the truth of it. Despite everything, his feelings for Jess felt right. Perfect. Clearly the forever sort, despite his best intentions to avoid them, especially with a woman who was not an emotional mill pond, but a crashing, unpredictable, beautiful ocean. Seeing that the damage was done and couldn't be undone, he might as well embrace it. He probably told her all that, too. He'd been very vocal. Tender, fevered, heartfelt words tumbling over one another because all capacity for rational, pragmatic and measured thoughts were gone.

He had brushed a tear from her cheek, a happy tear because she was smiling at him with such affection, and she had returned the endearment to him. In French of course, just to be contrary.

'Moi aussi, je t'aime.'

And then she had giggled and covered him in kisses and he had laughed along with her, marvelling in the moment, until the intense power of their joining overcame them and they'd thoroughly lost themselves in each other again.

It had been, for want of a better adjective, spectacular and Flint couldn't help feeling a little bit overawed as he gazed at her knotted in his crumpled sheets, that such a beautiful, challenging and maddening woman was his. If he ever met Cupid, he'd shake his hand and thank him for hitting the bullseye. He had had little sleep and by rights should be exhausted, but instead he felt completely invigorated and ready to slay some dragons in her honour. Or jump right back into bed and tumble with her again.

But he'd had work to do so he had crept out a little before dawn, clutching his boots, casting one last longing look at her sleeping and quietly closed the door. Several hours, many conversations and a thorough check of the castle's watertight security later and he was still disgustingly pleased with himself and starving.

'Good morning!' As it was still very early by society standards only his mother, two sisters and both their husbands were in the breakfast room with a very subdued Hadleigh. All except his mother were seated while she fussed around them all, loading plates as was her way. 'I'll have a bit of everything, please. Don't skimp, I could eat a horse.'

Flint sat down at the head of the table next to Ophelia who was watching him with interest, so he offered her a sunny grin.

'Somebody is cheerful this morning. Are you ill, Peter?'

He snapped open his napkin, reminding himself he was supposed to be the sensible, pragmatic and unemotional sibling, and schooled his features to their usual ironic-tinged blandness while the butler handed him yesterday's London newspapers. 'I am always perfectly agreeable in the mornings.'

'You are? Since when?'

'Since he brought a certain lady home, I've noticed his moods have become quite erratic,' said Portia with a knowing smirk. 'He's either fuming, mooning or grinning—and we all know what that means.'

He ignored her and his eldest sister's pointed *I told you so* looks to scan the headlines of *The Times*, pleased when he saw a story front and centre about the female traitor being held in the Tower. While they didn't name names, there were enough juicy titbits to give credence to Jess's incarceration there. The Marquis of Deal was named in another article outlining his arrest on suspicion of treason alongside a detailed account of the Excise Men's shocking discovery of a veritable arsenal on the *Grubbenvorst* in Folkestone—weapons bound for France and destined to help Napoleon's supporters raise another army. All stories planted by Lord Fennimore to fan the flames and give credence to Flint's decoy.

A plate was slammed down in front of him a moment before his mother clouted him around the head. 'Peter Othello Flint, I'm ashamed of you!'

Flint yelped as everyone else looked on stunned, while his mother sailed self-righteously to her own chair at the head of the table directly opposite him. She shot him a narrowed look which told him she knew exactly what had being going on.

Tomfoolery.

But being his mother, she would never embarrass Jess, so quickly composed her expression to one of pleasantness. 'Could you pass the salt, please, Portia?' A clear signal to all and sundry that she was not prepared to publicly discuss anything with anyone, but was going to flay the skin from her youngest child the second she got him alone. That was the way things were done in the Flint household. Understanding it, they all picked up their forks and continued with their breakfast as if nothing was wrong.

'Othello?' A grinning Hadleigh broke the tension.

'*That* name does not leave *this* room.'

Over the course of the next twenty minutes, the rest of the family gathered and the room became noisy, yet there was still no sign of Jess and he began to feel guilty for leaving her alone in his room, knowing full well she would have to leave it at some point and dart down the landing in just her nightgown to get to hers and dress. Too late, he realised he should have woken her before he had crept out and smuggled her back to her bedchamber before the house awoke. Perhaps then he would be spared what was likely to be the most awkward conversation he had ever had with his mother.

As the clock kept ticking ever closer towards ten, another thought began to plague him. What if she had availed herself of the hidden passageway and was already miles away? The idea that he would never see her again, when he was head over heels in love with the vixen, made his chest hurt with a vengeance. Surely she wouldn't make love to him, then leave? Not when last night had meant so very much to him…

When she suddenly appeared at the door, all wide-eyed, hesitant and guilty-looking, it took all the strength he had not to audibly sigh his relief.

'Good morning, Jess! I trust you slept well?' To his own ears he sounded unconvincing and hoped that he wasn't making it plainly obvious to every curious face around the table that they had both barely slept because they had been far too busy being naked.

'*Oui*… Yes…thank you.' Her eyes flicked to his, then dropped to his mouth and a delightful blush bloomed on her cheeks as she hastily turned to his mother. 'I am sorry I am so late, I didn't mean to sleep in.'

'You poor dear, you must be exhausted after your *ordeal*. Who could blame you for grabbing additional rest? It's obvious to all of us that you *need* your rest and, thanks to *my son*, you've not been getting nearly enough.' A loaded re sponse if ever there was one and one that made poor Jess's face burn crimson. 'Sit, sit. I shall fetch you a plate.' As his mother chose a path past him, Flint shot her some daggers in case she decided to clump him again. If she did, Jess would be mortified and the whole table would be left in no doubt that he had thoroughly rav- ished and ruined her.

Not that he was sorry. He sincerely hoped nei- ther was she.

Jess chose a chair well away from him and was soon commandeered by Desdemona and Hermia, who engaged her in a stream of mean- ingless, inane chitchat while she waited for her food. After that she concentrated intently on her plate, allowing the disjointed and effusive family conversation to waft around her. It took several minutes before she was brave enough to look up and allowed their eyes to lock. In that beau- tiful, scant moment that loaded, heated, equally longing gaze made him feel like the ruler of the entire world.

As soon as he got her on his own—

'Sorry to interrupt!' The door slammed open to reveal Gray, Lord Fennimore and two other King's Elite agents—Jake Warriner and Seb

Leatham. All four wearing matching grave expressions.

'What's happened?' Because something had. Something bad else they wouldn't all be here. Without thinking he left his chair and was immediately at Jess's side, ready to protect her.

'There has been a worrying development.' Lord Fennimore took in the sea of stunned faces around the table. 'Something best discussed in the privacy of your study, Flint.' He then addressed the table at large. 'Ladies and gentlemen, I would ask you all to stay here so that we can appraise you of the next steps as soon as we have decided upon them. Rest assured, your safety is paramount.' With that he stalked out.

Flint tugged Jess to accompany the men, not wanting to leave her alone nor leave her out of any decisions. This was all about her, after all. Fennimore did not blink an eye when she was ushered into the now quite cramped study and settled in a chair.

'There were several incidents last night. A well-armed gang marched on Newgate at midnight. Several guards were killed in the fray. Despite the remaining soldiers' best attempts to repel them, they were overwhelmed, and the prison was compromised. By the time the situation was back in our control, both the Marquis of Deal and Viscount Penhurst were murdered.'

At Jess's sharp intake of breath, Flint placed his hand on her shoulder to reassure her. 'It will be all right, Jess. They still don't know you are here.'

'Actually, I think they do.' Lord Fennimore's voice was matter of fact. 'At the same time as the incident in Newgate, another ransacked your bachelor lodgings, Flint. Hours beforehand we later learned witnesses who claimed to have seen you in London were brutally assaulted. At least two admitted they had not seen you for weeks and another, a high-ranking peer in the Foreign Office, confessed Lady Jessamine was not being held in the Tower when one of the cut-throats held his daughter hostage and threatened to slice her throat. If the smugglers know it was you who was her escort—and we have to assume that is now common knowledge—and they suspect you are not in town as we tried to make them believe, then it is only a matter of time before they come searching for you here. Even if they do not suspect Lady Jessamine is here hiding, they will suspect you know where she is—which makes you a target, Flint.'

'Saint-Aubin was in Plymouth.' Jess's voice quivered. 'He could be closer now.'

'Why would he move from the convenient escape route of the coast when the Boss would handle things in London? I certainly wouldn't.'

Lord Fennimore addressed his agents. 'We didn't bother disguising our arrival. In view of the imminent fear of attack, we came by gunship with a Royal Navy escort with as many men as we could muster at short notice. I'll tell you upfront that wasn't many. We've summoned the local militia—not that we expect them to be of much use, but they will be here shortly—and as we speak a whole battalion of marines should begin making their way from the barracks in Plymouth to Penmor.'

'Then proper reinforcements won't be here till late this afternoon!' And even that was with them setting a blistering pace. Flint's heart was racing. The local militia were a rag-tag disorganised bunch at best. Poverty-stricken farmers and fishermen mostly, in need of a little extra coin to feed their families, not trained soldiers. 'Penmor could be surrounded long before then.' She was in danger. Grave danger and he couldn't stand it.

'It was built to withstand a siege. We are ready for a siege,' Gray tried to remind him, but already Flint's mind was whirring. But for the first time in his life it wasn't thinking pragmatically or strategically. It was only thinking about how devastated he would be if he lost Jess. A whole flurry of terrible what ifs clouded all rational thought. Of course, Penmor was impenetrable. That's why he had brought her here. His unwanted new feelings towards Jess were clouding his judgement and warping his reality. He needed his legendary calm more than ever now, because without it he was no use to her.

'The first thing we need to do is bring all the men we have out on the moors inside. I'll round them up, then secure the front entrance.' Fortunately, Leatham stepped forward to take charge. 'The navy have the sea covered so we don't need to worry about a coastal assault. Warriner and Gray will organise what we have manpower and weapons wise around the battlements and in the courtyard. Once the militia arrive, we'll divide them up and share them around so at least we can direct them. Flint, find the safest place to secure Lady Jessamine Fane and your family— we don't want a lucky musket ball to fly over the battlements and find someone—then we'll see you outside. We'll need your knowledge of the castle to do this properly. Hadleigh and Lord Fennimore can guard them all.'

The sense of urgency and purpose brought all his emotions under check. 'If I put them all upstairs in the west wing, then there is only one narrow staircase to guard and they have a means of escape if the worst comes to the worst and the defences are breached. Which they won't be.' Why was he suddenly convinced these ancient walls weren't enough when they had always been more than sufficient? He willed the nagging, irrational doubt clawing at his gut away, but his beating, frightened heart knew the answer. It was her.

Ten minutes later, Jess found herself sat on the exact same four-poster bed Peter had made sinfully passionate love to her on just a few hours earlier. Except this time she was there with his mother, all five of his sisters, their respective husbands and children, the Crown Prosecutor, a curmudgeonly grey-haired man who was apparently in charge, and a trunk full of ammunition.

'Well, isn't this cosy,' said Lady Flint, pouring tea. 'We haven't done this in years, have we, girls?'

'You have done it before then?' Such a concept seemed quite bizarre. 'Napoleon?'

'Trewin, wasn't it, Cedric?' Lady Flint deferred to Lord Fennimore who was staring out the window, watching the courtyard like a hawk. 'Harry Trewin?'

'No—it was his brother John, I believe. Harry was the one clapped in irons. Nasty family. We had the devil of a job with them, as I recall. How long were we here for?'

'Three weeks.' She passed Jess a teacup, smiling. 'Cedric and my husband were Excise Men together back in the old days. Smuggling was rife in Cornwall then. Practically everyone was involved and didn't take lightly to having the source of all their income locked up in our cellar. John Trewin whipped them all up and brought them to Penmor with his gang of cut-throats to free his brother and we were stuck here until Royal Marines could disperse the mob outside.'

'That took them three weeks?'

'They were different times, dear. England was newly at war with Old Boney and most of the military were off supporting Nelson somewhere, so the smugglers were able to run riot. It was shortly after that Cedric and my dear husband set up the King's Elite.'

'Peter's father was a spy, too?'

'Oh, yes! It's quite the family business, although my husband was the first Flint to do it full time. Being here in Cornwall, where smuggling was at its most rife, and after the incident with the Trewins, it became quite apparent they needed a dedicated force to deal with the problem—and Peter's father was not keen on another similar siege at Penmor. We ran out of bacon, milk and cheese in the first week and it put him in a very ill temper for the duration. He hated his tea without a splash of milk. To be frank, I don't think he ever got over it.'

Jess couldn't quite believe her ears. Once again, the danger of her situation seemed to be overshadowed by the surreal. 'You ran out of milk?'

Lady Flint patted her hand. 'Fear not, dear. That won't happen this time. Once bitten twice shy, after all. I had some cows brought in and twelve haunches of bacon delivered by the butcher as soon as you arrived. This siege I am fully prepared for.'

Chapter Twenty-Four

The militia arrived shortly after three and, as Flint had expected, a shoddy, disorganised bunch they were, too. The commanding officer was a scruffy fellow with a deep Cornish accent and a uninterested manner who was more suited to netting pilchards than soldiering. If the man had been any more unconcerned he would be asleep. His platoon of forty men was equally as lackadaisical and ridiculously slow to follow instructions, treating the deployment as more of a nice day out than a matter of the utmost urgency. Leatham, Gray and Warriner did their best to mobilise them effectively, but they seemed more interested in eating the food his mother had insisted be delivered to them than manning their assigned posts. That's what happened when a ramshackle fighting force was made out of fishermen and farmers. Their presence did not make Flint feel better.

Anxiously, he paced the battlements looking for any signs of movement on the moors or the promised battalion of marines, but so far there was nothing to see but the still and tranquil sunny day.

But his gut told him danger lurked. As each hour passed, that feeling of impending doom grew stronger and stronger, although he couldn't put his finger on why.

'Stop pacing, will you?' Gray had been staring out to the horizon through a telescope, which he closed with an irritated snap. 'We've got the whole area covered. The moors are as desolate as they always are and even if they do come, they've got to either scale a forty-foot sheer cliff or jump over a forty-foot chasm to get here. And then they'll still need to breach the walls. You're making me nervous.'

'Something doesn't *feel* right.'

'He's worried about Lady Jessamine.' Warriner nudged Leatham and winked. 'She's made him go all peculiar.'

'I did notice the distinct *frisson* between them. Touching, I thought. Do you think that *frisson* is clouding his judgement?'

'Absolutely.'

'Definitely.' Gray pulled the telescope back open and glared through it again. 'And if you want my opinion, it's been a worrying trend of late. You've all gone soft. The lot of you. What happened to the merry band of confirmed bachelors I joined? The one where we were all perfectly content to remain blissfully single for ever? Avengers of justice, duty before all else? First Warriner discards his rakish ways for a life of eternal monogamy, then Leatham does the unthinkable and not only speaks to a woman, he marries her, and now Flint—the last bastion of everything sacred in the temple of the great unwed—looks like he's done for, too. It's a blasted tragedy, I tell you. Either that, or a strange disease has afflicted you all for which there is no cure. In which case, I'm off down to the courtyard to break up that useless bunch down there.'

He pointed to where a shabby group of militiamen were still stood laughing and gossiping around a water barrel when he'd only tried to move them on ten minutes previously. 'The last thing I want to do is catch your terminal ailment. It will be a cold day in hell before I fall foul of the parson's trap.' He slapped the telescope into Leatham's hand and stalked off, leaving them all silent. It didn't last long.

'The fact she's about to go on trial for treason is a sticking point in their relationship, to be sure.' Warriner continued to address only Leatham in a bid to annoy Flint. He had to grit his teeth not to bite back, knowing they'd have a field day if he did. 'The poor man must be in bits about that. Hadleigh says Flint's determined to prove the chit innocent, so much so I believe they've almost come to blows on the topic.'

'Proof indeed that he is in a quandary.'

'Not that he'll discuss it with us. His two *oldest* and *dearest* friends.'

'Indeed,' said Leatham, focusing the telescope and then pointing it directly in Flint's face. 'He's always been a very closed-mouth fellow. Why would he confide such an important conundrum to us, or, heaven forbid, ask us to help him in his noble quest, when he failed to appraise us of his middle name in all the nine years we have known him? Peter *Othello* Flint. Who knew?'

Oh, how Flint hated that name. 'I'm going to kill Hadleigh! And Jess is not a blasted traitor!' Like a fool, he was only adding fuel to the fire, yet couldn't seem to stop. He prodded Warriner in the chest. 'But that does not mean I've gone peculiar!'

'Right, you useless lot, back to your posts!' Gray's voice floated upwards and Flint decided it was better to watch him stalk across the court-yard than get into the sort of discussion his so-called dearest friends wanted to have. 'There is serious work to—'

The explosion sent Gray flying backwards. Then all hell broke loose below.

It took a few awful minutes of chaos for the shocking reality to fully sink in. Leatham was the first of them to discharge his weapon after spotting the militiaman directly behind Flint produce a blade from his belt. A blade that would have been destined to cut his throat had his friend not had the great foresight to kill the blighter first.

'Trojan horse!' Leatham yelled at the top of his lungs, as another of the militia aimed at one of the Invisibles. In the nick of time, their man lunged sideways, avoiding the deadly musket ball by a whisper.

Several men simultaneously rounded on the two remaining militia men on the battlements, overpowering them. Both were prostrate on the ground by the time Flint got to them. He grabbed one by the hair.

'*Salaud d'Anglais!*' The French insult chilled him to the bones.

'Where is Saint-Aubin?' Because his gut told him the bastard was here. The smuggler spat in response and earned himself a hard knock from Warriner.

'We've got this! You go protect your womenfolk!'

Flint didn't need to be told twice. With his

heart in his mouth, he grabbed two fresh pistols and flew down the stairs to the courtyard where a full-on battle was already being waged. There were dead on both sides, but he didn't have time to mourn his fallen comrades now. He had to get to Jess and see her safe. Like a man possessed he barged his way across the courtyard, mentally taking note of each unfamiliar face and trying to work out which one was Jess's abuser. In all the conversations they had had about Saint-Aubin, why had he never had the foresight to ask her what the bastard looked like?

As he reached the entrance he was relieved to see the well-trained King's Elite had obviously swarmed to the door to defend it the moment they had realised they were under attack. A bleeding Gray was in the thick of them, covered in a layer of dust from the explosion, one arm clearly out of action as the other wielded a sword.

'There are at least two Frenchmen among this rabble!' Gray read his mind, jabbing in the directions with his blade. 'Him and that one there!' The first was embroiled in the combat, the second, a dark-haired man with an angular, neatly clipped beard, seemed to be issuing rapid orders from the rear. That had to be Saint-Aubin. He had the air of the malevolent about him. And he was Flint's.

'Get Jess and my family out! We'll hold them off for as long as we can.'

At the thundering sound of the explosion, Lord Fennimore and Hadleigh had snapped into action, directing the male members of the Flint family to set up an armed barricade at the top of the stairs. Jess dashed to the window, only to be immediately dragged away by Lady Flint. 'We can't let them see you! If they get one inkling you are up here, then *here* is where they will come.' She lowered her voice and allowed her eyes to dart to her frightened grandchildren. 'And then we'll all be done for!'

While that made sense, and she certainly didn't want to be responsible for an innocent child being injured, Jess couldn't stand not knowing what was happening below and was sick with worry for Peter, wondering if he had been injured in the explosion, or worse, if he was already dead. The next ten minutes of frantic pacing were the longest of her life. His family were deathly silent, even the little ones seemed to understand the need to keep quiet, as they all listened to the sounds of a war being waged outside. Gunshot merged with the clash of steel and hand-to-hand combat.

When Gray stumbled into the room, covered

in blood and debris, and looking dead on his feet, Jess almost lost her breakfast.

'What happened?' Lord Fennimore kept one eye on the stairwell, his own pistol raised in readiness.

'The militia weren't the militia. Lord only knows what happened to the real ones, but that lot down there are smugglers and mercenaries wearing their uniforms and carrying their official papers. Mostly English, but quite a few French. All armed to the teeth. A situation we never anticipated.'

'We've been ambushed.' Lord Fennimore seemed to age in front of her eyes. 'Any sign of the marines?'

'Not yet, and if they come we aren't able to let them in. The smugglers hold the drawbridge and seem to want to keep it closed. Warriner has signalled the gunships, but as the castle has already been breached I'm not sure what use they will be. If they fire, we all suffer. But if they send men ashore, we cannot lower the drawbridge. Flint wants the women evacuated.'

'Peter is alive?' Please God let him be alive.

'Yes.'

Grateful tears filled her eyes. Then she saw Gray's subtle, almost imperceptive look towards his superior as he stalked to the wardrobe and terror gripped her. The situation was grave, very grave. Peter's life could very well hang in the balance. Something that was entirely her fault.

In seconds, Gray had the secret passageway revealed and was stuffing fresh pistols in his belt. 'I'll lead the way. Try not to panic. For now we have them held at bay downstairs. Flint and the others will hold them off as long as they can.'

As if they had practised such an evacuation every week of their lives, Flint's sisters gathered up the children and began to file into the narrow opening after Gray, closely followed by their armed husbands. The last of whom, Ophelia's, paused, waiting for her, Lady Flint hovering close behind him.

'No! No! *Mon Dieu!* We have to help him!' Jess's feet instinctively went for the stairs where Hadleigh caught her.

'You need to leave, too, my lady!'

'But Peter…'

'Needs to focus on the job in hand, not feel torn because you are there.'

'He's right, Jess. My son will do a better job knowing you are safe. It will be all right. You'll see. The Flint men are famously resilient. His father got shot on three separate occasions and survived every one. And Penmor will protect him.' Her serene calmness and absolute faith in her son's victory did nothing to ease Jess's terror.

'Then I'll stay! It's me they want!' If she surrendered to Saint-Aubin, then everything else would be all right.

'I am afraid that is out of the question, my lady.' The lawyer grabbed her as she lunged once again, then, holding her tightly by the arms, he marched her towards the tunnel, swearing audibly when she broke away and dashed to the window instead.

The scene below was horrifying. The small courtyard was filled with men fighting. Dotted among them on the ground were dead and wounded. As Hadleigh tried to pull her away, she gripped the sill, frantically searching for Peter until some sixth sense drew her eyes towards the area nearest the drawbridge and her heart literally stopped beating in her chest.

The man she loved was separate from his comrades, single-handedly hacking his way through the militia, his course obvious. Less than twenty feet away and safely surrounded by his customary band of lackeys was Saint-Aubin. Jess could only stand impotently and watch, her body slumped in defeat. Knowing Peter didn't stand a chance. 'He's all alone!'

Hadleigh took advantage of her momentary grief, manhandling her towards the passageway and handing her over to Lady Flint, who gripped her hand firmly. She turned to plead with him one last time and saw the despondency in his eyes. 'I'll do my best to keep him safe, ladies. You have my word.'

Then the shelves slid back into their proper position and he slammed the heavy oak door behind her. She heard the key ominously turn in the lock and then listened to his and Lord Fennimore's boots rapidly disappearing as they, too, went into battle on her behalf.

Why had she stolen her mother's ledger? That single, stupid final act of defiance had created a chain reaction she never could have imagined. But she had had to have the last word. Had to have her petty revenge.

Once more good men were dying—Peter might be dying—and it was all her fault. How exactly was she supposed to bear that guilt in perpetuity when already it suffocated her? How could she live on, knowing the man she loved was dead? A painful death he would endure because of her.

Listlessly she allowed herself to be dragged towards the spiral staircase to freedom, searching her mind for something, anything she could do. As they began to descend, the narrowness of the stone walls necessitated single file. Ophelia's husband blew out the last remaining candle in the passageway, plunging the corridor into a chilly darkness that was only alleviated by the dim light of the torch much further on.

That light was transient, disappearing each time Gray turned on the spiral, and it took all her concentration to safely place one foot in front of the other to follow it. Her companion was also concentrating. He had let go of her hand to brace his against the walls in case she stumbled and fell on the lethal, cold, damp stone.

If she did, it would be a blessed release. She didn't want the weight of Peter's death on her conscience. Didn't want to emerge into the daylight of the moors knowing that for the rest of her life she would live in darkness because he wasn't with her.

Her step faltered and she almost slipped, falling backwards on to the hard stone. She yelped in pain as step hit bone, and when her companions did not respond she realised she had lagged too far behind. The tears fell then and she let them, burying her face in her hands. Raw emotion choked her, forming tight bands around her throat and ribs, causing her to pause and pray for him. Asking that just this once God would answer her and keep him safe because Peter deserved to live. He was a good man. A kind man. A noble man and she loved him completely. Jess had never loved before and now knew without a single doubt in her heart that she would sacrifice herself willingly to keep him from harm.

Dear God, let him live. She asked nothing

more. Nothing for herself. Was that too much to ask God after all the obstacles she'd had thrown in her path? All the ordeals and pain she had been subjected to? Was the Lord so disgusted with her that he would allow her to taste love and then cruelly snatch it away? It wasn't fair!

It wasn't fair!

And she was damned if she was going to be beaten and allow it to happen!

Before her selfish nature surfaced and talked her out of it, she raced back up the now pitch-black spiral staircase, tripping and stumbling until she remembered he had told her to use Penmor's reliably sturdy stone walls to guide her. When she reached the top, she groped in the dark, feeling her way until she was convinced her toes were pointed back towards the stairs and his bedchamber was reassuringly behind her, checking, then rechecking to make doubly certain. She leaned against the right-hand wall, using her fingers to guide her, following it as it turned, taking her away from the stairs to freedom and closer towards what she hoped was Peter.

After an eternity, the flagstones beneath her feet no longer felt solid, they felt slimy. Coated in something soft and noxious that smelled quite foul. In the distance she could hear something rustling.

The bats.

By the amplifying sound there were hundreds of them and they were getting increasingly agitated by her presence, yet still she ploughed on, not knowing whether the draught on her face was from the outside or the angry flapping of their bony wings in the pitch-black passageway beyond.

There was no point thinking about the bats or the height of the ruined tower she was determinedly headed to, or Saint-Aubin's inevitable dreadful retribution when she confronted him and surrendered. The only thing that mattered was Peter and doing what was right.

Chapter Twenty-Five

Flint slammed the handle of his sword into the smuggler's face, felt the satisfying crack of bone and watched him crumple to the floor. Next to him Hadleigh aimed his gun and fired. For a man who ostensibly sat behind a desk, he was a surprisingly good shot. His bullet tore through the shoulder of a militia man who howled something French as he dropped his sword and collapsed to his knees.

He scanned the vicinity for Saint-Aubin and growled when he found nothing. He had lost him in the fray a good ten minutes ago and hadn't seen him since. He was probably hiding. Men like him, the sort who picked on defenceless women and hid in the shadows, wouldn't risk their own skin in an honest fight.

'I can't see him either.' Hadleigh hastily reloaded while Flint stood on point. 'I know it's not what you want to hear, but when we find him we need him alive.'

That would happen over Flint's dead body, but he wasn't going to argue with the lawyer now. It was always easier to seek forgiveness than ask for approval and if he was punished for the insubordination, so be it. Better that than risking the monster escaping while he languished in gaol awaiting trial and execution. Or worse, escaping capture because the King's Elite lost this battle. Saint-Aubin had certainly caught them on the hop and there was no denying Flint had never imagined bringing the fight within Penmor's impregnable walls. He had underestimated the Frenchman and now the King's Elite were paying the price.

Right now, they were holding their own. Just. A state of affairs that could change in a heartbeat if the smugglers had any more unexpected surprises up their sleeves. Leatham and his men had the entrance to the keep secured and had promised not to budge till they could be certain Gray and his precious charges were well clear of the tunnel—but even so, they needed more men. They needed those marines.

The Royal Navy gunship began firing warning shots into the ocean, letting the cut-throats know they were there. One hit the cliff below, causing the ground to rumble ominously beneath their feet and giving a few of the enemy pause for thought. While Flint was in no doubt each and every one of them was a smuggler, he suspected a goodly few were more loyal to the coin they raked in from free trading than they were to Saint-Aubin. As long as Flint's men could hold them at bay until the promised military reinforcements arrived, then maybe they stood a chance. He was banking on the Frenchman's little army fleeing to save their own sorry hides as soon as the redcoats appeared on the horizon, because while the King's men couldn't get in until Gray could direct them to the bothy, Saint-Aubin's couldn't get out. If it came to it, he would cheerfully blow up the keep, too, if it bought Jess and his family more time.

He cupped his hands and yelled through them up to Warriner and Lord Fennimore on the battlements. 'We need to reclaim the drawbridge!' Further encouragement to make the enemy leave. A nice, inviting, open path to freedom. Within seconds, musket balls rained down towards the smugglers who guarded it, clearing the way for him, Hadleigh and the brave Invisibles closest to charge forward.

Out of nowhere came what sounded like high-pitched screaming as a thick band of black surged out of the ruined tower. At first, the noisy density resembled a monstrous spout of oil until the whole began to separate into a vast, twisting, screeching mass around the keep, before swooping low to swarm the courtyard and then soaring back up to the sky.

Bats!

The cannon balls must have spooked them. They certainly spooked the smugglers who raised their arms in the air to swat them away. It was too good an opportunity to miss and he rallied his startled comrades. 'Kill as many as you can! Now!'

'Saint-Aubin! *Si tu me veux, viens me chercher!*'

Flint froze at the sound of her voice, frantically searching for her among the melee on the ground when Hadleigh nudged him and gestured up. There she was, stood precariously at the top of Cromwell's tower. Slim shoulders pulled back proudly, glorious dark hair tumbling all around her shoulders, the enormous murmuration of bats like a giant, ominous storm cloud above her head.

She edged further out on the ruined stonework, using her arms to balance herself like a circus tightrope walker, taking herself further way from the safety of the shard of ruined wall that protected the tunnel. He watched her glance down, blanch and wobble before she regained her footing.

'*Si tu me veux, viens me chercher!* Did you hear me, Saint-Aubin? If you want me, come and get me! I am here! Take me home!'

Flint was going to wring her blasted neck. Of all the times to prove to herself she was capable of grand, selfless, gestures, she had to choose now? When everything was at its absolute worst? Not only was she liable to fall or the unstable bricks crumble at any minute, she had made herself a target to boot. Her wholly unnecessary gesture shifted the smugglers' focus. Clearly, they had a prearranged plan to capture her as they began to surge en masse towards the base of the tower, attempting to form a wall around it. Their weapons facing outwards to pick off any who dared come near while those closest to the ruined wall formed a human scaffold to allow them to climb from the solid round base to the more haphazard and easier-to-climb shattered remnants of the edifice above.

Flint was about to charge forward and take on the lot of them single-handed, when he found his arm dragged back. Hadleigh held it in a vice-like grip. 'Wait! She might be giving us the break we need.'

'But Jess is all alone up there! Unarmed!'

'They won't dare hurt her. Jess is too important to Saint-Aubin. He wants her alive. Desperately wants her alive else he wouldn't be here.'

As if he could hear him, Lord Fennimore suddenly changed tactic, too, directing all the firepower from the battlements towards the base of the tower. Leatham abandoned the entrance to the keep, sending half his men towards Flint and Hadleigh as reinforcements while he disappeared with the others around the corner.

'Take cover! Shoot to kill.'

'Fire one more shot and she dies!' The French-accented voice came from within the closed ranks of the smugglers, but they parted at his command to reveal Saint-Aubin. Behind him, halfway up the Cromwell's tower, his weapon pointed decisively at Jess as he hid among the ruined stones was a sniper.

Jess's head was spinning so fast it almost drowned out the sound of the hammering pulse in her head. Each time she looked down, fear paralysed her, yet she had to look down to find Saint-Aubin among the thronging mass of men directly below. She could feel his presence, sense his fury. It did not take long to lock with his icy, malevolent eyes.

He was stood directly below her, staring up with such raw, unadulterated hatred she almost wavered and fled back into the tunnel, but then some sixth sense made her feel Peter close by, feel his love for her, his belief in her innocence, and that gave her all the strength and resolve she needed.

The courtyard fell eerily silent as close to a hundred pairs of eyes all came to rest on her. She could feel Peter's willing her to look at him and allowed herself one last indulgence, ignoring the desperate plea in his gaze with a tiny shake of her head. He wanted her to save herself. How could she? Not when only she held the key to everyone else's survival. His survival. Decisively she looked away, leaned out and spoke directly to her tormentor in French.

'There is a passageway behind me that leads well away from the castle. If you climb up here, I can take you through it to safety. Hurry.'

Saint-Aubin laughed. 'I am not a fool, Jessamine. Why would I trust you when you have betrayed me?'

'I didn't. I wouldn't dare.' Jess forced herself to look beaten. 'I am too frightened of you to betray you. I told them nothing. I swear.'

'Liar!'

'They knew about Deal already. It was only a matter of time before they linked him back to the *Grubbenvorst.* I kept trying to escape. I managed twice to stall them. You know that. You traced me back to the inn at the fishing village.' And almost beat the poor innkeeper to death. 'When they discovered you were in Plymouth they brought me here instead of London, thinking they were clever—but I knew you were cleverer and I knew you would come.'

'You stole from me!'

She shook her head vehemently, allowed the very real fear she felt for Peter to show on her face to allow Saint-Aubin to revel in his perceived power over her, realising at last that now she had something she loved more than her own life he no longer held that power. 'I had to destroy Mama's ledger—I knew it would ruin everything if the British got hold of it. But it is all right.' She tapped her temple. 'It is all here. I memorised it all. They know none of it, I swear it. Aside from Deal, they know nothing else. But they are not stupid either. A battalion of Royal Marines are due here at any moment...' She allowed that to sink in, hoping his desire for self-preservation would play into her hands. 'So we must leave immediately!'

'Jess, stop!' Peter pushed through his men at the front, oblivious of the line of guns which suddenly pointed at him. By the look on his face he was going to do something selfless and heroic and she couldn't let him.

'I am not your prisoner any more, Monsieur Flint.' She hoped the love and utter devastation at fate's cruel joke did not show on her face for all to see. 'I am no longer your responsibility. Thank God.'

'I will not let you do this!'

'Stand down, man! That's an order.' Lord Fennimore's voice came clear from his perch a few feet away, yet so hopelessly out of reach. His eyes darted to Jess's and she got the distinct impression he understood what she was doing even if she hadn't fully thought it through herself. 'I won't waste a good man for a traitor! We'll get them, lad. If the Marines don't get here in time, we'll get them another day. You'll still see them both swing.'

But typically, her vexatious protector refused to step back. Jess turned her head to avoid his unwavering stare, knowing that she wouldn't be able to hide her grief if she allowed herself to see his face. She had memories. Beautiful, precious memories which would sustain her for as long as she was allowed to breathe. That had to be enough.

Saint-Aubin ordered the men surrounding him to aim their guns at Peter and the silent English, then instructed his marksman to climb. Once the man reached Jess's narrow ledge, he stood behind her, his gun pressed into her neck. Only then did Saint-Aubin begin his assent up the ruined tower, keeping his body carefully within the sheltering confines of the outer wall.

The closer he got, the more the icy tentacles of fear crawled up her spine and suffocated her organs. By the time the gunman stepped aside to allow Saint-Aubin to press his blade into her throat, she was shaking with fear, yet oddly accepting of her fate. At least she could live with herself now, even though her life was destined to be short and painful. Secure in the knowledge that, thanks to her testimony, his days were numbered, too.

'Be in no doubt you will pay for your defiance once I get you home! But first, I shall allow you to watch that poor, deluded brave Englishman down there die.'

'No—please! No more killing! I beg you!'

She watched his expression change, his dead eyes amused. 'You care about him.'

'I don't!' But she knew she had given the truth away.

'Ki...' As hard as she could, Jess plunged her teeth into the hand that held the knife. His grip loosened, not enough to escape, but enough to let her turn around to spit in his face.

'*Salaud!* Go to hell!'

She braced her hands on his chest, ready to push them both over the edge to protect Peter, when Saint-Aubin reeled backwards in a spray of crimson blood.

* * *

Flint started running the second Hadleigh's pistol unexpectedly fired, ignoring the hail of bullets Lord Fennimore and his men mercilessly pelted into the remaining startled smugglers in the courtyard. He trampled over their dead and dying bodies, his sword cutting down anyone who dared to be in his way, then he scrambled up the walls towards her, pausing only long enough to check that Warriner's bullet had killed the sniper.

Oblivious to the new battle being waged below them as Leatham and the rest of the King's Elite charged the now scattered militiamen towards the drawbridge, he scaled the haphazard ruin to the top like a man possessed. All that mattered was getting to Jess and never letting her go again.

She was sat on the ledge, hugging her knees, her wide eyes staring straight ahead. Flint came to stand next to her, tugging her gently to her feet towards him and gathering her tightly in his arms.

'Is he dead?'

Flint leaned over to check Saint-Aubin's twisted, blood-soaked body on the unforgiving flagstones below. 'Completely.'

'Does it make me a bad person to be happy he is dead?'

'Of course not. He had it coming.' Although he still wished he'd had the pleasure of doing the deed himself. But Hadleigh had gone against his own directive and for that alone he would be in the lawyer's debt for ever. 'It's over, Jess. You are safe now.'

'I feel a bit dizzy. This tower is very high.'

'It is, sweetheart. Let's get you back on the ground, shall we?'

She allowed him to lead her back into the dark tunnel, through the narrow damp passageway, never once letting go of his hand. By the time they arrived back at his bedchamber, Lord Fennimore had reopened the concealed entrance and they emerged blinking into the light and saw a line of concerned faces who were there to greet them.

'There you are!' His mother bustled forward, pushing her to sit on the bed, using a handkerchief to dab ineffectually at the cobwebs and dirt marring Jess's lovely face. 'I had quite the fright when I realised you weren't behind us! What were you thinking?'

'She wasn't thinking. She was being selfless and typically maddening!' Just two of the many things he loved about her.

'He was going to kill you. I couldn't let that happen.'

'You didn't need to risk yourself—we had everything under control.'

'We didn't.' This came from Hadleigh. 'Your bravery saved us all, my lady. On behalf of his Majesty's government, I should like to offer our sincerest thanks. We are indebted to you, for both today and for your valuable testimony. I am dropping all charges against you. Something I had already decided upon last night when...' He paused, then glanced awkwardly at his feet. 'When new and conclusive evidence was presented to me. Your efforts on England's behalf today merely cemented my certainty of your innocence.'

Tears gathered in her dark eyes and her voice trembled. 'I am no longer a prisoner?' She gazed at Flint for confirmation.

'You are free to go whenever you want— although I hope you choose to stay. With me. I've grown rather accustomed to your presence.' Unashamedly, he sat next to Jess on the mattress and gathered her into his arms. She happily nuzzled against his chest, her hand resting perfectly over his heart.

'Oh, he loves you!' His mother clasped her hands to her bosom and sighed dramatically. 'All's well that ends well. I knew he wasn't arrow proof... Of course I saw it straight away. It was blatantly obvious he adored you the moment he brought you home. I said as much to the girls. He's so like his father—'

'The marines are here!' a voice shouted from the hallway below, interrupting his mother's effusive ramblings. 'And they have Gray and the family.'

'Better late than never—although rather a case of closing the stable door after the horse has bolted. I suppose I should go and see to them. It's a long march from Plymouth and they are probably hungry. And at least all that bacon won't go to waste.' Nothing galvanised his mother quicker than a house full of mouths to feed. 'Come along, everyone. Poor Jess is exhausted. She needs some hot tea, a warm bath and some sleep. Shoo, the lot of you.'

Unceremoniously, Hadleigh and Lord Fennimore were batted out of the door. Before she closed it behind her she turned back and pierced her son with a glare that could curdle milk. 'And while I'm on the subject of stable doors, don't get any funny ideas, Peter. I will be back in less than five minutes. There will be no more tomfoolery before the legalities!'

'Legalities?' Jess was staring up at him. 'But I thought Lord Hadleigh said all charges have been dropped?'

'She means the wedding. Our wedding. Assuming you'll have me.'

She relaxed against him, her hand snaking around his waist. 'Was that a proposal?'

'A very bad one, but no less heartfelt. Please say yes.'

'*Oui.*' She kissed him, smiling against his mouth and sending him tumbling back on to the mattress surrounded by the glorious riot of her hair. '*Define* tomfoolery.'

'It can't be defined.' He rolled her to lie beneath him, pouring all the love he felt into a kiss that left them both laughing and breathless. 'But if you've got all night, my love, and I can find a way to slip my irritating and interfering mother a sleeping draught, I'll happily show you.'

'*Non*, Monsieur Flint…' She twisted to reverse their positions, her beautiful hair falling to form an intimate cocoon around their heads. 'You are not in charge any longer. Show me now. *Tout de suite… Mon chéri.*'

Her kiss was passionate and earthy and perfect. Just like her. He didn't need further encouragement to do exactly as she commanded and probably never would. Against her smart, sultry mouth he found himself smiling at the excellent choice his heart had made. Lord save him from troublesome women…

* * * * *

MILLS & BOON

Coming next month

A DUKE IN NEED OF A WIFE
Annie Burrows

'I want a woman who will be a mother to Livvy and a duchess upon whom I can depend.' He turned and started pacing again. 'I hope that my Duchess will share my political views and support me in my aims.'

'And those are?'

Oliver paused, as though choosing his words carefully before starting to pace again. 'Because of my childhood I have seen how the underprivileged have to live. The means they must employ simply to put food on the table. And now I am one of the wealthiest men in England. I want to…I need to have a duchess at my side who will agree that something needs to be done to address the current imbalance.'

Golly. Sofia would never have guessed, from his haughty, forbidding manner that he could feel so passionate about reform. 'Golly,' she said out loud.

'What do you mean by that?' He came to a dead halt and looked at her intently.

She shook her head. 'Oliver, you clearly have very noble ambitions. But…what about love? Oh…' she put out her hand before he could give her a set-down '…I know you mistrust the emotion, but without it…' She took a step in his direction. 'If your wife cannot love you, she will be neither a good mother, nor a good duchess. If you must marry, you should find a woman who will love Livvy because she loves you. And who will support your work for the same reason. And more than that...' She took a deep breath, the way she would if she was going to dive into the lower lake, since she knew she was likely to get an equally chilling reception. 'You deserve to be loved. And don't say it's not true. *Everyone* deserves to be loved.'

'You...' He swallowed. 'You take my breath away. I never thought...'

And then suddenly he was right in front of her. 'Thank you,' he said huskily.

The next thing she knew, he'd put his arms round her waist and was kissing her. She was so surprised that she gasped. At which point, he deepened the kiss.

Even though she was amazed he was doing this, even though a part of her knew it was wrong to be kissing a man, in the dark, in a secluded part of the estate, it felt so amazing that she made no protest whatsoever.

Her first kiss.

Continue reading
A DUKE IN NEED OF A WIFE
Annie Burrows

Available next month
www.millsandboon.co.uk

COMING SOON!

We really hope you enjoyed reading this book. If you're looking for more romance, be sure to head to the shops when new books are available on

Thursday 24th January

To see which titles are coming soon, please visit
millsandboon.co.uk/nextmonth

LET'S TALK
Romance

For exclusive extracts, competitions
and special offers, find us online:

- **f** facebook.com/millsandboon
- 🐦 @MillsandBoon
- 📷 @MillsandBoonUK

Get in touch on 01413 063232